# "I take it I'm breaking another rule."

His mouth curved up in a half smile. "Let's see. I should have seated both of us facing backward."

Juliette laughed. "Now you're just being silly, Mr. Jameson. No, you certainly broke all sorts of rules from the moment we met in the street. But the biggest one, I would say—" She stopped, suddenly feeling she was about to tread on dangerous ground. She felt his thigh against hers, warm and hard, and when she looked into his eyes, she felt her breath catch and then disappear.

"The biggest one is that a gentleman should never seat himself like this beside a lady," she said. "Unless, of course, they are married or engaged to be married."

At this, Thomas Jameson smiled, then grinned, then burst out laughing. When he stopped, he shook his head. "No wonder I'm meant to live in America. What is the thinking behind all these rules? That if I sit next to you, with my leg against yours, I'll get ideas that a gentleman shouldn't have about a lady?"

"I—I suppose so, yes," she said, feeling as if she had forgotten how to speak.

Thomas Jameson laughed again. "I hate to tell the purveyor of all these rules, but I've had those 'improper' thoughts about you from the moment I saw you in the shop last week. I could be in Australia and I'd have those thoughts about you."

The American's words had literally taken Juliette's breath away. She felt a silken, languid heat forming deep inside, a delicious warmth tingling from her loins all the way down to her toes.

Other *Leisure* books by Elizabeth Clarke:

**LUKE ASHCROFT'S WOMAN**

# The BARE TRUTH

## ELIZABETH CLARKE

LEISURE BOOKS  NEW YORK CITY

*To Bert Gippert, Cindy Stein, and Norma and Nina Rodriguez—the best fans I could ever hope to have.*

A LEISURE BOOK®

March 2007

Published by

Dorchester Publishing Co., Inc.
200 Madison Avenue
New York, NY 10016

ISBN 0-8439-5672-0

The name "Leisure Books" and the stylized "L" with design are trademarks of Dorchester Publishing Co., Inc.

Printed in the United States of America.

Visit us on the web at www.dorchesterpub.com.

# The BARE TRUTH

# Chapter One

*Just pretend you're telling the truth,* Juliette told herself as she waited outside the morning room to be interviewed by Lady Olivia Whitehall.

The butler was looking down his nose at her as if he knew all her fibs and lies and bendings of the truth. *You've never been a lady's maid,* it looked as if he was thinking. *You've barely worked in service, and you've lost every job you've ever had because you can't keep your opinions to yourself.*

Juliette shook her head, trying to shake her negative thoughts away. The butler couldn't truly know anything of the sort. Even though she was only pretending she had been a lady's maid, she *had* had a job in service.

"The applicant has arrived, milady," she heard the

butler say, in a voice that made it obvious, at least to Juliette, that he thought Lady Whitehall clearly would be wasting her time by interviewing her.

*You can do this,* Juliette told herself as she walked into the room and saw two women surrounded by the most beautiful furnishings she had ever beheld. It seemed as if everything was either brocade or cut glass or rich, dark wood, and Juliette knew right away that these people were far, far wealthier than the other family she had worked for.

The younger woman, a fine-featured beauty with blue eyes and gold-streaked light brown hair much the same color as Juliette's, was already smiling at Juliette, and she motioned for her to sit down opposite them in a beautiful baize-covered chair. "I'm Sarah Whitehall, and this is my mother, Lady Olivia Whitehall. Your name is Juliette, you said in the letter?"

"Yes, milady," Juliette answered, realizing she didn't know exactly how to address the daughter. "Juliette Garrison, and I have quite a good bit of sewing experience and years in service as well."

She held out the letters she and her ailing mum had written the night before, one from a Madame de la Tour and one from a Mrs. Brooke, a barrister's wife in Herndon. "Here are my characters, milady. Unfortunately, Mrs. Brooke has since passed away, and Madame de la Tour is traveling in Italy at the moment, I believe, but you'll see that I have fine references from both."

Lady Whitehall murmured, "I see," but as she scanned the letters, she raised a brow in a daunting manner: Was it so obvious that Juliette and her mother had written the glowing references themselves? Had she gone on too much about her "exceptional skills and excellent manners that would be a credit to any household in all of England"?

"You were a house parlor maid and then a lady's maid?" Lady Whitehall asked without raising her eyes from the letters.

"Yes, milady. I took a break in between to go back to the sewing trade—I suppose needlework will always call to me, whether I'm in service or not."

"Quite unusual, to say the least," Lady Whitehall said, handing the papers to her daughter. "Most of our better servants have spent their working lives exclusively in service—except for my personal maid, of course, who apprenticed to some of the best dressmakers in London before coming to me. But to have jumped around—"

"Oh, Mama," Miss Whitehall interrupted, saying "Mama" with the second syllable more strongly, exactly the way Juliette had heard her employer's daughter pronounce it the one brief time she had actually worked as a maid for three excruciating weeks. "If Juliette has seen fit to see a bit of the world outside of service, why should we let that become a problem? She'll be working for me, not for you, and I would much rather hire a girl with a bit of spirit in any case."

Juliette was amazed to see Lady Whitehall's cheeks darken, and she had the feeling Lady Whitehall and her daughter clashed often. "Whomever you choose will be your first personal maid, my dear. I should hope you shall choose wisely. An experienced maid can guide you in your decisions. An inexperienced maid can cost you dearly."

Juliette felt a familiar feeling of recklessness catch at her heart. This was the enthusiasm her mum had tried to teach her to quiet because it was what always ended up getting her fired from her jobs. A habit of speaking out of turn wasn't a quality, apparently, that any employer was looking for, and it had landed Juliette out on her ear too many times in the past few years.

"But I do have experience, Lady Whitehall, and I have ever so good an eye for fashion and hairstyles—" She sighed, realizing that she had interrupted Lady Whitehall and spoken when she hadn't been spoken to directly.

Lady Whitehall's lips were compressed into a thin, angry line. It looked as if she were about to speak, but suddenly Miss Whitehall spoke up instead. "Oh, please, Mama. The other applicants have been simply dreadful. I'd rather do all my own sewing and dressing than be dressed by any of those dour, dried-up old spinsters—"

"Sarah Whitehall! I will not allow that sort of rudeness to be uttered within the walls of this room!"

"But you *know* what I mean, Mama. The others might be all right for you, but when you were my age, would you have wanted someone like that as your maid?"

Again, Juliette saw Lady Whitehall's cheeks darken just the tiniest bit, and she had the feeling Miss Whitehall had won the argument.

"Very well, Sarah, but on one condition," she said, her voice suddenly as firm as if she, rather than Miss Whitehall, had won the argument.

"Yes, Mama."

Lady Whitehall looked Juliette up and down. "You're quite presentable, Juliette. I'm sure if you hadn't found employment here, you would have found it in another suitable household quite easily. In any case, presentable though you may be, the fact is that you lack what I consider to be an acceptable amount of experience. Because of this, I shall require you to serve part time as an under house parlor maid—"

"But, Mama—"

"I'm not going to yield on this, Sarah, and in any case, that's exactly the way *my* first maid began, and the experience stood her in good stead for years of exemplary service. Juliette will thank us in the end, I can assure you."

"But then Mrs. Winston will be her supervisor. A lady's maid should report to the lady she's aiding and to no one else!"

"My dear Sarah. We have the finest servants in London—I can't tell you how many acquaintances of mine have confessed that they positively covet our staff—and one of the reasons everyone works as well as they do is that we recognize people's talents as well as their faults. Mrs. Winston began as a kitchen maid for my mother and worked her way up to being one of the finest cooks in all of London. She prefers to run the household on her own terms rather than to have to share any areas of responsibility with a housekeeper— hence, she's both, which suits her as well as it suits us, highly unusual though it may be."

"But, Mama—"

"I've told you I won't yield on this point, Sarah. You shan't need a maid all that much; the rest of Juliette's time can be well spent learning other skills she might eventually need elsewhere."

Miss Whitehall gave Juliette a look which in that instant made Juliette certain she would like working for her. It was as if she was pleading with Juliette to agree to the terms, and she felt like blurting out that she would do almost anything at all just to spend time in this lovely house. In all her years on the London streets as a girl, freezing and nearly starving in the seemingly endless winters, she had never dreamed she would even set foot in a house so fine.

"Very well," Miss Whitehall said. "If Juliette is game, of course."

Juliette felt like hugging Miss Whitehall. "Yes, of course," she said. "I'd be delighted to start immediately."

The happiness in Miss Whitehall's eyes was unmistakable, and even Lady Whitehall seemed somewhat pleased. "Very well, then, if you do mean right away, I'd like you to begin immediately, and we shall arrange to retrieve your belongings another time."

For a moment, Juliette felt a rush of panic. She didn't truly know what a lady's maid did, except the very few details she had observed at the Rowleys'. She certainly knew how to sew and clean various kinds of fabric, and she knew what she thought looked good as far as hairstyles went, but would she know enough to please Miss Whitehall?

"Come along, Juliette," Miss Whitehall said, standing and preceding Juliette toward the door. "I'll ring for Caroline, and she can show you to your room."

"Caroline?"

"She's the head house parlor maid, and she can show you what's what. You'll quite like her, and she has years of experience," she said as she closed the door of the morning room.

"Thank you, milady," Juliette said.

Miss Whitehall was looking at her carefully. "You'd better beg Caroline to teach you quickly, Juliette, if you don't want my mother to give you the sack. If you had as much experience as you said, you wouldn't be calling me 'milady.' It's 'Miss Sarah.' "

*Don't let me lose this job before it's even begun,* Juliette said to herself.

"You do know about all the things you've promised, I hope—sewing and hairstyles, that sort of thing?"

"Oh yes, Miss Sarah. I promise. My mum has always said I could sew an evening gown a night in my sleep if I wasn't so tired."

A change came over Miss Sarah's face, and Juliette could see that she was willing to take a chance on her. "Very well, then. I think we'll be quite happy with each other, Juliette. But just be sure you don't make any horrid gaffes when you're working as a housemaid. My mother's standards for her staff are extremely high."

"It's quite more than all right here," Caroline was saying as she stretched the sheet straight and flat on the bed. "It's certainly the best job I've ever had in service, and I would never have any desire, I don't think, to go somewhere else unless I were to leave service altogether."

Juliette kept working, but she looked at Caroline for a long moment before she spoke. She knew that Caroline had worked hard and steadily for eight years in the Whitehall household, since she had begun at the age of sixteen as an under house parlor maid. Yet, aside from being extremely pretty, with blond-streaked, long red hair and beautiful almond-shaped blue eyes, she didn't look a day beyond seventeen. The women Juliette had grown up with, all of whom had lived on the streets as she had for years, looked at least ten years older than their true ages. And although Juliette didn't think she looked too much older than her twenty-four years, she had scars and vestiges of frostbite on all her extremities that made it impossible for her to forget, even for a day, those nights without a roof over her head. From the way Caroline looked, Juliette had the feeling that having a roof over her head every single night of the year was going to be very appealing.

Just to be in this house, with all the magnificent fabrics covering the walls and furniture, all the deep, rich colors and beautiful finishes, was going to be wonderful. "I can see that it will be lovely just to be surrounded by all this beauty."

Caroline laughed. "Don't forget *you're* the one's going to be shining it up and keeping it beautiful," she said. "We have it rather easy compared to scullery maids and some of the other girls, but you wouldn't even want to think about what 'all this beauty' would look like without the servants. Still, I don't complain. My mum and dad retired and bought a pub in Brighton to run, and it was all with money they saved from being in service."

"They must have worked a lot of years," Juliette said, thinking about the fact that she had never stayed in any job for more than six months because of her apparently inevitable clashes with her bosses. But that was her dream, to stay with a job long enough that she could save heaps of money and open her own dress shop someday.

"Yes, they did. But they're still enjoying life," Caroline said, smoothing out a beautiful embroidered coverlet. They were working in one of the Whitehalls' many spare bedrooms; Juliette couldn't wait to see what Miss Sarah's room looked like. "It's what I'd love to do someday with Martin, if things go the way I'd like. He's footman to a family that's quite good friends with the Whitehalls." She laughed again. "Probably a complete fantasy, and Lord knows the Whitehalls would have a fit if we saw each other as much as we liked, but I like to dream. What about you? Any men who'll be knocking surreptitiously at the door?"

Juliette followed Caroline out of the room and into the next bedroom, which was much grander than the first.

"This is Miss Sarah's room," Caroline said. "You'll be spending a great deal of your time in here and in fact will be doing this room on your own most of the time. So what about you and followers? Will Mr. Blake, the butler, be blowing a steam gasket because you have a series of men coming to see you?" she asked, kneeling by the fireplace and handing Juliette a small shovel.

Juliette laughed. "Hardly. I haven't known many men in my life, Caroline—it was just me and my sister and our mum growing up. I never—" She stopped. She was embarrassed that she had no stories to tell, no followers, not even a tale of an unrequited love. But the fact was that in all her factory and dressmakers' jobs, she had worked with other women. And when she had briefly been in service at the Rowleys', she had spent just about every waking moment trying to fend off the master of the house. "I guess I've spent too much time working," she finally said.

She began scraping ashes up in the shovel.

"Apparently not as a maid," Caroline said, taking the shovel from Juliette's hands and showing her how to scrape up the ashes without scattering them all over. She looked at Juliette with eyes that suddenly seemed keenly intelligent. "Exactly how long have you worked in service, Juliette?"

Juliette felt her cheeks grow hot. "Not very long," she said. "I exaggerated my experience rather extremely to the Whitehalls. And Lady Whitehall thinks I was a lady's maid as well as a housemaid, which isn't quite the truth."

"Ah, 'not quite,' hmm? A character reference from a faraway land, perhaps?"

"One from a faraway land and one from someone who would have died—if she had ever lived," Juliette said with a laugh. "I think the only reason Lady Whitehall agreed is that Miss Sarah seemed to truly want to hire me."

Caroline raised a brow. "That may be, my dear. But I can tell you right now: It may have seemed as if Sarah always gets her way with her mother, but believe me, she doesn't. And if Lady Whitehall sees that you don't know what you're doing, you'll be out on your ear before the week is out."

Juliette thought of the situation she had left when she had set out that morning: her mum unable to work anymore because of consumption, their flatmates kind enough but none promising to keep paying Harriet's rent forever, and a landlord who had said if the back rent wasn't paid immediately, they'd all be out on the street again.

She thought of the strangely elated feeling that came over her each time she entered a new room at

48 Epping Place, and her heart sank at the thought that she might be sacked. She had already vowed that she would keep her opinions to herself, even if it meant biting her tongue until she wanted to scream; yet now, Caroline was telling her she could lose her job simply because she had talked her way into it and didn't know what she was doing.

Later on, Juliette felt more confident as she helped Miss Sarah dress for dinner and fixed her hair in a flattering chignon. "This business of my sharing you with the rest of the household is going to be quite ir-ritating," Miss Sarah said to Juliette in the mirror as they put the finishing touches on her hair. "But then again, I suppose I should be happy I have you at all. How do you like it so far?"

"I love it," Juliette said without hesitation, because surprisingly, she did. She had sought a secure job out of a desperate need for money, but she had found a job that, so far, she truly did enjoy.

Miss Sarah smiled. "Good. I'm glad. Just be on your toes tonight for dinner. One thing Mama can't abide is any sort of mistake when we have company."

"And tonight you have company?" Juliette asked, her stomach already jumping.

Miss Sarah rolled her eyes. "Nobody *I* care about, though Mama wishes I did. Some dull-as-can-be earl Mama has the utterly irrational idea I might wish to marry."

"Can she force you to?" Juliette asked, smoothing Miss Sarah's chignon one last time so that not a hair was out of place.

Miss Sarah stood up. "A few of my friends have been steered quite firmly, I suppose you could say, into marriage, but I can tell you quite honestly I'd rather live on the street than be forced into a marriage I don't want."

Juliette couldn't help smiling. "Forgive me, Miss Sarah, but you don't know what it's like to live on the street until you've experienced it."

"And you have?"

"It's probably the main reason I'm here rather than in a factory job or at a dressmaker's. There's something deeply appealing to me about knowing I'm going to sleep in this beautiful house every night, and eat downstairs morning and night, and not to have to be fighting with a landlord or have no landlord at all." She looked at Sarah and suddenly had an idea. "If this earl who's coming tonight has never seen you before, would you like me to make you look as unappealing as possible?"

Miss Sarah started to laugh. "Can you imagine? I'd love it if it weren't for the fact that Mama does know how I ought to look." She stood up and gave Juliette a hug. "Do your best tonight, Juliette, for both of us. I do think I'm going to thoroughly enjoy your company."

An hour later, Juliette stood at the side of the dining room beside Caroline and the butler, Mr. Blake, who still looked none too pleased she had been hired.

She could see why Miss Sarah had no interest in a future with the Earl of Whatever he was, no matter how wealthy he might be. He was handsome in rather a humorless way, reminding Juliette more of a carved, perfect-looking statue than of a man. He was also as stiff and lifeless as a wooden carving, and even from the short time Juliette had known Miss Sarah, she knew her mistress needed a man with more spirit.

Juliette could tell that Miss Sarah was ill at ease; she was speaking at twice her normal speed, telling a long story that Juliette had missed the beginning of, but it had something to do with a visit to the Swiss Alps.

Everyone was listening quite raptly except, it seemed, for the earl, who was cutting up the duck on his plate as if it were the most interesting activity he had ever performed.

"It was quite spectacularly beautiful," Miss Sarah was saying, "really the most amazing view I've ever seen. And the family that had fascinated me because they seemed so perfect were looking out at the view. The man had one of those new little cameras one can buy."

"An odd concept, taking pictures of whatever strikes one's fancy," Lord Whitehall said.

Lady Whitehall shot her husband a warning look. "Sarah is in the middle of a story," she said in a voice that could have cut glass.

"Yes, of course, dear, how right you are. Go on, Sarah."

Juliette had the feeling Lady Whitehall was trying to will the earl to at least pretend to pay attention to Sarah, but he seemed oddly fascinated with the food on his plate.

"Thank you, Papa," Miss Sarah said. "In any case, they seemed to be a fairy-tale perfect family—the mother, the father, the girl, and the boy—and suddenly the two parents started arguing about how to take a picture. The man was telling the woman to back up more—and then she was gone. She had dropped right off the face of the mountain."

"Oh my goodness," Juliette said.

Suddenly everyone in the room seemed to freeze, and Juliette realized why. She had spoken, because

13

she had been listening to Miss Sarah's story as if they had been upstairs together in Miss Sarah's room.

But they hadn't been.

Lady Whitehall began to talk quite loudly and quickly, asking if the woman had recovered from her fall—which she had.

But the furious look on Mr. Blake's face, and even the surprised expression in Caroline's eyes, told Juliette she had made a huge mistake.

# Chapter Two

It was all thanks to Caroline, Juliette thought as she neared the confectioner's shop in Barrington Street. If it hadn't been for Caroline's nearly 'round-the-clock teachings, she knew she would have been out on her ear after that very first evening.

But now, nearly six months later, Juliette had settled in amazingly well to a job she actually liked. Mrs. Winston and Mr. Blake, the butler, could be difficult at times, and Lady Whitehall's unyielding snobbery grated at Juliette's soul—she was quite sure that if Lady Whitehall knew she had been a match girl and a crossing sweeper and had sold watercress and flowers as a child, she wouldn't have dreamed of keeping her on. But so far, Lady Whitehall hadn't cared one whit about much beyond placing Miss Sarah in a suitable situation for marriage, and since Juliette had apparently done a good job making Miss

Sarah beautiful, which was easy and fun, her position was safe.

She wished she could buy chocolates for Caroline, but every farthing was already spent twice over before she earned it. Right before she entered the sweet shop, she caught sight of her reflection in the shop's window, and she was surprised at the sight, as she always was when she ventured out in her mistress's cast-off clothes. How right and proper and wealthy she looked, the fine Liberty lawn such a far cry from the tatters she had worn as a young girl. And she had fixed her long, dark blond hair much as she would have Miss Sarah's, in a French twist. The clothes were a bit tight, as her waist was plumper than Sarah's, and her arms more muscular. But they fit well enough, and Juliette was happy her mum would be able to see her in finery that was certainly beyond their wildest dreams when Juliette and her sister and mum had slept in tunnels down by the Thames all those years before.

She had heard stories of mistresses who mocked their servants for trying to look nice when they went out, for "putting on airs" and trying to look like young ladies, but Miss Sarah was the complete opposite. She had even given Juliette the black and print dresses and aprons she worked in, rather than insisting Juliette pay for them herself, as was the case in most households.

As she stepped into the confectionery, Juliette breathed in deeply, giving herself up to an aroma that had to be one of the best on earth. It was one of the reasons she would never be as fashionably tiny-waisted as her mistress. She was quite sure that if she had the money to buy all the dark-chocolate-covered nuts she craved, she would be as large as a house.

"I'll also take a pound of those dark-chocolate walnuts and pecans," came a deep voice just ahead of her. Juliette turned to see who shared her taste so exactly.

Crowded as the shop was, Juliette was amazed she hadn't noticed the man right away. The voice had sounded strong, deep, and American, and the man who had spoken definitely looked foreign, with bold, handsome features, dark hair, and a tall, muscular frame that looked almost comically out of place in the tiny shop.

Juliette didn't want to stare, and she didn't want to lose her place in the disorganized semi-queue, but there was something about the man that caught her.

She suddenly felt something brush against her side. A tiny, emaciated girl, probably no more than five or six years old, had slipped past her. At a glance, Juliette could guess the girl's circumstances, much like her own at that age: She was hungry, she didn't know when or where her next meal would be, and she probably worked at whatever she could, all day and every day, and cried herself to sleep every night.

Juliette was about to offer the girl a piece of the chocolate she was going to buy for her mum when the girl slipped off into the small crowd of people, heading for the door.

"Not so fast, yer little varmint," came a gruff voice, and as the crowd parted, Juliette saw that the shopkeeper, a portly, pasty-faced, mustachioed man, had grabbed the little girl by the back of her shirt. "Now let's see what your sticky-fingered little hands got a hold of," he said.

"You will unhand the girl this instant!" Juliette heard her voice ring out, loudly and imperiously.

For a moment, she could hardly believe she had spoken, and in a voice that was much more like Lady Olivia Whitehall's than her own. Everyone in the shop was staring at her.

The shopkeeper, completely surprised that the little girl was with Juliette, made a bow in front of Juliette and hastened to speak. "Begging your pardon, milady, but I thought—I didn't know the child was with you," he said, still holding on to the little girl, though more gently.

Juliette was furious. Though the man claimed to believe her, he clearly didn't believe her one hundred percent. Why else would he still be holding on to the girl, stolen chocolate or no stolen chocolate?

Juliette drew herself up and realized she had nearly popped a button on her dress. "I am Miss Juliette Whitehall. My footman is just outside, and I strongly advise you—again—to unhand the child this instant," she said, holding her hand out for the girl to take.

The shopkeeper let the girl go, and Juliette took hold of her tightly, wondering what the little girl was thinking. She reminded Juliette of a mouse, quick, thin and hungry, and she probably wished she had chosen to steal a boring old apple from a costermonger instead of stepping into an expensive confectionery.

"Not that I'm under any obligation to tell you this," Juliette said to the shopkeeper, "but this child is part of a social-welfare project I'm involved in, and I had specifically instructed her to choose a sweet."

"I do apologize, Miss Whitehall," the man said. "And tell me what you would like today as well."

Still holding tightly to the little girl's hand, Juliette

asked for an eighth of a pound of dark-chocolate-covered walnuts and pecans, paid for them quickly, and led the girl through the crowd and out onto the street.

She let go of the girl's hand. "I can remember—" she began, planning to tell the girl how many times she had been caught in just this sort of trouble.

But the girl bolted and ran.

"Wait!" Juliette called out, beginning to run.

But the child had already disappeared, skilled, no doubt, at just this sort of escape after a lifetime's worth of practice.

Juliette thought of what she had been about to say, that she could remember so much about a childhood that had been just like the little girl's—the gnawing hunger that had spurred her to do things she knew were wrong; feeling she would do nearly anything on earth just to have a warm, dry place to sleep for one night—and she realized the little girl wouldn't have wanted to hear any of those things, because her life, unlike Juliette's, would quite likely not change for the better.

"I would have thought your footman would have helped you in your chase, milady," came a low voice from behind Juliette.

The words had been spoken in an American accent, and Juliette was almost certain she knew who had said them before she turned around to see.

Her heart skipped a beat; her guess had been right: The tall, handsome man who had been in the store was now looking at her—indeed, taking her in from head to toe in a bold sweep that was more direct a look than any Englishman had ever given her. Were all Americans so bold, she wondered, or just this tall, unnervingly handsome man?

"I beg your pardon?" Juliette murmured, shaken by the stranger's daring gaze. Her eyes met his—dark, penetrating, intelligent—and the words he had spoken flew out of her head.

The man smiled, and the corners of those daring eyes crinkled in a most attractive way. "I said I would have thought your footman would aid you in your chase, milady," the man repeated, drawing close to her and looking around. "Has he already run after the little girl?" he asked.

He looked down at her, and his eyes locked with hers. Juliette knew she had to move away from this man.

And once again, she had forgotten what he'd said.

The man began to laugh. "I know you speak English because I heard you in the store," he said. His eyes narrowed then. "Am I breaking another ridiculous rule of English etiquette by addressing you out here in the street? What is it—a man isn't allowed to address a woman on an odd-numbered day of the month? Or I can't talk to you because the sun is shining so brightly on your hair that it looks like spun gold? Or because you're so pretty that I'm not supposed to address you directly?"

*Speak!* Juliette commanded herself. She had already proven to be a scatter-headed harebrain. But if she spoke now, there was at least a slight chance she could redeem herself.

She took a deep breath, tried not to think about the effect his words had had on her, and spoke. "I—" She stopped. "It's of no importance to me, sir, whether you've broken any rules. I have the feeling you're in the habit of breaking whatever rules you choose to break. But since I—" She stopped again, and tried to ignore the way she had felt when he'd said she was pretty.

"I'm actually in the rather awkward position of telling you—a stranger—that I've broken rather an important rule myself, by venturing out without another soul." She took a deep breath. "And I would be grateful to you if you didn't share this information with anyone."

His eyes lit up with interest. "Why would I share with anyone but you, Miss Whitehall?"

Miss Whitehall. She had said that her name was Miss Juliette Whitehall. Why hadn't she used an entirely false last name?

But it was probably of no importance, she reasoned. The Whitehalls never frequented the confectionery, and this stranger—

"I must go," she murmured, and she took off at a run that was unladylike indeed in order to catch the approaching omnibus to East Hanford Street.

She hopped on board and moved to the upper level. She caught sight of the tall, handsome stranger as she was pushed toward the rear of the omnibus.

The American was walking along in her direction, and he looked as if he was smiling about something private and quite comical.

And then a thought struck her. She had assumed, without even thinking about it, that the American had believed she was Miss Juliette Whitehall, a slightly plump but certainly genuine member of London's aristocracy.

But what if he hadn't? What if he had merely been toying with her? What if he was laughing now because she had made an utter fool of herself?

As she sat down, she felt her face redden with anger and embarrassment. The truth, not that the stranger would ever know it, was that she wasn't the least bit ashamed of what she was: personal maid and part-time housemaid as well. Her mother had taught her a long time ago that if a woman could make her way in the world by any decent means, supporting herself without the help of a man, she had much to be proud of indeed.

Perhaps that was the reason, Juliette had often thought, that she had been sacked nearly immediately from her one other position in service: She hadn't been able to be subservient enough.

At the East Hanford Street stop, Juliette hopped off and a moment later was letting herself in to the rooms her mum shared with four other workers at the Dressler Sheet Warehouse. She knew her mum had been ailing—many days she had been too tired to get out of bed, with a cough that had been deep and rough and draining—but when Juliette walked in to the bedroom and saw her mum's face, pale and drawn and wrinkled, she couldn't help crying out and covering her mouth.

Her mother stirred, smiled wanly, then closed her eyes again.

*I'll leave her the sweets and the rent money and be off,* Juliette said to herself, heading for the nightstand. She set the chocolates down, and suddenly her mother reached out and grabbed her by the wrist. The wan smile was now a full-fledged grin. "Now just where do you think *you're* going, my dear one?" she murmured, her eyes glassy with fever.

"You're burning up," Juliette said as the heat from her mum's hand burned into her wrist.

Harriet, always one to argue if an argument was to be had, didn't say a word. Juliette saw the corners of her mother's mouth turn down and then force themselves into a smile. "Aye, 'tis grave," she said quietly. "But Polly was burning up for three days with consumption, and on the fourth woke up feeling as fine as a healthy young girl."

Juliette knew that her mum was just saying the words. True, some people could live with the illness for months, even years. But those were, for the most part, people who could travel to warm, blissful climes like Sicily and Greece. If her mum had to return to work in the crowded back room at the warehouse, it was an entirely different thing.

"I wish I could have brought you a year's worth of wages instead of this," Juliette said, opening the bag of chocolates. "But they *are* your favorites."

Now appeared a true smile on the sweet, lined face Juliette loved so much.

"That's my girl," Harriet said, propping herself up in bed. "Now tell me about your work. You've still held on at Epping Place?"

Juliette laughed. "Oh, come. Do I detect a huge amount of surprise in your voice? I actually still have the job, Mum. And I enjoy it as much as ever. Sarah Whitehall is day-and-night different from anyone else I've ever heard of in that group," Juliette said. "Her mum, Lady Olivia Whitehall, is true-blue aristocracy. But I think Miss Sarah is so happy to have me that she quite looks the other way when I make a mistake. She can't bear some of the things she has to do in her position and talks to me until the wee hours about all the adventures she wishes she could have."

An odd expression had come over Harriet's face.

She set down the bag of chocolates and opened her mouth to speak, then shut it. It reminded Juliette of when her mum had had to tell her that her older sister, Grace, had died; her pain and confusion had been so deep that for a few moments, she had been unable to speak. Juliette wanted to take her in her arms, as she had back then, but she knew she had to keep her distance because of the danger of becoming infected herself.

Harriet took a deep breath and began to cough, then patted her chest and looked into Juliette's eyes. "There's something I must tell you, and I believe now is the time to do it."

"What is it?" Juliette asked, as tears began to fill her mum's eyes.

"You know how much I love you," Harriet said softly. "You know how much I loved Gracie," she went on. "How we both cried rivers when she left us."

It was a memory that had haunted Juliette every day of her life, how her sister, Grace, had died when she was twelve and Juliette ten. She and her mum had nearly gone mad with grief, and she could remember that neither one had eaten a scrap of food for days.

"What you don't know," her mum went on slowly, "what I agreed not to tell you until you were old enough, dear, is that I'm not your mum."

Juliette felt as if she had been punched in the stomach. "What?"

"You were but six months old when your mum died, and we were the best of friends, she and I. Like two peas in a pod, we were, and always bound for a heap of trouble because we never quite fit any of the molds we were supposed to fit into—"

"But who was she?" Juliette interrupted, immediately sorry she had cut off the woman she would always consider to be her mum.

"Your mum was named Kate Claypool, and she was house parlor maid in the Banford household on Glendynn Place. And your father, my dear, was the only son—the only child, actually—in the household: William Banford, the son of Sir Roger and Lady Edith Banford."

Juliette was shaking her head, though she felt as if the room were spinning.

"Your mum lost everything—it was a dramatic time, filled with troubles, and all the result of a love affair that I do believe was true and deep for both." She propped herself further up and then reached into her night table. She pulled a maroon, velvet-covered book out of the drawer and handed it to Juliette. "Here is her diary, dear. She wanted you to have it when you turned twenty-five, but I believe twenty-four is close enough, and you're a wiser and more mature girl than she might have known you'd be at the time of the promise."

A diary. Written by a woman Juliette didn't remember in any way, written by the woman who had given birth to her.

She opened it, and a photograph fell out, of two young women, laughing at the camera, their arms wrapped around each other's waists and shoulders. She recognized Harriet, a pretty, red-haired, freckle-faced young woman whose beauty Juliette could still see now.

"That's me and your mum on holiday at Brighton, before things got tough for both of us. I hadn't yet met Grace's father, an inn owner I should never have laid my eyes on. But she was quite the beauty, your mum was, wasn't she?"

There was no denying that Kate Claypool had been a great beauty—with pale blue eyes; a full, lush-looking mouth; and high cheekbones. Her light-colored hair had probably been the same dark blond as Juliette's, and there was something in her smile that Juliette knew was like her own.

But Juliette felt like a child at that moment, as if she would be betraying the woman she had known as her mother for her whole life if she expressed her thoughts. "You were both beautiful," she finally said, meaning it.

Harriet wrapped an arm around Juliette and drew her in as close as she would allow in her condition. "I know it's a mountain of feelings to take in, dear. Your mother's life was as dramatic as any matinee playing at Drury Lane. And I know you'll always think of me as your mum. You don't have to prove it or tell me or act any different from how you always have. But Kate—your real and true mum—was as fine a person as they come, and as true a friend, and she loved you to pieces. It was a terrible thing, her dying when she did and you being only a baby. Then your father—not that he ever knew you—died of the cholera fever with his wife when they went to India not too very long after. No great loss to the world, if you ask me, them who have everything treating others like dirt." She shook her head, clearly even now not thinking much of the man. "Now, you get to know your mum through this diary, dear, and you let me rest. Come to me next week if you can, and we'll talk some more."

Juliette blew Harriet a kiss and fought tears she knew would come no matter what. "I love you, Mum," she whispered before she left. As she walked out into the street a few moments later, her heart ached for the woman she loved and the woman she would never know, the life she had known and the life Kate Claypool had never gotten to lead.

When she returned to Epping Place and stood outside in what was known as "the area" and knocked at the servants' entrance, she felt almost as if the afternoon had been a dream. "Miss Sarah wants to see you right away, Juliette," Mr. Blake, the butler, told her as he hurried her into the kitchen. Juliette suspected that Mr. Blake had a kind heart, but he was still more of an authoritarian than she would have liked. In his early fifties, he no doubt saw himself as something of a father figure to the others. Juliette felt he was more interested in their personal lives than he had the right to be. A handsome man, with strong, even features and a smile that could turn a stern-looking face kind in a moment, he seemed to be nearly jumping out of his skin over the fact that Miss Sarah, never one to use Juliette as much as Lady Whitehall used her own maid, needed Juliette's services on her afternoon off.

"Thank you, Mr. Blake," Juliette said, moving past him and heading up the back stairs to her room. She would put the diary away in a safe spot until she had time to read it. On her way home in the omnibus, she had been afraid of dropping it or being jostled, and so had done no more than glance through the pages, handwritten in a script that was surprisingly, eerily like her own.

She put the diary in the drawer of her night table, then took it out and looked at the photograph one more time. Two happy young women, looking as if neither had a care in the world. She thought of all the struggles both had had to endure afterward, and she wondered what choices they had each regretted, and which had been the right ones. Harriet had always taught her there was at least one fork in every road. ("There's *always* a choice, dear, whether you know it or not," she had often said.) But had her mother always had a choice?

Suddenly remembering that Miss Sarah needed her, Juliette put the diary back in the drawer and hurried downstairs. She knocked on the door to Sarah's room, and not half a moment later, Sarah flung it open and pulled Juliette inside. "You must tell me *everything*, Juliette, and if you leave one detail out, I shan't ever forgive you."

"Details about what, Miss Sarah?"

"Sarah, please," her mistress said, looking exasperated and beautiful at the same time. She was one of those women Juliette suspected would always look good—her skin never creased from sleep, her eyes never reddened or dark-circled from too little rest. "Every time you call me Miss Sarah, I feel as if I'm an old, wrinkled spinster."

"All right. Sarah, then. But details about what?" she asked again. Surely there was no way Sarah could know about her mother.

"The American! According to my father, a 'rugged, rather handsome, strapping American' went to his club this afternoon. And do you know why?" she asked, her eyes glinting with excitement. "He was asking after Miss Juliette Whitehall. And naturally, my father said that neither his daughter nor his wife went by that name, and that my name, his daughter's name, is Sarah."

Juliette sighed. "And now I'll be sacked by your father without a character reference, I imagine," she said, feeling a rush of disappointment and dread. She could just imagine what Lady Whitehall's reaction would be to her having foolishly and pointlessly used the Whitehall name.

"You've no need to worry on *that* account," Sarah said, "thanks to your handsome American friend. First of all, I wouldn't let Papa or Mama sack you, no matter what you had done. But the American covered rather gracefully for you, apparently, saying he must have gotten the name wrong." Sarah's eyes glittered. "A stranger lying for you, Juliette? I'm impressed. Apparently he was due to meet with Papa to discuss a possible investment in his shipping venture—but he called on him early, and seemed, according to Papa, much more interested in discussing the Whitehall daughter than any details about the business."

"It's rather mysterious," Juliette said as Sarah sat down at her dressing table. Juliette moved behind her and began undoing her hair, which had been in an elaborate French twist that Juliette was rightfully proud of creating.

"On the contrary," Sarah said. "It sounds quite straightforward. The man was obviously taken with Miss Juliette Whitehall. So please tell me, Miss Whitehall: Was the American handsome? I think Papa would have acted quite differently about the mystery if the American had been a bent-up, gnarled gnome of a man, though I can't explain why."

Juliette laughed, and she couldn't help feeling a sudden, deep yearning as she thought of the tall, strong-looking American with the smooth, low voice and eyes that had seemed to lock with hers in a gaze that felt more like a touch. She thought of how he had looked her up and down in a way no polite Englishman would have done, a definite assessment of her womanly qualities. But far from finding it rude, she had felt alive and desired and appreciated, as if the American had held a mysterious, silken power over her. "I can tell you quite honestly, Sarah: I believe the American was the handsomest man I've ever met—not that his features were perfect, mind you: I'm not even sure he would look that good in a photograph. But he has a presence, a way of looking at a woman—"

Sarah made a mock swoon onto her dressing table. "It's just too unfair. I never meet anyone who has any more presence than this hairbrush, and of course the less presence a man has, the more my parents think he'd be the perfect husband for their only daughter."

Juliette smiled. "Maybe the American will be the perfect husband for you. Don't forget, he thinks I'm Miss Juliette Whitehall, Sarah. I'm sure he isn't seeking to wed a lady's maid during his stay here in England." She suddenly stopped, thinking about all that her mum—or Harriet—had told her that afternoon.

"What's wrong?" Sarah asked, turning to face Juliette. "You look as if your heart just broke in two."

"I'll tell you tomorrow," Juliette said, starting to comb Sarah's hair again. She couldn't face even thinking about Harriet and her illness. And all the details of the past she had never known; she certainly wasn't ready to talk about that. She felt guilty having experienced such a rush of pleasure thinking about the American stranger. But then she told herself it was silly to feel guilty about something that had been no more than a passing fantasy: Certainly this stranger, if she ever saw him again, wouldn't take kindly to her deception. He would inevitably remain a fantasy for her, and nothing more.

# Chapter Three

*Dearest diary,* Juliette read, lying motionless in her bed so as not to disturb Caroline, who was still sleeping, exhausted, as she always was, from her work as head house parlor maid. It wasn't even dawn yet, and they both would have to get to work in five minutes, but Juliette knew Caroline needed every minute of her sleep.

*It is now ten o'clock at night, and I should be asleep, but I'm writing this because I cannot contain my excitement any more.*

*The rules in the Banford household, my employers for nearly eight months so far, are strict, and the consequences for breaking them are severe. Get caught with a forged character reference or look at the housekeeper, Mrs. Green, the wrong way, or the butler, Mr. Merton, and you will be on the wrong side of a wall you can never climb back over. You will be sacked soon enough—or you will wish you had been sacked and will quit before the day is done. Poor Effie Gray, the under housemaid, fell into a trap set by Lady Edith and is now out on the street. Apparently Lady Edith is in the habit of hiding three or four farthings in various places a good maid would find them—in the crack of a settee or under a tea cloth—and if the hapless maid doesn't turn them in, she's given the sack by the end of the day because she's either not a good enough maid or she's dishonest. Poor Effie had the 'gall,' as Lady Edith said, to pocket the money, and she's now out on the street, without home or possessions or anything at all to call her own.*

*Despite all this, I like my job. Twenty-four Glendynn Place is a beautiful house, and it is exciting to help out at the large dinner parties the Banfords always seem to be having—handling the fine, shining silverware and lovely linens and eating the delicious leftovers. Most of the girls who work here come from the Midlands like me, and every day is a bit of excitement we'd never find back home, even if in the end, we're all so tired we're asleep the moment our heads hit the pillows. The other morning, one of the maids fell asleep while she was scrubbing the stairs!*

*Dear diary, here is my biggest bit of excitement and the reason I've begun writing, because I always said I wouldn't write in you without a dramatic reason. So here it is:*

*William Banford, Sir Roger and Lady Edith's son, seems to have taken a huge and surprising interest in me ever since the day he caught me in the morning room reading the illustrated newspaper that comes to the house.*

*And, diary, I know that these dashing young aristocrats love nothing better than to toy with the hearts of their innocent female servants, that usually their attentions mean nothing more than a petal on the wind.*

*But William Banford is a different sort altogether from the men I've seen at the family's dinner parties. When we are serving, we are supposed to perform our duties as if we cannot hear the conversations of the diners, and we are supposed to be perfect. Step forward with the food, clear the table, etc. etc. as if we are deaf, and blind as well, I suppose, except as far as the food is concerned.*

*I suppose I was nervous because William Banford is so extremely handsome, and he's often away for months at a time in the army. Well, I was holding a dish of asparagus, and some of it slopped out and splashed on his sleeve, and do you know William jumped up and apologized for knocking into me? I know Lady Edith was about to light into me, but he cut her off right at the pass. And then, in front of everyone, it was as if we were the only two people in the world. 'Please accept my apologies for my clumsiness, Kate,' he said softly.*

*Diary, I didn't even realize William knew my name! I could hardly sleep last night . . .*

Juliette had read more than half the diary by the time the bell from Sarah's room rang. She set the diary on her bed, then put it under her pillow. She didn't want to take the chance of anyone finding it. She could just imagine if Rachel, the kitchen maid, ever found it, although now that she thought about it, she didn't know if Rachel could read more than a few words. But if she could, Juliette could picture Rachel screaming the news in the servants' hall: "Juliette is part *upper class,* Mrs. Winston! She's higher level than even you!"

Strange that Miss Sarah had rung so early, Juliette felt, but she had discovered in the six months that she had been working in the Whitehall household that the only predictable aspect of Miss Sarah's personality was its unpredictability.

A few moments later, as she walked into Sarah's room and opened the curtains, she saw that she wasn't the only one who had awoken early. Sarah was already up, sitting at her dressing table and combing her hair. "I didn't want to wake you, Juliette, but I couldn't sleep any more, and I need your help with the dashed corset. How I wish no one had ever invented it. Surely it was a man, don't you think?"

"Without a doubt," Juliette said, taking a lace-trimmed corset out of one of Miss Sarah's drawers and laying it on the bed. "Did you want to wear morning dress or carriage dress, Miss—Sarah?" she asked, looking through the enormous closet that held only a portion of her mistress's clothes.

"Oh, you decide. Please. And forgive me for not asking about your mum, Juliette. Is she any better at all? Would you like me to send Dr. Robertson 'round to see her? I feel absolutely horrid that I didn't even think of her."

"Oh, she's—" Juliette hesitated, not knowing where

to begin. She knew that she wanted to tell Sarah and Caroline what she had found out about her origins. But when?

She looked into Sarah's eyes, expectant and curious and beautiful, and decided to take the plunge. "She's still very ill. I was wondering if I could advance my afternoon off so I might go back sooner than in a fortnight."

"Of course," Sarah said. "Just let me know when, and I'll make a point of telling my mother. I think even *she* will understand if your mum's as grave as you say."

"Yes. Well. It's rather a long story, if you have time. She *is* very grave, and—" She hesitated again, but knew that she had to go on. "It turns out that my mum—well, Harriet—isn't my mother at all. She raised me after my mother died. My mother was Kate Claypool, under house parlor maid in a house on Glendynn Place."

Sarah's hand flew to her mouth. "I don't believe it," she murmured. "What an enormous shock that must have been to you. And here all I could do was go on and on about Thomas Jameson."

Juliette couldn't help smiling for a moment. She knew she had to keep going, that she should reveal all she had learned to Sarah. Who knew where all this information would lead? And Sarah was an ally of hers; of that she was certain. "Yes. Well, there's more, actually."

Sarah's eyes lit up with their usual fire, and Juliette once again counted herself lucky almost beyond imagining that she had such a wonderful mistress.

"Actually," Juliette went on, "it turns out that my father is dead, that he died several years ago. He was a member of the Banford family—Sir Roger and Lady Edith's only child, William."

Sarah looked amazed. She smiled and sank back down onto the bed. "How perfectly—" Her eyes met Juliette's. "Are you absolutely sure of this?"

Juliette nodded. "My mum—Harriet—gave me a diary my mother wrote. She had asked Harriet not to give it to me until I turned twenty-five, but Harriet felt that since she's doing so poorly . . ."

"Does Sir Roger know about you? Do you know that he and my father are quite chummy? They're all members of the same rather small circle, and we've known them absolutely forever."

Juliette was shaking her head. "Apparently Sir Roger knew that a child had been born, but he didn't know my name or what happened to me."

Sarah narrowed her eyes. "I recall having heard something about William," she murmured. "He and his wife died of cholera when they went to India."

Juliette nodded. "That's what Harriet told me. But the Banfords completely forbade William to marry my mother. And he was a far weaker man than my mother had known, because he gave in to their demands."

Sarah shook her head. "Horrible," she said. "I *will* say about my parents that even though I sometimes think my mother would rather die than commit the tiniest faux pas, at least she would do the right and decent thing if I had a brother and he got one of the servants into that sort of trouble. At the very least, the child would be supported." She sighed. "I'm sorry to put it like that, Juliette, but you know what I mean."

Juliette did, though she didn't know that Sarah was correct in her estimation of what her mother might do in those circumstances. Juliette could just imagine how Lady Whitehall would react even if Juliette made her own news public at an "inappropriate" moment: Juliette would be out on the street in less time than it took to say "without a character."

Sarah turned to face her. "So when are you breaking the news to Sir Roger?" she asked. "Of course, I'm already thinking of myself and how dreadful it would be to lose you, but you must follow through with this, Juliette. Especially because your mum left you a diary. Does she say what she would have wanted for you?"

Juliette felt a rush of sadness—and guilt that she hadn't yet finished the diary her mother had written with obvious great care. But every sentence brought new emotions and more questions than Juliette could ever have imagined she would have about her own life. "I don't know what I'll do," she said honestly. "First finish the diary, obviously."

Sarah was suddenly smiling. "Do you know, I think the scandal of it all will kill Brenna Banford, your half-sister. She is as conventional as they come, and I think she'd rather die than admit the truth, if it came to that."

"If it were you in my place, what would you do?" Juliette asked. She thought of the days, all the weeks and months, when she didn't know where her next bite of food would come from; all the nights she'd had to sleep in din-filled rooms or worse, out on the street; the cold, late afternoons in the biting London wind, sweeping up the horse manure in the streets for people who looked down at her as if she were an insect; watching her beloved "sister," Grace, succumb to consumption; and she knew she would do anything to protect what she now had: a secure roof over her head, three delicious meals every day, a skill that could earn her enough always to get by—and to support her beloved Harriet now that she was ill. "I don't even know these people—"

"You will soon enough," Sarah cut in. "We always invite Sir Roger and his granddaughter to our autumn hunt at Hampshire, which is in less than a fortnight's time. By then, my dear, I'm sure you will have finished the diary, and perhaps let me read it as well, and we shall have our plans for revealing your surprising past thoroughly and quite perfectly laid out."

It was his last stop of the day, and Thomas felt like packing it in, going back to Gregory Chiswold's house and downing a couple of beers instead. Wasn't England supposed to be famous for its fine ales and fish and chips?

He didn't know what it was about the country—or maybe it was just London rather than England as a whole—but he just couldn't get used to it. He had never seen so many inhibited, self-conscious people in his life.

Or maybe it was just the prospects he had lined up to visit. It was a small group of people in London that Chiswold had told him about, and according to Chiswold, they were all friends. "It's the so-called upper, upper crust you're dealing with, Tommy, and you might save yourself some time and talk 'confidentially' about your shipping company to just one of them. By the end of the week, the whole group will know what you're proposing."

Thomas hadn't seriously considered Chiswold's half-joking suggestion, but now, as he knocked on yet another imposing-looking door of yet another imposing-looking house, he wondered if he should have. Supposedly the so-called master of the house, Sir Roger Banford, was quite good friends with the whole Whitehall family, and Thomas could have saved some time and aggravation by meeting just with Lord Whitehall and letting the "secret" details trickle out over the next few days.

Lord Whitehall's daughter, Miss whoever she was, was the one he would have liked to talk to, but he had the feeling women weren't involved in too many business decisions in England. Not that he had especially wanted to discuss business with her—but there was some mystery there, because she had said her name was Miss Juliette Whitehall, yet Lord Whitehall had said his daughter's name was Sarah.

*Leave it alone, and forget all your questions about her.*

He had come to England to gather investors, not to make love. And if he did become involved with Miss Sarah Whitehall, he'd lose out on Lord Whitehall as an investor, because the British, at least the upper-crusters he was dealing with, didn't take kindly to men like him giving their women the kind of attention he had in mind.

It wasn't only her looks that had made him notice her. He would have noticed her just for that, he knew—but when she had saved that little girl from the shopkeeper, he had been intrigued, whether the girl was really part of a social-welfare project or not.

*Forget about Miss Sarah Whitehall. You're too rough for her anyway.*

His existence had been the opposite of hers, and when his parents had died on their way to America when he was five, his life had changed even more.

He'd had to make his own way in the world from that day on, and he probably had as little in common with Miss Whitehall as a beggar had with a queen.

The door opened, and a butler who looked amazingly like every other butler he had seen that day—gray-haired, in his fifties, with a haughty, dour expression that made it clear he didn't appreciate Thomas's rough, windblown looks, said, "Good afternoon."

"Good afternoon. Thomas Jameson. Here to see Lord—Sir Roger Banford."

"Sir Roger is expecting you, Mr. Jameson," the butler said with a little bow. "Follow me, please."

Thomas felt he could have followed the butler with his eyes closed, because all the houses he had visited so far seemed to have been designed the same way. They crossed the foyer to the morning room, and the butler opened the door and announced that Thomas had arrived.

But when Thomas walked in, he saw not just Sir Roger Banford—a gray-haired man who was smoking a pipe and dressed quite differently from the other men Thomas had met, in a colorful tweed jacket and loose-fitting pants; but also, sitting down on a couch, a young woman who at that moment had her head bowed over a pad of some sort. To Thomas, it looked as if she was trying very hard to look casual and candid, as if she were concentrating so hard on whatever she was drawing or writing that she hadn't heard him come in.

But he could have been wrong, he realized, because when she did finally look up at him, she looked surprised, all the features of her pretty face shifting into a look of shock. She set her pad down, ran her hands through her hair, and stood.

"Brenna Banford," she said, extending her hand.

He had seen a lot of hands in his life, but never one that looked so . . . *unused* was the only word he could think of. Brenna Banford was a beauty, no question about it: pale blue, almost turquoise eyes; smooth, perfect skin; auburn, almost-red hair; and a body that would keep any red-blooded man awake at night.

But she looked as if she had been protected in a display case her whole life. Even when she spoke, he felt as if a doll were speaking to him.

"I had no idea my grandfather's guest would be so—" She shook her head. "I don't know where to begin. Young, for one thing."

Thomas had to laugh. "I'm thirty-five if I'm a day, Miss Banford."

"You don't look it," she said, circling him as if he were a trophy her grandfather had won in a hunting tournament.

"Brenna, you're being quite rude to our guest," Sir Roger scolded. "Where are your manners?"

"I apologize," Brenna said, sitting down again on the sofa and patting the spot next to her. "Do sit down, Mr. Jameson, please. It's just that my grandfather's guests, especially when it comes to business matters, are usually quite old and uninteresting."

Sir Roger laughed and shook his head again. "Maybe you'd better go finish your drawings somewhere else, Brenna. I imagine you'll be quite bored when we begin talking about Mr. Jameson's business."

"What sort of business are you involved in?" Brenna asked as Thomas sat down.

"Shipbuilding," he said.

Brenna shot her grandfather a look. "You know I love the ocean, Grandfather. How could you have

41

thought I wouldn't be interested in Mr. Jameson's proposals?"

"Interested or not, Brenna, I'd like you to give us some privacy. Now, take your sketchpad and leave us."

She sighed and picked up her pad, but not before Thomas had gotten a good look at it.

He had thought Brenna Banford might be a good artist—a lot of these young women were well-schooled in all the arts, Chiswold had told him, since they didn't have to learn any sort of practical or money-making skills.

But the drawing he glimpsed as Brenna stood up looked as if a child had done it. "I know better than to argue with my grandfather when it comes to business," she said, "but I do hope we'll meet again. I'd love to see one of your ships."

"I'm sure we could arrange that," he said. "And I can certainly show you some sketches of my ships sometime."

"I'd like that," she said.

Chiswold had told him some of the rules he had to know about—"I can tell you've broken rules all your life, so I'm not going to delude myself that you will actually follow most of them," he had said, "but there are some you simply can't break if you don't want to get run out of town."

His usual behavior with women, he knew, would never do. It was completely different here, Chiswold had said. A society woman's reputation could be ruined forever if she were even seen alone in a carriage with a man.

Now, Brenna Banford was giving him signals that in America would have meant just one thing.

But she wasn't his type, beautiful as she was. Something about those hands, maybe, or how . . . *idle* she was.

He had come to talk to her grandfather, anyway, someone who he hoped was going to be one of his most important investors.

*You're never going to be able to follow all of these English rules. Never in a million years.*

He presented the details of his proposal to Sir Roger and, surprisingly, found the man to be one of the more interesting people he had met so far in England. When he talked about the part of his company that was his passion—building yachts that would compete in the America's Cup races rather than the steamers, ferries, and schooners that were the more predictable part of the business—Sir Roger's eyes lit up with enthusiasm and understanding. "Of course, those must be your passion," he said, offering Thomas a brandy as he spoke. "I've seen them sail, and they're magnificent—absolutely magnificent. Any chance I've seen one of yours perform?"

"The *Artemis* was ours and the *Pisces* in Ninety-seven."

"Good God, man. That was a beauty. I'm not a sailing man, but I actually remember that one. Magnificent—absolutely magnificent." He looked at Thomas carefully. "And it's your company and yours alone?"

Thomas shook his head. "I have a partner," he said, still surprised at the words, even though he had made the deal more than a month earlier. He had sworn since the age of ten that he'd always work alone, so it still chafed at him to admit he had a partner. "Cyrus

Compton is his name. He's been in business since Sixty-nine."

Sir Roger nodded. He leaned back in his chair, drew on his pipe and gave Thomas another long, careful look. "Impressive," he said. "Still, you strike me as more of a loner. Not the partnering up sort."

Thomas had to laugh. "Now it's my turn to be impressed. You're the first person who's ever said that to me, and you're a hundred percent right."

"Then why the partnership, if you don't mind my asking? When I invest in a company, I don't tolerate mysteries."

"Understandable," Thomas said, nodding. "I've always worked on my own—and I never thought I'd buy into another company. But one of Compton Lines' builders was—is—one of my oldest friends, and that led to the partnership. I knew I could trust at least most of the employees—"

Sir Roger raised a brow. "Just most?"

"I never completely trust anyone other than myself and Hank," Thomas said truthfully. "You might as well know that right now. But it is a good group of workers, really the best group I've ever had. I treat them right, I pay them better than any other builder, and they're pretty much always at their best. And when I need them to work extra or around the clock, they do it."

Sir Roger drew on his pipe. "What type of schooners have you built?"

"Mostly centerboard steel-hulled," Thomas answered. He had the feeling Sir Roger knew more about ships and boats than anyone else he had spoken to so far. "I can show you some sketches and designs if you'd like to see them right now," Thomas said.

"Very much," Sir Roger answered, sounding so enthusiastic that Thomas felt he could probably count on his first British investor.

Sir Roger asked incisive, knowledgeable questions about the sketches, and Thomas was amazed that the man recognized almost all the innovations he and Hank had come up with.

When the meeting was over, Thomas took a cab back to Gregory Chiswold's house and felt he had finally had a good day here in England: He had met an intelligent, enthusiastic man he was almost certain would invest.

He saw that a cable had been dropped in the post box, and he wasn't surprised. He had been cabling every day since he had arrived with various questions about how things were going back at Compton and Jameson, but he had received either no response or vague ones to each cable he had sent.

He opened the cable and was about to pour himself a drink when he glanced at the first words—and then all thoughts of food or drink flew from his mind.

*Extremely urgent,* the cable read, and he skimmed to the bottom and saw that his faithful secretary, Enid, had signed it.

*So sorry, have been researching, hoping mistaken. Compton gone. We've discovered debts of several hundred thousand dollars so far. Wish were wrong, but financial disaster becoming clearer by hour. More tomorrow.*

He set down the cable and poured himself a tall drink. If Enid was right—and as far as he knew, Enid had never been wrong—his company, even with all the ships in inventory, was worth less than nothing.

Less than nothing. They were the words Kyle McClintick had screamed at him on his first night at the

McClinticks', when he was ten and Kyle's father had decided to give Thomas a home in exchange for work. "I hope you know you're not going to be part of this family, Tommy Jameson. You're a worker—less than nothing to us."

He picked up the cable again and read it one more time. Fool that he was, he still hoped he had missed something the first time he had read it.

But, of course, the words were the same. *Financial disaster becoming clearer by hour. More tomorrow.*

# Chapter Four

"If these problems continue, Caroline, Lady White-hall is going to axe you without a moment's thought to all your good years here. I shouldn't have to be telling you this, my dear," Mrs. Winston said.

Juliette ceased her scrubbing in order to hear the conversation better. She was in the ironing room next to the kitchen, trying to get mud stains out of the hem of one of Sarah's silk dresses by rubbing dried bread crumbs on it, but she dearly wanted to hear how her best friend was going to reply to Mrs. Winston.

"I know, Mrs. Winston," Caroline said quietly. "I promise it won't happen again."

"Leaving the linseed oil in the morning room, forgetting to polish the stairs?" Mrs. Winston cried out. "These are mistakes a girl would make in her first week—not after eight years."

"I know, Mrs. Winston. I do apologize. Truly."

There was silence, or as much of a silence as could exist in a kitchen that was almost always in use. In the background, Juliette could hear Rachel washing the dishes from breakfast; Grant, the footman, polishing boots and humming; and Mr. Blake berating Grant for "dilly-dallying" when there was so much work to be accomplished before the Hampton visit.

"You know, dear," Mrs. Winston said in a soft, motherly voice, "if there are troubles you want to discuss with me, I'm here to listen. I didn't get to be fifty-four years old without learning a few things about life, and if you have a sad tale to tell or questions—"

"I'm fine, thank you," Caroline answered quietly. "I've been distracted, Mrs. Winston, but it won't happen again. I promise."

A few minutes later, when Caroline passed Juliette as she headed for the morning room with her cleaning supplies, Juliette could see that Caroline was crying.

Folding Sarah's dress over her arm after she tossed the bread crumbs into the waste trough in the scullery, she headed up the stairs. She hung Sarah's dress in her own room so she could work on it more—the stains still weren't completely out—and then she found Caroline in the morning room, dusting and sobbing.

They talked every night before they went to sleep, so Caroline already knew about Juliette's "real" mother, and Juliette knew that Caroline had fallen in love with a man named Martin Capshaw, footman for a family who lived a few streets away. Was Martin the reason she was crying?

"Quick, before someone comes in, tell me what's wrong," Juliette said.

Caroline shook her head, her eyes squeezed shut

against tears that came anyway. "I'm such a fool," she muttered, opening her eyes and wiping them with the back of her hand. "Do you remember what Martin said the last time Lady Foxcroft came for tea?"

"He told you he loved you," Juliette said, her heart sinking. In truth, she didn't think she had ever seen any two people as in love as Caroline and Martin, and Caroline had seemed over the moon with happiness.

Caroline nodded. "He told me he was in love with me, that he was thinking of his future in an entirely different way because of me." Her lower lip began to quiver, and her beautiful skin, what Juliette thought of as the perfect peaches-and-cream complexion, was streaked with tears. "This morning he sent me a note—delivered by the milkman!—that said we needed to talk, but that he didn't know when it would be, and that we had to 'rethink' everything we had talked about. He said that if he was to keep his job, chances were good that we would have to 'end our relations,' which was something he didn't want, not at all, but that he couldn't afford to lose his job."

Juliette was stunned, though she knew she shouldn't have been: Most employers were quite picky indeed about the private lives of their servants. Some were realistic enough to permit "followers," though many didn't allow even that little bit of contact with the outside world; even those who did allow romance limited visits to certain times and places. And this wasn't much of a gift when you considered the fact that quite often, you would lose your job if your so-called follower ended up marrying you.

Caroline was shaking her head and trying not to cry. "I realize that Martin is in quite a visible position," she said. "As footman to the Foxcrofts, he couldn't hope to get another position in service if the Foxcrofts let him go without a character. But he could do something else, couldn't he? Learn a trade, go to America . . . I would do anything I had to in order to be with him."

Juliette thought about what she had seen of Martin so far: Every time he had even glanced at Caroline, it looked as if he felt she had hung the moon. At the time, Juliette could remember thinking she had never actually seen a man look at a woman that way; certainly no man had ever looked at *her* that way.

And now he was telling Caroline they had to end their relationship? If he indeed meant what he had written, Juliette was convinced it was only because he was desperate to keep his job; perhaps he truly needed every cent he earned to help his parents and sister, as Caroline had told her earlier.

She wondered, as she often had, if these masters and mistresses who made such rules for their servants had any idea how they were hurting them. Was it because they had never experienced that kind of love themselves? From what she had seen of Lady and Lord Whitehall's relationship, it seemed as if they were friendly enough but certainly not in love. Sarah yearned for the kind of love Caroline and Martin had, Juliette knew that for a fact because Sarah had told her as much. She had said that in her family's circle; one married for all sorts of reasons that had nothing to do with love, but that she was determined to be the first to break free of that trap.

"We'd better first see why Martin said what he did, Caroline. Maybe he wrote the letter because he felt he had to, but he's since changed his mind. He obviously—" She had been about to say that Martin obviously loved her when the door to the morning room opened, and Lady Whitehall walked in, followed by Sarah.

"Oh, good," Lady Whitehall said. "Caroline, tea will do for the moment, and see that the tea is hotter than it was yesterday."

"Of course, milady," Caroline said, moving past her silently and swiftly, as all the servants had learned to do with "their betters," no matter what their own moods or thoughts might have been.

"Mama, couldn't you see that Caroline was crying?" Sarah said. "Is she all right?" she asked, looking at Juliette.

"She'll be fine, Miss Sarah," Juliette said, knowing better than to discuss anyone's private affairs in front of Lady Whitehall.

Lady Whitehall shook her head. "She had better get over whatever is making her suffer before Friday night, or I'll have to speak with Mrs. Winston. I can't have the girl weeping into Lord Hargrove's soup."

"Oh, good Lord, Mama," Sarah cried, sounding furious. "Did it ever occur to you—"

"Enough, Sarah, and right now," Lady Whitehall snapped. "Stop this minute, or you'll be sorry indeed."

"But, Mama—"

Lady Whitehall rose from her chair, then must have remembered that a servant was still present. She sank slowly back down, glanced at Juliette and then looked at Sarah and said something in French.

"Oh, Mama, honestly," Sarah said, sounding annoyed. "But that does remind me: Juliette," she called out, "I thought you were taking the day off today."

"The afternoon off, Miss Sarah," Juliette said. "Not until two o'clock, as usual."

Lady Whitehall looked surprised that Juliette had dared to correct Sarah.

"Weren't you away Tuesday past?" she demanded.

"I *asked* you, Mother, and you said it would be no problem today," Sarah said quickly. "Remember that Juliette's mother is quite ill?"

"Ah, yes. Consumption, is it?"

"Yes, milady. At rather a serious stage, I'm afraid."

"What a shame your mother can't situate herself in the Mediterranean region for a short period. It did Lady Woolrich a world of good." She turned away from Juliette as if the matter were settled, then turned back abruptly. "Are we to receive our tea before nightfall, Juliette?" she asked sharply.

"I believe Caroline is bringing it, milady, but I'll go check right away."

She stepped out of the room and was just shutting the door when she heard Lady Whitehall say, "Honestly, Sarah, you're quite out of control—arguing with me in front of the servants. And Juliette's poor manners do not reflect well on you as her mistress."

Juliette couldn't hold the door open any longer without eavesdropping, so she shut it, wondering whether she was on the verge of losing yet another job, a job she truly wanted and needed to hold on to.

The rain had begun lightly when Juliette set out walking for the confectioner's shop. By the time she came out, having bought a quarter-pound of Harriet's treasured favorite, the gentle sprinkle had turned into a heavy, drenching downpour.

There was no question of turning back, Juliette knew. Every day that she saw Harriet was a gift, she felt, something not to be taken for granted. If she got drenched waiting for the omnibus, which she most surely would, well, what of it?

She bent her head down against the rain, tightened her bonnet and stepped outside.

But almost immediately, a parasol appeared over her head.

Juliette looked up to see who had stepped forward, and the moment she saw the man's strong, powerful frame, she knew: It was the American, Mr. Thomas Jameson.

"You're a determined, passionate chocolate lover, Miss Whitehall. I didn't really believe you'd keep to a schedule to satisfy your need for chocolate, but I'm glad I took the chance."

She had forgotten how handsome he was—well, not really forgotten, but she had forced it from her mind, assuming she would never see him again. His eyes, dark in a tanned, wind-blown face, had a knowing, penetrating quality that took her breath away. And she knew she was crazy for imagining it, but when she looked at his mouth, she couldn't help wondering how his lips would feel on hers.

"I try to keep to a schedule to visit my . . . friend," she said. "She's quite ill, and on my day—" She had been about to say "on my day off," but something had stopped her.

She knew it was absurd—for one thing, she wasn't ashamed in the least about being a maid; for another, what difference did it make what this stranger thought about her? But she felt it was simply easier to leave the truth alone for a bit. He apparently thought she was Miss Whitehall, and as far as Juliette could see, it was easier not to correct the man's impressions; she didn't need to explain herself to someone she would probably never see again.

"On whatever days I can spare the time, I like to go see her," she finally said.

She saw a flash of intelligence and challenge in those dark brown eyes, at once soft and sharply observant. "Surely you could have picked a more appealing day, Miss Whitehall. But maybe your schedule is as busy as mine." He held out his arm. "Please. Let me take you wherever you're going in my cab. There's no reason for you to get drenched."

She looked down at his arm and felt color rush to her face.

She knew it was absurd: All he had done was offer his arm. But something about it—the fact that she knew how strong it would feel, and warm, and firmly muscled—made a river of warmth rush through her body.

When she looked up at the American, she could feel that her cheeks were hot. An amused look came into his eyes.

He smiled. "Now don't tell me I'm breaking yet another rule just by offering you a ride in this damned pelting rain."

Suddenly his arms were around her and he was leading her—almost pushing her—toward his carriage. "Do you know what I've discovered about your English rules, Miss Whitehall? They don't mean anything to me. Now get in before you catch your death of cold!"

His arms were around her waist, his warm, strong hands nearly burning through the fabric, and Juliette couldn't believe that her feet even knew what to do as she stepped up into the carriage, too dazed and self-conscious and . . . *something* to argue with the American.

He stepped up and seated himself next to her as if he had known her his whole life. "I take it I'm breaking another rule," he muttered, turning toward her.

Juliette opened her mouth, but no words came out. He had seated himself as close as he could to her without having her sit in his lap or vice versa, and she could feel his thigh against hers, his hip against hers, could nearly feel the movement of his chest as he breathed in and out. "I—" she began, knowing she had to say something. "Well, yes, of course you're breaking a rule. That does seem to be your specialty, from what I can gather."

His mouth curved up in a half smile. "Let's see. I should have seated both of us facing backwards."

She shook her head and smiled. "Close, but that's not it."

From his expression, she could tell he was enjoying the question-and-answer period. "Hmm. First tell me where I'm taking you, so I can direct the driver and we can be on our way."

Juliette told him Harriet's address, he spoke to the driver, and as the carriage lurched to a start, Thomas Jameson held up his finger as if a brilliant idea had just struck him. "I believe I have the answer, Miss Whitehall. I shouldn't have asked you to sit facing north on an odd-numbered day of the month."

Juliette laughed. "Now you're just being silly, Mr. Jameson. No, you certainly broke all sorts of rules from the moment we met in the street. But the biggest one, I would say—" She stopped, suddenly feeling she was about to tread on dangerous ground. She felt his thigh against hers, warm and hard, and when she looked into his eyes, she felt her breath catch and then disappear.

"The biggest one—" he prompted.

She knew she had to go on, or her dangerous ground would become even more dangerous. "The biggest one is that a gentleman should never seat himself like this beside a lady," she said. "Unless, of course, they are married or engaged to be married."

At this, Thomas Jameson smiled, then grinned, then burst out laughing. When he stopped, he shook his head. "No wonder I'm meant to live in America. What is the thinking behind all these rules? That if I sit next to you, with my leg against yours, I'll get ideas that a gentleman shouldn't have about a lady?"

"I—I suppose so, yes," she said, feeling as if she had forgotten how to speak.

Thomas Jameson laughed again. "I hate to tell the purveyor of all of these rules, but I've had those 'improper' thoughts about you from the moment I saw you in the shop last week. I could be in Australia and I'd have those thoughts about you."

The American's words took Juliette's breath away. She felt a silken, languid heat forming deep inside, a delicious warmth tingling from her loins all the way down to her toes.

She tried to think how she would have reacted if she were truly Miss Whitehall instead of Juliette Garrison, but she was convinced, though she didn't know why, that almost any lady would have felt what she was feeling at that moment.

She didn't know Thomas Jameson, only that he was wealthy and American and one of the handsomest men she had ever seen. He was deeply masculine and strong-looking and somehow . . . well, rather animal-like. And she knew, instinctively, that when he talked about having ideas that a gentleman shouldn't have about a lady, almost any woman in the world would feel what she did right then: breathless, pulsing with a desire she would have loved to let him satisfy.

*He thinks you're Miss Whitehall,* Juliette told herself, trying to cool her thoughts and her body.

*He's flirting with you because he has no idea who you truly are.*

She realized, at some level, that these thoughts were probably true, and she knew that it was way past time to tell him who she really was.

But at some other level, when she looked into those deep, dark eyes and caught a whiff of his scent, she just wanted to make these moments last, because they would probably never happen again. No one had ever looked at her the way Thomas Jameson was looking at her right then.

"What about you, Miss Whitehall?" he asked softly. "Do you think sitting this close leads to improper thoughts?" Thomas Jameson asked, his voice rough and low.

"Really, Mr. Jameson—"

"By the way, how did you know my name?" he asked. "Since I broke yet another rule by not introducing myself."

"Isn't it obvious?" she asked. "You *did* go see my father at his club, did you not?" *Oh, are you in deep water,* she warned herself. And now, she knew, would be a good time to tell him the truth. But she would look like such a fool if she did, or at the very least a liar, when truly she had never set out to lie at all. And what was the point of telling the truth now, she asked herself, if she was probably never going to see him again?

*Change the subject!* an inner voice cried, and Juliette looked out the window of the carriage, scanning desperately for an interesting sight to point out. "Oh, dear," she said. "Your driver should have turned back there," she semi-lied. "Although the next right would lead to East Hanford Street as well, I think."

Thomas Jameson looked at Juliette with an intensity that was even greater than before. "Good. Then that will make for a longer ride," he said softly, apparently not caring whether she arrived at Harriet's or not. "I have the feeling, Miss Whitehall, that your life is filled with far more mysteries than you can share with me. But now that we're nearly at your destination, don't think you'll escape without telling me at least one thing about your life."

"One thing?" she asked, amazed she could even find her voice or speak words that were intelligible.

"Anything you'd like to tell me about your life, other than—let's see, other than the fact that you love dark chocolate with nuts, and that you're in charge of a social-welfare project for children, and that you have a friend you like to visit even on stormy days when most women of your class wouldn't dream of venturing outside. . . ." His voice trailed off. "Now it's your turn," he said softly.

*You're Sarah or Juliette or Someone Whitehall, she told herself. You're a member of one of the wealthiest families in all of England, and you—*

"I love the theatre," she blurted out, for Miss Sarah certainly did, and even Lady Whitehall did as long as she wasn't forced to attend anything other than the opera (everything else being "hopelessly vulgar").

He tilted his head. "Then the theatre it is. You tell me what night you're free and what you'd like to see—choose anything at all, I haven't ever seen a play in England. I'll get the tickets and pick you up."

Juliette had to laugh. "You would have to get a ticket for my chaperone as well, Mr. Jameson. I can't go to the theatre with you alone."

He looked amazed, and then angry. "Do you know how much I wish I had met you in America?" he asked.

The carriage came to a halt, and Juliette realized they had reached Harriet's address.

"I must go," she said, gathering her things. At least the rain had stopped, so chances were good that Thomas Jameson wouldn't feel obligated to walk her to the house. "And please, Mr. Jameson, for reasons I can't go into, I *must* ask you to keep this . . . this meeting just between us. I must ask you not to tell my father that I left the house once again by myself, and please don't attempt to contact me."

The American's eyes glinted. "A woman with secrets," he murmured. "Very, very appealing. Very intriguing. But if you think you can get me to promise not to contact you—"

"I'm counting on it," Juliette said, opening the door of the carriage, jumping out and then turning to face Thomas Jameson. "Please, Mr. Jameson. Respect my wishes," she said, and she turned and ran.

A few moments later, she began walking up the long flight of dingy stairs that led to Harriet's rooms. What a different world this was from the one she lived in day to day, and how different from the world Thomas Jameson thought she was part of.

*You should have told him the truth,* an inner voice scolded.

59

She knew that the voice was correct: She had resisted because it had been fun, for one thing, just to pretend for a bit, and then it had seemed almost too late to suddenly say, "Oh, by the way, I'm actually Miss Sarah Whitehall's *maid*. It's just a minor detail, I know, but one I thought you might like to know."

But it probably didn't matter one way or the other. If he had business to conduct with Lord Whitehall, he would meet with him at his club, and she would probably see him again only in her dreams.

# Chapter Five

*Dear diary,*

Juliette read, a subtle pain gnawing at her insides. She had felt it earlier when she and Harriet had talked about her real mother this afternoon, and now, looking at her mother's handwriting, so oddly like her own, she felt it more strongly.

*I have been missing William since he went to India, more than I would have ever imagined. I would love him if he were working the land or running an inn or doing something quite different, instead of being the son of one of London's wealthiest bankers. He says he is determined to marry me when he returns from India, and then we might both be working the land or running an inn or doing something quite different, penniless but happy with each other!*

*I guess there is a part of me that still doesn't believe it, partly because our relationship has been conducted entirely in secret. But in his letters, William has promised his love for me dozens of times over, and swears he cares nothing for what his family will think.*

*Diary, I hope in the end I'm not proven a fool. But this is where we are today, on a beautiful day in June, 1876."*

Juliette set the diary down and thought about what Harriet had told her. Things had ended so sadly for her mother, yet, because she'd had Juliette and had been able to keep her, her heart had been, as Harriet had put it, "wounded but not broken. She loved you to the skies, dearie, though she became bitter as a root about men. But then, who could blame her for that?"

Harriet had then looked at Juliette in that long, careful, motherly way that had usually preceded some sort of lecture. She had stayed true to her pattern that afternoon, even ailing as much as she was. "You're the picture of your mother sometimes, Juliette. And that can lead to trouble of the worst kind. Don't you get trapped by troubles of the heart the way your mum did."

Juliette had smiled and tried to laugh off Harriet's probing stare.

"I can see you already have some sort of secret," Harriet had said, still giving Juliette a long, careful stare.

"Believe me," Juliette had said, "I don't have any secrets, Mum. Believe me," she had repeated. Because even though thoughts of the American had kept her tossing and turning at night, she certainly wasn't foolish enough to think he would end up as any sort of secret in her life.

The bell to Sarah's room rang, and Juliette put the diary back in her drawer and went downstairs to see what her mistress wanted.

As soon as she walked in the door, she could see that Sarah had been crying. She knew that Sarah wanted to be treated as a friend, that she genuinely valued Juliette's opinions. But Juliette didn't think she could go put her arm around her the way she would have done with Caroline or Harriet.

"Is everything all right?" she asked as Sarah, still in her bed but sitting up against the beautiful silk-covered headboard, wiped at some new tears.

"I'm so mad I could scream," Sarah said, swinging her legs down to the floor and standing up. "Honestly, Juliette, sometimes I'm just tempted to get up and walk out of this house and never come back."

"What happened?" Juliette asked as Sarah sat at the dressing table. It had become a pleasant routine with them. She and Sarah had some of their best conversations when she was brushing Sarah's hair or helping her get dressed.

"Oh, it's Mama again. Of course," she said with feeling. "First off, she can't seem to stop perseverating about Caroline and her 'inappropriate behavior,' as she puts it. Apparently Caroline was 'still sniffling,' as my mother said, during dinner last night, and Mama said if Caroline falls apart one more time during a meal, she'll be out the door."

Juliette shook her head. "I shall have to speak with Caroline."

"Please," Sarah said. "I will too, but maybe she'll

listen better to you. I wish I didn't have to say anything because I'm actually ashamed to have to do it, but I don't want to see Caroline lose her job."

"Of course not," Juliette said.

"And then there's me, and the argument I'll never win unless I do leave home," she said, sighing. "Do you remember Gavin Hamilton, the gentleman who came to dinner the other night with the Foxcrofts?"

Juliette nodded. He had been extremely handsome and, Juliette had thought, rather charming. "He's quite good looking," she said.

"Yes, without a doubt," Sarah said. "But that, my dear, is where his appeal ends for me. He's quite good looking, and he knows it, and he expects women to fall at his feet when he walks into a room because of those looks and the fact that he's one of the wealthiest men in London. And even though I made it clear to Mama that he's completely unappealing to me, she's still trying to match me up with him with all her considerable talents in that area."

"Do you know him at all?" Juliette asked. "Maybe he's a better person than you think."

"He's probably far worse," Sarah snapped. "And whose side are you on, anyway?" she asked with a half smile.

"It just seems a waste, all those good looks," Juliette said, laughing. She thought of the American, Thomas Jameson; he was undoubtedly the handsomest man she had ever seen. And no doubt he was as full of himself as this Gavin Hamilton was, supremely aware of his effect on every woman who was lucky enough, as he was sure to express it, to cross his path.

"Well, then, *you* go to the theatre with him," Sarah

said. She turned around to face Juliette. "Have you decided yet how you're going to approach Sir Roger?"

"I don't know that I will," Juliette said.

"Oh, come," Sarah said, standing up. She opened her armoire and began searching through her clothes. "Are you saying that you're actually considering not telling anyone other than me? Have you told any of the servants, by the way?"

"Just Caroline," Juliette answered, "and she's sworn to secrecy. Not Mrs. Winston," she went on with a laugh.

"That would be a sight worth seeing. She's a good person deep down, I think, but God help the poor servant who doesn't hop to it within a millisecond of one of her orders." Her face lit up. "You must promise me I can be there when you tell her, Juliette."

"I'll do no such thing," Juliette said, trying to imagine any other mistress to whom she could say such words. "And as I said, I still haven't decided."

"Whenever you're ready, I can discuss it with Papa, you know. He'll be much more clear-thinking and less . . . hysterical than my mother will be."

"And I'll be out of a position, Sarah. You know that."

"I don't completely know it," Sarah said. "I think Mama could be reasoned with if my father were in on it." She turned and looked into Juliette's eyes. "But . . . not to be too personal, but with all your skills and talents, if the so-called worst came to pass and Mama did sack you, would that truly be so terrible? Of course for my sake, I hope you stay with me forever—I'll quite need you when I'm fat and unmarried and trying to fit into a gigantic corset. But we both know you won't be with me forever, and you could go back to working in a factory or with a dressmaker if you chose to."

Juliette raised a brow. "If I chose to make no money to speak of after paying all my living expenses," Juliette said. "Harriet and her friends manage to get by if all goes well, but look at Harriet now, while she's unable to work. If it weren't for me, she would have nothing. And that's after a lifetime of skilled work. She would do better at a dressmaker's, but I think she'd run into the same problems I usually ran into—she's too outspoken and too independent. When I worked for Madame Dupont in Essex Street, she told me right before she sacked me that I had a better eye for clothes and a finer stitch than any girl who had ever worked for her, but that she'd rather hire a clumsy-fingered, completely inexperienced man than have to listen to my 'saucy tongue,' as she put it, for even one half hour more."

Sarah laughed. "Well, her loss and my gain, so I should be grateful for that. And I am. But if you do want me to talk to Papa, I think now would be a better time rather than at Hampton."

"I can't rush it, Sarah. Perhaps next week . . ."

"Have it your way, Miss Stubborn as a Mule. But keep in mind that you might be quite distracted yourself at Hampton."

"Well, I know it's a different atmosphere, of course, and you'll be changing your outfits at least three times a day, from what I've heard—"

Now Sarah was laughing. "You don't honestly think I'm going to be a slave to that ridiculous custom, do you? You'll have a bit more free time than the other maids, Juliette, because I'd rather be a peasant than change my clothes as many times as my mother."

Juliette smiled, knowing that Sarah was not quite as independent as she would have liked to think. Though she prided herself on having her own principles and standing up for them at every opportunity, she was also no one's fool: Juliette had seen Sarah compromise when she found that giving up her noble principles led to her receiving what she wanted. She had no doubt that when they were actually at Hampton, Sarah would do what her mother expected.

"You'll have some free time, but you'll have plenty on your mind," Sarah said, her eyes gleaming. She looked like a mischievous child at that moment.

"I would imagine," Juliette began.

Sarah was shaking her head. "I don't think you can," she murmured. "The American is going to be one of Papa's guests."

"So Enid was right," Thomas said to Gregory Chiswold as Chiswold packed his valise. Thomas knew that Chiswold was different from most English aristocrats—he had almost no servants, and he liked to do things for himself, by himself, without acting as if he couldn't tie his own shoes.

And he could also be trusted to give good advice. "So then you're quite without funds?"

Thomas still didn't even know the full extent of his debts, but the situation was completely different from the one he had thought he was in when he had arrived in England.

He wondered how he could have been so wrong.

Granted, he hadn't been looking to go into partnership with anyone, but Hank had insisted it was the right move.

Could Hank, his oldest and closest friend, have known that Cyrus Compton was not to be trusted?

The truth was that since Quentin McClintick had died, Thomas had trusted no one; he had been a loner since the age of ten, and it had felt right.

But he had trusted Hank, and instinct now told him Hank had been as ignorant of what had been going on at Compton and Jameson as he had been.

"All I know is that it's bad," Thomas said.

"Which you will tell no one, of course," Chiswold said, closing his valise.

"I don't know what I'm going to say. This is the part of being in business that makes me remember why I never went into business with anyone before. I'm a shipbuilder; I could build an America's Cup yacht with my eyes closed. Dealing with all of these people, figuring out what the hell to say about my partner—" He shook his head. "Truthfully, I'd walk right away from the company and go out on my own again, but all my men are counting on me."

He thought about Hank, between Boston and Madrid at that moment, and how disgusted he would be when he found out about Compton—and how he would feel responsible for putting his two friends together. But Thomas had walked into the deal with Compton with open eyes. It was his own fault he had gone against his principles and taken a partner.

So here he was, probably penniless, having already presented himself to half a dozen members of this upper-crust clique, and about to present himself to a dozen more at the Whitehalls' country estate, Hampton.

He had been surprised that Lord Whitehall had invited him, and Lord Whitehall had apparently sensed his surprise. "One of my hobbies is introducing foreigners to some of our customs," he had said, "and I daresay you've never been invited to a hunt week, so why don't you come on board with us, so to speak? You can meet far more prospective investors—good ones—than you would on your own."

Thomas had said yes immediately, partly because he liked the idea of meeting so many prospects at once, partly because Lord Whitehall had already told him Sir Roger would be there, and Thomas had enjoyed Sir Roger's company enormously.

But mostly he had agreed because Lord Whitehall had said that his family would be there too—and that meant that Thomas would get to see the young Miss Whitehall again.

*He was more of a brother to Quentin McClintick than Quentin's own brothers were, and Thomas, even though he was only ten, knew this as well as he knew his own name. He knew that when Quentin, who was also ten but couldn't speak, needed something, he gave a signal to Thomas. And if Thomas guessed wrong, at least they laughed about it afterwards.*

*Quentin's brother Kyle was fourteen, and Richie was fifteen, and to Thomas, they seemed like men. All four boys were supposed to help their father, Mike, who worked at building wooden boats from early in the morning until late at night. The boys sawed wood all day some days, and other days moved logs, and other days pounded nails into the boards until they couldn't hear and their hands were numb.*

*Richie and Kyle complained a lot, but Thomas kept his mouth shut. The only reason he was living with the McClinticks was because he was a worker—Mike McClintick had watched him work for days down on the docks. If Thomas didn't work, he wouldn't have a reason to sleep in the McClinticks' house or to eat their food.*

*But today was different; today was Sunday, and even Mike McClintick, the hardest-working man Thomas had ever seen, rested on Sundays.*

*Thomas liked the Sundays when he and Quentin could go off together by themselves. They'd walk down to the docks and see what floated the best of the objects they had picked up on the way, or they'd walk out to Connor Street Park to look at the dogs people had.*

*But today, all four boys were together, and already Thomas didn't like it. Kyle and Richie seemed to be mad at both of them for some reason, and Thomas wished Mike hadn't said they all had to stick together.*

*"It's all your fault," Richie said, shoving Quentin.*

*Quentin tried to look defiant—Thomas always knew he was mad when he squinted his eyes and jutted out his chin.*

*"Chicken," Richie taunted.*

*"Just leave him alone," Kyle said. "Let's just live with it; it's only for the morning. Who wants to go to the docks?"*

*Nobody said anything, but they all began walking in that direction, so Thomas knew it was agreed.*

*The docks were deserted at that time of the morning, and Thomas realized he felt happy to be there.*

*The sun looked all shiny and low on the water, and Quentin's face was lit up as it was only sometimes, when his brothers were actually being nice to him.*

*"Look at that rig over there," Kyle said. "That wasn't there yesterday."*

*"It's Dobson's," Thomas said. "He brought it in yesterday right before dark."*

*"It's taller than anything in the harbor," Richie said. "I can't believe Dobson has the tallest rig here."*

*"Imagine jumping off that into the water," Kyle said. "You'd have to be braver than brave." He looked at Quentin. "Are you that brave?"*

*Quentin looked scared. Thomas knew he wasn't used to having his brothers talk to him unless they were teasing him. According to them, their mother favored him something fierce, and he was used to being bottom dog with the other two.*

*Suddenly Quentin nodded, and pointed to his chest with his thumb.*

*"Don't be crazy," Thomas said. "You don't even like to climb Mike's ladders."*

*Quentin shook his head and pounded his chest.*

*"You're not that good a swimmer," Thomas said. "No one is, Quentin. Those waters are rough."*

*"Why don't you shut up?" Kyle said. "If he wants to do it, let him do it."*

*"Then you do it first," Thomas said. "I know you can't."*

*"Why don't you mind your own business, stupid? Who do you think you are to come into this family and try to boss us around?"*

*"Your father's the boss of the family," Thomas said, suddenly feeling as if he could hardly breathe. "You can't tell anyone else what to do."*

*"Why, you scheming, filthy orphan,"* Kyle said. *"I'll show you what I can do."*

*Thomas had always thought of himself as a street fighter—he'd had to take care of himself for five years, and his strong fists and lack of fear had made him a good fighter. But Kyle was four years older than he was, bigger and stronger and faster. He grabbed Thomas and pinned his arms behind his back, and no matter how hard he struggled, he could feel he wasn't going to be able to break free.*

*"I know you can do it,"* Kyle called out to Quentin. *"Your loyal 'friend' here doesn't think you can, but I know you can. Just show us. And I'll let Tommy go."*

*"Quentin, no!"* Thomas shouted.

*But Quentin had put on his serious face, and Thomas knew what that meant. He was going to show Kyle and Richie he could do something hard, and this once, he was going to be a hero for Tommy instead of the other way around.*

*He began climbing the rig, and he climbed it faster than Thomas had thought he could—probably because he wanted to get the whole thing over with, Thomas realized.*

*Up at the top, he clung to the wood, and Thomas had the feeling he would chicken out and climb down. Quentin hated heights, and he wasn't that strong a swimmer.*

*"Kyle, you'd better tell him that's enough,"* Richie said. *"I will if you won't. He can't swim that well."*

*But with a sound—it sounded almost like a baby crying—Quentin jumped.*

*Thomas shoved at Kyle and broke free, then ran to the dock.*

*He had seen where Quentin had landed—there*

*were still huge waves—and he waited to see Quentin's head or maybe an arm or a leg.*

*But there was nothing.*

*"Guys, come help!" he called out.*

*Kyle and Richie had come running.*

*"I'm going in. You tell me if you see him," he said, and he jumped.*

*The water was so cold, he felt as if it had stopped his heart for a minute. He held his breath and plunged his head down, but all he saw was darkness.*

*"Do you see anything?" he yelled when he came up for air.*

*Kyle and Richie both looked scared.*

*He plunged his head in again and saw nothing but blackness. He felt himself start to cry, and he came up for air. He looked around for Kyle and Richie, but they were gone.*

*He didn't know how long he stayed in the water, but when he climbed out, he knew that his friend was dead, and he was crying like a baby.*

*He didn't know how long it took him to walk home, back to the McClinticks', but it felt like forever, because everything had changed in that same huge way it had after his parents had died.*

*When he reached the house, he saw Kyle and Richie's shoes, so he knew they were home. He opened the door and right away saw Glenda sobbing at the kitchen table. The boys were nowhere to be seen.*

*Mike had been sitting down comforting his wife, but when he saw Thomas, he stood up.*

*"Get out," he said. "Take your things and go and don't ever come back."*

*Glenda raised her head—her face was covered with tears, streaked red with misery. "I knew Mike never*

73

*should have trusted you," she said. "I knew it, and now we've lost our boy."*

*"I tried to save him," Thomas said. "Kyle and Richie were the ones who dared him."*

*"Oh, they said you'd try to wiggle out of it," Glenda hissed. Her face and voice were so twisted by pain and rage that Thomas knew there was no sense arguing; she believed that he, rather than her own sons, had tricked her favorite boy into doing something crazy because she needed to believe it. And even in his ten-year-old's heart, he understood.*

*He looked at Mike, and he had the feeling Mike knew the truth. What he saw in his eyes was love, and that he felt sorry for Thomas.*

*But he didn't open his mouth until he said, "Do what she says, Tommy."*

Thomas woke up drenched in sweat, and for a second, he didn't know where he was.

Usually, after dreaming about that day, he could feel good about what he had done with his life. The sea had taken the people he had loved most in his life, but it had also given him his passion. It had drawn him in and taught him well, and he could always think about all the ships he had built and the wealth he had gathered, what he had learned to share with the sea, his mysterious, huge partner.

But now he thought about what he had learned about Compton and Jameson; he had been pulled back to the starting gate. He must begin all over again, from nothing, and he had the feeling it was going to be even more difficult this time.

# Chapter Six

"You'd do best to understand your time here will be busier than at Epping Place, Juliette," Mrs. Winston was saying as the carriage pulled in to a long, tree-lined road that looked as if it belonged in a fairy tale. After the discreet, easy-to-miss wooden sign that said *Hampton*, they had turned onto a road that was covered by a living arbor made up of thick hedges and equally thick, mysterious-looking vines. "Many a young girl has met her downfall at places just like this," Mrs. Winston went on, "thinking she's far enough from the real world that nothing bad can happen to her."

Juliette let Mrs. Winston prattle on about the dangers of nature and isolation, only half-listening as they rode up the path to one of the most beautiful places she had ever seen in her life.

The ride out from London had been spectacular in

and of itself—lush, rolling countryside, undulating meadows and colorful hedgerows, rushing brooks and all manner of animals dotting a countryside that truly looked like a page torn from a child's book. True, she had only once before in her life left London, when she and Harriet and some friends had taken a trip to Brighton, but she knew that this part of England, these lands owned by the wealthiest of the empire's aristocrats, were undoubtedly among the world's most beautiful.

". . . And that goes doubly for girls like Caroline, whose heads are turned by every handsome young man that stops at Epping Place."

Juliette was about to defend Caroline, whom she knew had been in love with Martin for almost two years, but Mrs. Winston went on. "And you mind that you don't put on airs with any of the guests, Juliette Garrison. When Miss Sarah was a young lass and she snuck out to go fishing with her governess, and that governess, I think her name was Gillian, had specifically been instructed to keep Miss Sarah clean, the woman was out the door before the sun set. And it didn't matter one whit that Miss Sarah cried a river of tears. Do you understand me?"

"Yes, Mrs. Winston," Juliette said, knowing it made more sense to continue agreeing with Mrs. Winston— forever, if necessary—rather than speak her mind. Mrs. Winston had been with the Whitehall family for so long that Juliette had the feeling she probably held at least as much influence as Miss Sarah did, if not more, when it came to hiring and firing.

Mrs. Winston looked as if she were struggling with herself over her next words. "I just feel I have to give you some friendly advice that you'll quite likely need, given that you've got a fetching way about you when you're not in an argument. More than one servant has been dismissed by Lady Whitehall after hanky panky and all manner of goings on. And don't forget you must be at your most conventional and proper. Never speak out of turn and don't be seen by the guests if you can possibly help it. And just between you and me—" she began, but apparently realized, as the carriage came to a stop, that there would be no more privacy for whatever confidential words she was about to offer. Grant, the Whitehalls' footman, who had been riding in the front of the carriage with the coachman, had already opened the carriage doors and was holding out his arm to help Mrs. Winston disembark.

Juliette wished that she owned the photographic equipment a man had brought to the National Gallery one day last year, when he had taken pictures for the *Illustrated London News* of the crowds at the museum.

"I wish I could take a picture of this so I can remember it forever," Caroline murmured.

"Oh, there'll be a photographer by and by," Mrs. Winston said. "The Whitehalls commemorate the occasion every year. They even take pictures of the servants!"

"I'd like to have a picture of this house," Juliette said, "and the gardens and all the grounds. I don't need a picture of our miscellaneous crew, nor of anyone else's!"

Mrs. Winston shook her head. "Now, there you go again, my dear, trying to rise above your station in life. There's nothing wrong with owning a picture of yourself with your coworkers on a special trip—"

"And there's nothing wrong with owning a picture

of a beautiful house, Mrs. Winston. I shall make it my business to get one for myself."

Half smiling but harrumphing at the same time, Mrs. Winston shook her head again. "No one could ever accuse you of neglecting your own interests, my dear. Well, give it a try and now be on your best behavior and look sharp—I see some guests are already arriving."

Most of the servants at Epping Place had come earlier to help the Hampton servants ready the house, and Juliette saw that other carriages were arriving behind them, apparently bringing members of the Whitehall family and some early guests.

Juliette saw a familiar-looking couple emerge from one carriage, and she was surprised they had arrived so early: Lady Florence Cornelian and Lord Charles Cornelian. She was a nice enough acquaintance of Lady Whitehall's, and he, from what Juliette had seen, a loud-voiced, grabby boor. He was the kind of man who always made Juliette question how anyone could call him "Lord" anything, unless it was to call him Lord Admirer of His Own Personality.

She gripped her suitcase tightly, wanting to get settled in as quickly as she could so she could begin getting her and Miss Sarah's rooms ready. She began walking more quickly than she wanted to, following Mrs. Winston, who had already muttered, "Now, follow me, dear. You don't want to be using the front door. Come with Grant and me and keep your head down, dearie, and do all that I do as you enter Hampton House."

Juliette sighed, wanting desperately to look around and take in every detail of this truly amazing place. The path on which they were walking, made of some sort of white stone, glittered in the rays of the sun, and Juliette suddenly smelled lavender as strongly as if she were breathing in a sachet. The whole path, she realized, was lined with stone urns of the lovely gray-blue plant that was so headily fragrant. Beyond the path, the formal garden, arranged in an elaborate pattern made by boxwood and yew plants, made Juliette want to race down each path and smell each urn of flowers and touch each artfully designed fountain and bench.

"You'll mind what I say, Juliette, or you'll be out on your ear, pet of Miss Sarah's or no."

"Yes, Mrs. Winston—" she said.

But her gaze had strayed. She had looked at the coming carriages and the guests who were emerging, and she had stopped unconsciously to see who was getting out of the carriage that had just arrived.

She knew—even when she could see only his hands, then his arms—who it was. She would have known that strength anywhere; there was something about him that was completely absent from the men who came to Epping Place.

The American had arrived, with his strong-looking arms and dark, dreamy eyes and voice that tormented her even in her sleep.

*Look away!* she told herself, because here she was, carrying a valise and heading to the servants' door—not, she knew, that she would be able to fool the American forever. She had never meant to fool him, to lie. But now that she had, she wanted to prolong the ruse, for reasons she couldn't explain even to herself.

*Maybe because of the way he looked at you,* an inner voice said. *Maybe because of how you felt when he said you were pretty and that the sun made your hair look like spun gold.*

*Maybe because you want to feel those things again.*

*No,* she told herself.

She wasn't going to put herself in that position. Mrs. Winston had warned her about the girls "what got themselves into trouble" on outings like this. Juliette had seen hundreds on the streets of London who had started out in good jobs, ended up "in trouble" because of the master's son or a drunken guest, and out on the street they had been thrown, into the workhouse, a life of prostitution, or both.

And what about her own mother, who had felt certain she was loved by a man who had ended up turning on her right when she had needed him most?

She would stick with her dreams and mind her own business. And if she did cross paths with the American, well, she would simply maintain her distance.

Oh, who was she fooling, anyway? The American probably had grand plans with half a dozen beautiful ladies, liaisons and meetings, hunts and dinners and teas.

Before following Mrs. Winston into the servants' entrance, a beautiful stone-and-wood doorway framed by purple-flowering vines, Juliette allowed herself one last look at the American.

He was standing by yet another carriage that had arrived, this one evidently having brought a man, whose back was turned to Juliette, and a woman, who was talking animatedly to the American. Juliette couldn't see much—only that the woman was young, very pretty and well dressed, and seemed to know the American quite well.

And she shook her head at her earlier folly as she

walked in through the servants' door, wondering how a maid entering the grand estate owned by her mistress's family could have entertained such outlandish thoughts for even a moment.

"It simply won't do!" Juliette heard a woman say. Juliette was in Sarah's dressing room, unpacking her mistress's clothes, and Sarah and a friend had apparently just come in to Sarah's bedroom. "I said to Grandfather, what am I supposed to do without a lady's maid for an entire week? Grandfather said Charlotte *claims* she's ill, but that he also thinks Charlotte's in love and wants to stay back in London to be with some man— can you imagine? The poor girl is at *least* thirty-two years old if she's a day; I don't know *whom* she could possibly have in mind. But Grandfather said he saw her looking all dreamy-eyed at a tradesman last week. And now here *I* am. But the surprise will be on her when she finds herself out of a job next week."

"I thought you liked Charlotte," Juliette heard Sarah say. "Just last month, I think, you said she was the best dressmaker to ever walk through your doorway."

"Well, she may *be,* Sarah, but she isn't much use to me if I'm out here without a maid, and she's in town, now is she?"

"But she might indeed be ill, Brenna," Sarah said. "And if she is, I certainly don't want her here. She's better off by herself, I daresay, resting. And we're better off without her."

Brenna. So the woman who was complaining was none other than Brenna Banford. It was a strange thought—extremely strange, Juliette felt, thinking that in the very next room was the half-sister she had never met.

"Good Lord, Sarah, you sound just like Grandfather. It was his idea to let Charlotte stay back in London. But *he* isn't the one without a servant, is he? I daresay I shall manage on my own at night, but who's going to help me with my grooming and my clothes? I certainly shan't be able to do my hair the way I'd like, nor look the way I'm accustomed to when I dress for dinner or even for tea—all because of a lovesick little maid."

There was a silence, and Juliette thought in those moments that if Sarah offered her services to Brenna, it would be the first time in the Whitehall household that she felt a sense of humiliation, and anger at Sarah that she wouldn't be able to forgive.

But Sarah wasn't going to let her down, she discovered, for her mistress said, after a very long pause, "I'll talk to Mama about your predicament and see what she can do. Miss Porter, my mother's lady's maid, is a bit too old-fashioned for you, I fear, and in any case, I'm quite sure Mama would be completely unwilling to share her. And I wouldn't part with Juliette for even a second. But we've brought more staff than we usually do for the coming weeks. Perhaps you could have Caroline, our head house parlor maid."

*Not Caroline,* Juliette thought. The poor girl was having a hard enough time already.

"But does she know anything about clothes or hair? Of course, she'll know how to clean my room and empty the slops, but any maid would do for those things."

There was another long silence. When Sarah finally spoke, Juliette was surprised at the undisguised anger in her mistress's voice. "You're welcome to try to find someone else, Brenna," she said in a clipped tone that sounded more like that of Lady Whitehall. "As you know. But if not, then I daresay you'll use whomever we can find for you and be grateful for their services."

"I suppose," Brenna said, sounding uncertain. "Truthfully, I feel as if I can't even think straight. The American—Mr. Thomas Jameson—has made me positively mindless."

Sarah laughed. "You scoundrel, Brenna. Aren't you engaged?"

"Well, in a manner of speaking," Brenna said after a pause. "But it's really a marriage of convenience. Randall's my cousin, you know, and since he is part of Grandfather's various businesses, lending and so forth, it makes sense to both of us to keep everything in the family."

"I'm surprised at you," Sarah said, sounding almost angry. "You're not even being steered the way I am, and you're throwing away your freedom."

"There's a lot to be said for financial security, Sarah. And anyway, who knows? If the American is interested in me . . . Have you met him yet?"

"I haven't had the pleasure. But I've heard—" She stopped, and Juliette realized that she'd stopped working. If Sarah or Brenna Banford happened to peek through the doorway to the dressing room, it would be completely obvious that she had been eavesdropping for the entire conversation.

"What have you heard?" Brenna asked, her voice coming closer to the connecting doorway. "I'm dying to know what people think of him. He's positively . . . I wouldn't say handsome, actually. More . . . magnificent. That's the best word I can think of to describe him—"

With a crash, Juliette knocked over a china water pitcher. She thought she had been standing stock-still, but she supposed that when she had heard Brenna Banford describe the American as "magnificent," her body had reacted.

*As your body reacts every time you're with the man who indeed can only be described as magnificent.*

"What on earth—" said Brenna Banford.

Juliette had stooped to begin collecting the shards. When she looked up, Sarah and Brenna Banford were looking down at her from the doorway. Brenna was the pretty woman she had seen outside in the entry road, and now she was looking down at Juliette and laughing with undisguised condescension, as if she were watching a foolish child.

She shook her head and walked back to Sarah's room. "Servants!" she said with another laugh. "I sometimes wonder how they get anything done without our guidance."

"Did you not just finish saying you wouldn't be able to get through a day without one?" Sarah asked sharply.

"Yes, yes, of course," Brenna said. "But imagine if they had to live on their own. If they weren't taught what to do."

"I do believe, Brenna, that I should reconsider my offer to lend you one of our servants. You're a guest in this house and I consider you a friend, but I have to think of the feelings of my servants as well—"

"But I didn't mean it," Brenna said. "Rather, I did, but I didn't. Oh, *you* know what I mean, Sarah dear!"

"I'm afraid I don't," Sarah replied, again in that clipped tone that was so reminiscent of her mother's. "But I suppose we can give it a try. And if it doesn't work out—for Caroline as well as for you—then you shall be quite on your own."

There was a silence, but Juliette could hear rustling, and she guessed Brenna was giving her mistress a stiff, oh-so-aristocratic hug. "Thank you," Brenna murmured. "I'll be ever so grateful. And ever so nice to this . . . whatever her name is."

"You *are* incorrigible," Sarah said. "Now let me speak with Mama, and if all is well, I shall send someone to help you unpack."

"Thank you—again," Brenna said. "And I shall keep my promise to you, Sarah. I'll do virtually anything if it means having assistance this week."

Sarah laughed. "And that even includes being civil to a servant? This shall indeed be worth witnessing," she said, as Juliette heard the door to Sarah's room open and then shut.


Juliette had read this part before, but after hearing Brenna's voice—her half-sister's voice, the voice of a person whose existence she had never even suspected—she felt the need to visit their strangely shared past again for just a few minutes.

*Dear Diary,* she read. *Well, William came back from India and was true to what he had promised after I wrote that we were expecting a child.*

*I had feared the worst but had forged ahead and written him—I needed to share this momentous news.*

*"And, diary, he truly seems delighted. He took me in his arms and said he shall tell his parents tonight. No matter what Sir Roger and Lady Edith say, we shall run off together, if nec-*

*essary, and have a delightfully large family. And he gave me the most beautiful necklace I have ever seen—India sapphires, he said, a symbol of our future together.*

*He is so different from his mother that sometimes I find myself not quite believing him, but he did seem truly happy to see me on his return.*

There was a space, with a smudged, crossed-out line of writing, and then the next entry, which Juliette could remember knowing was going to be bad when she had read it for the very first time because of the way her mother's normally beautiful handwriting had changed.

*"Oh, how very wrong I was about everything. I'm so heartbroken I haven't even wanted to write in you, diary.*

*I was serving at dinner a few nights ago and Miss Hazel Crichton was the guest. I knew from before William went to India that she was sweet on him. She and William seemed to be quite the couple during dinner, and when I found him afterwards—which was quite a difficult feat in itself—and asked him about it, he laughed nervously and said his mother is pushing him to marry Miss Crichton. He promised me he wouldn't dream of it, but there seemed to be something different in his eyes.*

*"Have you told your parents about us?" I asked, thinking I already knew the answer. If he had, I would certainly have seen a change in their reactions to me.*

*"In time, darling," he said. "I have to choose the right moment."*

*Well, tonight at dinner, Lady Edith mentioned plans for "the wedding," and it became clear she was talking about William and Miss Hazel Crichton. I can remember looking across at William—I was holding a platter of peas in cream sauce—and he looked away from me. He actually looked away from me, and in that moment I knew, although I still hoped I was wrong—don't ask me why.*

*Do you know that later on, I decided to knock on William's door—I estimated I had nothing to lose at that point—and I think he was actually hoping I would go away. When he finally opened it, there were tears in his eyes. "I'm so sorry," he said. "I hope you know I do love you—more than I can say."*

*I was so stunned, all I could do, fool that I am, was run back to my room. There is so much I would like to say now, but I know there would be no point.*

Juliette set the diary down and hid it back among her clothes.

So the father she and Brenna shared had been a coward at best, an uncaring liar at worst.

And now, she wasn't yet sure to what extent, she would come to know the half-sister she had never guessed she had.

Juliette hoped she was headed for the sewing room, which she knew was well below stairs, along with the wine cellar, the root cellar, and the pantry.

But was it through the door she had just passed, or was she to descend another level? Mrs. Winston had told her that the downstairs was quite large, with various cellars and rooms a story below the kitchen.

Doubling back and folding Sarah's dress more carefully over her arm, she ascended the stairs and turned the crystal doorknob.

Hmm. Now she was faced with two other crystal-knobbed doors—one in front of her and one to her right.

She opened the one to her right and found herself, surprisingly, in a large room that seemed to be a sitting room but also some sort of storage area. There were big trunks, with lids that were closed, and tall, precarious-looking stacks of linens. So she was probably, she imagined, on the correct level. She carefully shut the door and opened the other one, and found herself, this time very surprisingly, in what clearly was the main entrance hall to Hampton.

*Wonderful,* she thought. She would have to learn the design of this magnificent mansion much better if she wasn't going to lose her job. It simply wouldn't do, as Lady Whitehall would put it, for Juliette to barge in on Lord and Lady Whitehall or their guests because she thought she was heading for the sewing room.

She was just turning to retreat into the stairwell when she felt a presence—later, thinking back, she would remember that she had felt the American's presence as clearly as if he had called out to her.

And then, in fact, he did call out to her. "Miss Whitehall!" he said as she stepped toward the door.

She turned.

When she turned and first saw the American, she realized that even though she had thought she remembered how handsome Thomas Jameson was, especially when Brenna Banford had described him, the truth was that she had forgotten. There was something about the way his dark hair hung over his forehead and his mustache grazed his full mouth, how his features were strong and bold, yet his eyes seemed to look right through you. . . .

Juliette realized she didn't even know how long she had been staring at Thomas Jameson, only that her mouth was hanging open and she probably looked like a dog waiting for a treat. "Oh," she finally said, trying to pull herself together physically and mentally. "Mr. Jameson. How nice."

He closed the distance between them in less than a moment, took her hand and kissed it.

He looked into her eyes then, and Juliette thought she would melt. She wanted to touch the spot on her hand that his lips had touched, and she realized that meant she was crazy, that this . . . this attraction was even deeper than she had imagined.

"I have our tickets," he murmured.

Tickets? she wondered, looking around and wondering what tickets he was talking about.

His mouth was curved up in a handsome half smile. "I reckoned that if you're not free on the nineteenth, I'll convince you it will be worth your while to break your other engagement."

At this, Juliette had to laugh as she remembered Mr. Jameson's promise of theatre tickets. No, she wasn't free, but certainly not for the reason he thought!

She knew that danger was just around the corner—a member of the Whitehall family or a guest.

But she couldn't resist playing along—*just one more time,* she told herself—because even though Thomas Jameson thought she was Lord Whitehall's

daughter, the look in his eyes, an obvious apprecia-
tion of her appearance, made her feel deliciously
weak in the knees.

"I think that after the theatre, Lady Whitehall, I'll
kidnap you and take you out on one of my ships—
you'd look just right up on a deck with the wind
blowing in your hair." He reached out and brushed
the hair back from her face, and the heat of his hand,
and his nearness, and the look in his eyes took her
breath away. "And I just might not bring you back to
your family," he murmured.

She let herself imagine—she couldn't have fought
the thought even if she had wanted to—how it would
feel to be kidnapped by this man, held prisoner by
arms that were no doubt as strong as steel, hands
that could be rough yet tender, lips that looked so
kissable she could almost feel the sensation at that
very moment.

She felt a warmth and a rush of desire between her
legs that nearly buckled her knees.

And as if he knew, as if he could feel what she was
feeling, he reached out and steadied her, touching
her hip with a hand whose firmness she needed,
though she had never been touched by any other in
quite that way.

"You look as if you like the idea as much as I do,
Miss Whitehall," he said, his voice raspy with desire.
"Do you know that I was kept up half the night with
thoughts of you?"

"I—" she began.

The front door flew open and Mr. Blake, the butler,
stood glaring at Juliette as if she had been caught
standing naked in the front entryway for all the world
to gawk at.

"I do believe you've lost your way, Juliette," he said quietly but firmly. "The sewing room is one story further down, through that door right there."

Juliette opened her mouth and closed it without a word. Then she swept past the two men, murmured, "Thank you, Mr. Blake," and quickly descended the stairs, feeling more the fool with every step she took.

# Chapter Seven

"She doesn't want to do it," Juliette said to Sarah, combing her hair out with long, soft strokes. "She was very upset, nearly in tears at the first mention of it."

Sarah shook her head. "I can't think of anyone else unless it would be you, but I wouldn't do that to you or to myself. I understand that Sir Roger has promised that Charlotte, Brenna's lady's maid, will arrive by coach tomorrow evening at the very latest, so it would only be for a short while. And Brenna isn't all that bad if you don't take her too seriously. She means less than half of what she says."

Juliette looked into the mirror at Sarah's eyes. "In other words, you're not actually presenting Caroline with a choice."

Sarah's features, always quite beautiful in Juliette's estimation, shifted and softened. "Juliette. Please. I hardly think I've been unfair—ever—to you or to Caroline. This is one task that will last less than two days' time. I would have thought Caroline might even find it interesting, and that she would be relieved not to be performing her usual tasks."

"Then you would have thought wrong. Caroline knows her duties as well as you know your piano and singing and French. She isn't comfortable with helping Brenna Banford, and I don't think you should force her to do it."

Sarah stood up and headed for the door. "Then I think you should adjust your thinking, Juliette, because it's going to happen whether you like it or not, unless you'd like to see Caorline lose her job. When these hunt weeks don't go smoothly, there's hell to pay from all sides, and I won't be the cause of a problem that shouldn't exist in the first place. So you can tell Caroline, if you don't want *me* to tell Caroline, that she must do it or leave our employ without a character reference. And those are positively my last words on the subject. Do I make myself clear?"

Juliette was stunned. She had known, of course, that she was a maid and that Sarah was her mistress. But she had always thought they were friends as well, that she could speak honestly to Sarah and that Sarah would listen and respect her concerns.

"Yes, Miss Sarah," she said, unable to stop herself from putting special emphasis on the "Miss." "You've made yourself more than clear. Now, if you don't need me any more this afternoon, I'll go check your ribbons on the line outside. If I have your permission, of course, Miss Sarah."

"Are you being sarcastic with me?" Sarah asked, her voice sharp.

"Of course not, Miss Sarah," Juliette answered, still

unable to believe how her relationship with Sarah had gone so askew.

"Juliette, listen to me," Sarah said. "I *am* sorry. I shouldn't have spoken to you like that. But there are things about—well, about how these grand hunt weeks work and families like mine operate in the world that you probably don't yet understand. I *am* sorry, but I do need Caroline to perform this one extra duty."

Juliette could see there was no point in trying to press the issue any further; Sarah obviously wasn't going to budge. It was clear she was sorry for her autocratic words; regret filled her eyes and her voice.

But the incident had made Juliette's position in the world that much clearer, illustrating something she often forgot because of her mistress's unusually generous and open nature: Juliette was a servant, in the home of people rich enough to buy all the dreams of every servant who worked for them. Yes, Sarah was by far the most caring and generous mistress Juliette had known, but she was still her mistress, and Juliette was still a servant, employed to do whatever the Whitehalls wanted. She was not Sarah's friend, whether or not Sarah enjoyed pretending otherwise.

The realization reminded her of a moment earlier in the day when she had watched the photographer the Whitehalls hired every year to commemorate the week. Nearly every guest's picture was taken either individually or in small groups—evidently the photographer usually tried to supply the region's newspaper with pictures of famous guests at Hampton. But when it came time for a picture of the staff, all the local and visiting servants were grouped together. They were not thought of as individuals with their own hopes and dreams.

Juliette had accepted Mrs. Winston's scoldings: "There isn't nobody going to be interested in a picture of a scullery maid, Juliette, and you know that as well as I do. But when the Prince of Wales himself visited—well, now, even you would have to admit that that was what they call newsworthy, my dear."

Now, Juliette walked down the back stairs and out into a narrow hallway, hoping she wouldn't commit another breach of etiquette and end up where she didn't belong. As she walked, she thought of her beloved Harriet and how even when they hadn't known where their next meal was coming from, there had been love in whatever rooms they had been in and caring for each other and for those around them. She did like the Whitehalls, and certainly they were so much fairer and more generous than most other families in their circle. But she just couldn't feel the way Mrs. Winston did, that "them upstairs" were her "betters."

"Not to put too fine a point on it," she heard Mrs. Winston say as she walked through the busy kitchen, "but do you know where you're heading, Juliette? Miss Sarah's trimmings are doing quite fine on the line, if you're wanting to check them."

"I did want to check them," she said, "and then to gather some mint for Miss Sarah's hair wash. I understand the herb garden isn't too far from the lines."

Mrs. Winston made a face. "Depends what a body means by 'not too far,' I daresay. You'd want to have your wits about you and not interrupt any of the guests, nor venture out there after dark."

"I'll be careful, Mrs. Winston. Do you need anything for the kitchen while I'm there?"

Mrs. Winston made a face. "I do my picking at dawn, child, and you'll want to learn to do the same soon enough, so as not to disturb none of the guests. Be quick about you, and come back along the outer paths."

Juliette nodded and moved past Rachel, the kitchen maid, who was scrubbing the floor with a mixture of turpentine and clay. "Good morning, Rachel," she said as she passed, and the girl's face lit up as if she had been given an armload of chocolate. Rachel had been assigned extra duties since arriving at Hampton, fixing up some of the guests' rooms with the two local housemaids, and she looked exhausted.

"Morning," she said softly. She looked briefly at Juliette, and Juliette knew that beneath the work-reddened face and grease-laden hair, Rachel was a pretty girl, with beautiful, long-lashed hazel eyes and a soft-featured, lovely face. Would she spend the rest of her life as a kitchen maid, or, after a series of promotions, work herself up to the position of cook or housekeeper, but always in service? Or would she fall in love with a tradesman and settle happily somewhere out in farm country?

Outside, Juliette thought about how girls like Rachel, who probably came from countryside just like this, were pretty much confined to the house during visits to Hampton. How unfair and unjust that Rachel would be limited to the back stairs and the kitchen and the occasional upstairs bedroom when she was so temptingly close to an outdoors that was no doubt part of her deepest nature.

For her part, Juliette felt she was London-born and

London-bred inside and out, and just smelling the light, flowery-fresh air and seeing the huge sweeps of perfectly green lawns and manicured gardens made her feel as if she had found a new passion. How could a girl like Rachel come here and stop herself from just running outside and rolling in the grass?

In an area that was completely closed off by tall hedges, Juliette checked Sarah's silk ribbons, which were hanging on the drying line. She had mixed gin, honey and soap to wash the delicate trimmings of Sarah's bonnet, and they would look lovely and fresh when they were dry—but not yet. She glanced at Lady Whitehall's lace collar, which was pinned on the line next to Juliette's washing projects. She wouldn't have dreamed of touching it, since Miss Porter would have thrown a fit, but she could see that it would need more sun before the stain was gone.

She walked out past the formal gardens, wishing she could follow all the paths in the labyrinth of yews and boxwood. Maybe tomorrow morning she would get up even earlier than she had to. Certainly none of the guests would be up, and she could explore to her heart's content.

She saw what had to be the herb garden up ahead, another arrangement of formal beds lined by tall shrubs that created a natural fence. Mrs. Winston had told her it had been one of Lord Whitehall's father's favorite gardens, and he had always prided himself on the fact that no manmade materials marred its natural beauty.

Juliette squeezed between two tall yews and entered a place that could only be described as magical. She didn't know the names of all the herbs—she had never seen anything like this in her life—but she recognized thyme and mint growing between flat stones and edging many of the paths, and huge plants of lavender and rosemary potted in stone urns. The silvery grays and deep lush greens, set against the beautiful gray stone walls, urns and paths, were spectacular.

"Amazing, isn't it?" came a low voice from behind her.

Juliette jumped and turned.

She had known whose voice it was; for as long as she lived, she knew she would never forget that low, smooth voice that reached her somewhere deep inside.

But even though she recognized that the voice belonged to Thomas Jameson, she was still surprised. How had he known she was here, and exactly when had he followed her?

"Oh," she said. "It's you." She couldn't help remembering what he had said to her what now felt like a lifetime ago, that he would like to kidnap her and take her out on the high seas and never bring her back.

What a fool she had been to lead him on. Somehow, she had let her heart soften toward this handsome stranger; she had let herself believe the fantasies, had dreamt of them and been kept up at night by them. And now, she had to stand here, trapped in a garden she would forever associate with humiliation and the embarrassment that came from a stupid mistake she had made and then even more foolishly maintained.

"What's wrong?" he asked, moving close to her—so close she could smell his scent, so close she could feel the heat of his body in front of hers.

She knew that she was forever done trying to fool this man, because it had led to nothing but trouble.

"Isn't it obvious?" she asked. "If you've come out here to gloat over the fact that I'm a maid rather than a member of the Whitehall family, you might as well save your energy, Mr. Jameson. I did what I did for reasons that have nothing to do with you, and now the sham is over. I would only ask, once again, that you keep what happened to yourself. If Lady Whitehall finds out—"

"Hush," he whispered, putting a finger against her mouth.

In that moment, she felt as if she never wanted to move again. She felt as if the earth had dropped out from beneath her feet, as if her heart were racing so fast it would burst out of her chest, as if she would melt between her legs if he touched her for even one more second.

He moved his hand away and instead drew her toward him, his warm, strong hands holding her tightly at the waist. She could feel his body in a way she had never—ever—felt a man's body before, and now she truly was in danger of melting.

"Why on earth do you think I would say anything to anyone about what we have together?" he murmured.

"What we have together?" she asked, her voice a half squeak.

He leaned down and brushed his lips against hers, then drew back and looked at her with eyes that had already hypnotized her. "I told you I haven't stopped thinking about you since that day I first saw you," he murmured. "Do you really think it matters to me whether you're Miss Whitehall or a housemaid?"

"I'm not a housemaid—" she began.

He pressed his mouth over hers, drew her in tightly against his body, then parted her lips with his. He slid his tongue in slowly at first, teasingly, and then he kissed her more deeply. She heard herself moan.

She knew she would never be able to think clearly as long as she was in this man's arms, and she knew she was already in way over her head. What was she doing, making love with a stranger in the middle of her ladyship's herb garden? Was she *trying* to lose her position on her first day at Hampton?

She pushed at Mr. Thomas Jameson's chest, which felt powerful and broad and warm beneath her fingers.

Surprisingly, he moved back as if she had burned him. "What's wrong?" he asked.

It took a moment for her to gather her wits. Even though she had wanted to push Mr. Jameson away, of course at some level she hadn't wanted that at all, and now, she felt bereft, as if she were missing a part of herself.

But she had to remember who she was, and where she was, and that mistakes like the kind she was tempted to make could cost a young woman everything.

She suddenly realized, as her mind was beginning to clear, that Mr. Jameson seemed quite forward—quite forward indeed—now that he knew she wasn't a member of the nobility. When he had thought she was Miss Whitehall, had he grabbed her and kissed her?

"I have no intention of being sacked because you've lost a few hours of sleep," she said. "Did you think it was fine and dandy to pull me into your arms because I'm a servant, but not when you thought I was Miss Whitehall?"

Thomas Jameson began to laugh. He laughed, and as he laughed, Juliette grew angrier and angrier. Did he think she was a fool as well as being fair game?

Suddenly he stopped laughing, and his eyes were

dark and serious and full of feeling. "Wild horses couldn't have kept me from pulling you into my arms, Juliette." He reached out and cupped her face in a hand. "Tell me you didn't feel that."

"Feel what?" she asked, her heart racing.

"What's between us. What could be between us if we let it happen."

"We won't, Mr. Jameson, I can assure you," she said, tearing herself away and then walking off. She hurried down the pebbled path, lined with pots of lavender on one side and tall, headily fragrant pots of rosemary on the other, and wished desperately that she could focus.

Mint was what she had come for. Mint, which was at the other end of the garden, but rosemary would do as well, and of course lavender; she could mix them with olive oil and nutmeg to help thicken Sarah's hair, and use the lavender and rosemary for the final rinse as well. She took out her scissors and snipped off huge hunks of each, knowing she was cutting too drastically from the plants but unable to concentrate. What had the book said? Cut so it didn't look as if you had cut the plant at all. Well, she hadn't followed *those* instructions well, but it was too late.

"Juliette," he said softly.

She turned.

"Do you believe in fate?" he asked. "Most women I've known believe in it without question."

She thought of the mysteries in her own life, how strange and disquieting it was that she hadn't even known who her true mother had been, how this very week she was staying in the same house as her half-sister and her grandfather. Surely fate had to have been involved somehow.

And why did Thomas Jameson, a man whose presence had struck her like a thunderbolt that very first day she had met him, keep reappearing in her life, even though she had done her best to avoid him?

She looked up into those dark, thick-lashed eyes and knew that for some reason, she was destined—or more likely damned—to tell this man the truth from now on; certainly lying had only gotten her into trouble.

"I suppose I do," she said softly.

He raised a brow. "I know *I* do," he said. "I'm not fool enough to believe I got where I am today on my own strengths. Any man who doesn't give luck its due is a fool, I always say." He drew a long, slow, deep breath, taking her in from head to toe with a fiery gaze that made Juliette feel as if he were touching her with warm, hungry fingers. "Don't ever let anyone tell you we weren't meant to meet, Juliette." He came forward and enveloped her waist in his hands. "If you can convince me you feel nothing for me, I'll leave you to your rules. You tell me you don't want more. I know I won't sleep until I've tasted every inch of your body. Now say you don't feel the same way."

She was too aware of the heat coming from her own body and from his to speak. She was too caught by a warmth and a need that pushed aside all the rules she had been brought up with, all the carefully laid out plans she had made for her life.

Oh, this man was truly magnificent. She could feel his hard length against her, insistent that she tell the truth. She could smell a scent that spoke deeply to her, see lips whose sweet softness she yearned to taste again.

She would have to tell him, once again, to leave her alone.

"I don't know how I feel," she whispered instead.

"I do," he murmured, and he closed his lips over hers.

Juliette gave herself up to the kiss for a few moments—*just a few seconds more,* she told herself again and again.

Finally she broke away, breathless and needy, shaken and confused.

This was crazy. Thomas Jameson was a guest of the Whitehalls, a man she barely knew; it couldn't go on, and it wouldn't go on.

She quickly cut off another handful of lavender, silently apologizing to the helpless plant for her roughness. She could hardly think, and her hands were shaking.

She looked back at Mr. Jameson, who was smiling—no, laughing at her, actually—and then she hurried out of the garden, furious she had let herself talk to the American even once.

# Chapter Eight

"They're your betters, Rachel, and if they say the plate is dirty, Lord help you for the rest of your life," Mrs. Winston was saying. "Why can't I get it through that pretty little head of yours that you must do your best every moment of the day, whether I'm hanging 'round your shoulder or not?"

"Do you really think I'm pretty?" Rachel softly asked Juliette.

"Now, Rachel, is that what I've been berating you about for the past fifteen minutes?"

Juliette ran a hand across Rachel's cap and down her hair, which was a rich-looking, lustrous reddish brown. "You're positively beautiful, Rachel, and if you were upstairs, dressed in upstairs finery, you'd have every man in the house wanting to pursue you."

Rachel's creamy-white skin darkened as if someone

had splashed rose-colored ink across her cheeks. "Thank you, Miss Garrison. Do you really think so?"

"I know so, my dear. And pardon me for disagreeing, Mrs. Winston, but don't you think the idea that the people upstairs are 'our betters' is just a bit antiquated? And actually completely wrong?"

Mrs. Winston shook her head, looking as if she were about to scream. "What I think, Juliette, is that someone has put ideas into your head that will end up leading you to doom and downfall. And here I thought you had been so well-raised. Properlike, with all them sewing skills and fine ways. But you're lacking a good and proper dose of humility, my dear."

Juliette smiled, knowing there was no sense arguing with Mrs. Winston over an issue like whether people such as the Whitehalls were "their betters" or not. But with Rachel, there was a chance to open the girl's eyes before she ended up a lonely spinster with no prospects other than a continued life of solitary service. "Yes, Miss Winston," she murmured, leaving the kitchen and heading upstairs with Sarah's silk tea gown, which was now free of grease spots thanks to the secret concoction Mrs. Winston had told Juliette about, fuller's earth mixed with fowl's dung, vinegar, and onion juice.

Juliette thought about how she had broken away from Thomas Jameson, and she still couldn't believe she had managed, couldn't believe the words he had said to her. Did he truly believe that fate had brought them together? Or were those simply the words of a man who was clearly accustomed to getting his way with women, whether they were members of the nobility or in service or anywhere in between?

She thought about her mother's diary, the excitement Kate Claypool had felt over William Banford's feelings for her, their apparently passionate affair, and then all that had followed, and knew that she certainly didn't want to go down the road her mother had taken.

But would she even have the chance, if she had wanted it? Or was Mr. Jameson simply a hopeless, shameless flirt, one of those men who used his considerable charms on every woman who happened along, then waited to see who responded?

When she entered Sarah's room, she found her mistress already half dressed for dinner—though her corset and blouse were still unfastened—and sitting at the dressing table with her combs and brushes neatly laid out in a row.

"Well?" Sarah asked, turning and smiling at Juliette as she walked in and closed the door. "Do you approve?"

"Of what, Miss Sarah?" Juliette asked. She still felt wary after their last conversation, her feelings about Sarah dramatically and perhaps permanently altered.

"Oh, would you please stop with the 'Miss Sarahs'? I apologized, didn't I? And I meant it. I *am* sorry, Juliette. You can't expect me to forget completely all the things my mother has told me, can you? If I had my way, I'd be out in the world, earning my own money and making my own decisions every minute of the day. I can't make such a sea change overnight, but this is a start, wouldn't you say? I'm *nearly* dressed, and I could do my own hair if I wanted."

Juliette laughed. "I thought you *did* want to. Let's see what you can do, then."

She was surprised to see Sarah's cheeks actually

the truth is going to make me unhireable, it's hardly worth it; it doesn't achieve anything good at all."

"It *would* put you in rather a peculiar position," Sarah agreed. "And it isn't as if you would be guaranteed any sort of inheritance whatsoever from Sir Roger." Her eyes flashed. "But think of the drama! Sir Roger *is* your grandfather, after all, and by all accounts wealthier than half the so-called earls and marquesses who think they're better than he is because their blood is even bluer."

"It still won't bring any good to anyone, will it?" Juliette argued. "I don't know *what* I want to do; I only know that I don't simply want to blurt out the facts as if I expect Sir Roger to hand me something. But then when I think of doing nothing, there's something deep inside me that balks at that idea as well. My mother wanted me to know my history, and she was definitely wronged by that family, in my mind."

"I believe she was, as well," Sarah said. "And I believe it's a wrong that should be corrected."

Juliette had to laugh. "And I believe, dear Sarah, that you're relishing the idea of scandal and drama for the mere sake of those two things. I won't make a hasty decision about something that might change my life forever."

Sarah stood and gave Juliette a little hug. "You're so right, of course. As usual. Do you know, sometimes I wonder how you've acquired all these perfectly useful skills and talents and insights with virtually no education to speak of, while I, having been sent nearly around the world for *my* schooling, seem to have none of the skills I truly need."

Juliette was about to say that she had received more formal education than Sarah thought. She had been sent to dame school when she was little, and she and Harriet and Grace had read stories and periodicals to one another nearly every night by what little light they could find, usually candlelight. Tired as they had been, the stories had taken them to other lands and other times, if only for a few minutes each night, and they had treasured them all. Once again, as so often happened, Sarah was thinking narrowly as she'd been taught all her life. Juliette was in service; therefore she was virtually uneducated. Yet it wasn't worth explaining; it was just another example of how there would always be an unbridgeable gap between the two women.

These stairs, Juliette thought, would be the death of someone someday, what with their steep pitch and their dark, sudden turns. It reminded her of a flat where she had lived in London with Harriet and seven other people, cramped and dark and constantly damp. She wondered, feeling a tightness in her chest at the thought, whether Harriet had even made it through all these days since Juliette had last seen her. She was a determined, strong woman, but how many other people, with wealth and the finest of doctors, had succumbed to that terrible disease?

*But at least if I were rich I could send her somewhere warm,* Juliette thought. The wealthy did indeed fare better in that regard.

*Someday, when I have my own dress shop,* she thought as she opened the door to the second floor, where most of the grander bedrooms were, *I shall send Harriet to the famous Mediterranean.* But would Harriet still be alive?

"No, sir! Please!" she suddenly heard. It was a

small, frightened young voice she knew was Rachel's, coming from one of the bedrooms.

"Shh. Now stop your complaining and lie back and enjoy what so many before you have said is one of the finest swords in the land."

"No, sir, please. I truly am not interested. I've never—"

"Shut your mouth unless you plan on using it on me, missy. Now lie back here, and I'll close the door, and we'll have a wonderful time while the rest of the house is downstairs playing those pointless games."

Juliette thought briefly of all she was about to give up—if Lord Cornelian told some sort of lie about her, she would be out the door by morning, no doubt. But Rachel! There was no way in the world she would let that poor girl succumb to Lord Cornelian's disgusting advances.

The bedroom door began to shut, and Juliette raced ahead and shoved it open. It must have banged into Lord Cornelian, because Juliette felt it hit something, and she saw that Rachel, her cheeks flushed and her eyes dark with fear, was standing back by the bed.

"What the devil—?" cried Lord Cornelian. His eyes were blazing and his normally ruddy cheeks were nearly purple. "What the devil are you doing? You'll leave my room at once, or I'll have you dismissed on the spot."

"Then go ahead," Juliette said. "Summon Lord Whitehall if you wish. Please. In fact, I could go get Lady Whitehall, or Miss Sarah if you'd like, or all three of them if you prefer."

Lord Cornelian opened his mouth to say something, but then he evidently saw someone behind Juliette, and his whole demeanor changed. He drew himself up and faced Rachel. "As I said, miss, the room lacks so many things, you're lucky Lady Cornelian hasn't complained to the Whitehalls. But you'll see that the problems are corrected at once, will you not?"

Rachel fled from the room, running past Juliette and out to the stairs.

From out of the shadows, the American appeared, and Juliette could feel the heat and anger emanating from his body as clearly as if they were pulsing from her own. "Does it give you a thrill to force your attentions on young girls, Lord Cornelian?" he asked, his voice rough with rage. "Because if it does, this house isn't big enough for both of us."

Lord Cornelian laughed, but he shook his head nervously and looked as if he was searching for a route out of the room that wouldn't require him to pass Mr. Jameson. "You have some very odd ideas, Jameson, if you think you can come here and dictate what you bloody wish." He began to walk toward the door, but Mr. Jameson stepped quickly to the left, so he was standing right in front of him. "If you don't let me pass—" Lord Cornelian began.

"Then what?" Mr. Jameson asked. "Will you summon the police? I'll help you out if you'd like."

"You'll be lucky if you receive a shilling from any man in this house after I'm done with you," Lord Cornelian seethed.

"Do I look as if I care?" Mr. Jameson asked, his voice low with contempt. He reached out and put his hand at the base of Lord Cornelian's neck. "I wasn't born in a grand house like this one, Cornelian," he said. "In fact, I didn't even have a home when I was a boy. Nor a family. What that means to you is that there are things I know how to do that you've probably never even imagined." He took a deep breath. "With one move of my thumb, I can end your life. Now, if you don't want that to happen, I suggest you listen to me. Hands off that poor girl and any other female in this house who doesn't want your attentions. Understand?"

"I should have you thrown out," Lord Cornelian said.

"So then you don't understand—" Mr. Jameson began.

Lord Cornelian reached up and tried to move the American's arm, but it was like watching a child try to move a huge tree. "Unhand me and I'll be on my way."

"When you agree to my order—and it is an order."

"Who do you think—"

"I repeat: It's an order. I would give it to Lord Whitehall himself if I caught him trying to ruin a young girl like that."

"Then you're a fool," Lord Cornelian said, "because you have no idea how things work in England. You'll be the laughingstock of the manor before the week is out, Jameson; of that I can assure you. But to humor you, I'll agree to your terms."

"Not to humor me," Mr. Jameson said through gritted teeth. "Because you mean it."

Lord Cornelian sighed. "Very well, then. Because I mean it. It will never happen again."

Mr. Jameson let him go, and Lord Cornelian touched his neck where the American's hand had been. The movement made Juliette think of when Mr. Jameson had kissed her lips, and afterwards, how she had touched herself, wanting to relive the moment. No doubt Lord Cornelian felt quite the opposite; but clearly, Thomas Jameson had a deep physical effect on people, whether they wanted him to or not.

113

"I'll thank you two to leave my room," he said, looking at Mr. Jameson. When he turned to Juliette, his eyes locked on her for what she felt was a beat too long. He opened his mouth, closed it, then shook his head, and a moment later, shut the door firmly behind them.

Mr. Jameson laughed as he and Juliette walked down the hallway. "'I'll thank you two to leave my room,'" he mimicked, laughing again and shaking his head. "Since I was a young boy, Juliette, whenever I've set my mind to understanding something, I've done it, even if it's taken me ten times as long as I thought it would. The first time I saw a great, grand ship in Boston Harbor, it was as if something grabbed me by the throat that wouldn't let go. But I'll tell you: understanding you English—I don't think I'll ever be able to do it."

He slung an arm around her waist and continued walking along the hallway with her as if it were the most natural thing in the world. He stopped in front of a doorway at the end of the long, grand corridor. "This is my room," he murmured. "And any time you want to come in, Juliette, day or night, I wouldn't care if the whole world knew about us."

She had to laugh. "So then you wouldn't care if I lost my job?"

He didn't say anything. He inhaled slowly, and the look in his eyes made her feel it might be worth it.

He opened the door, and a crooked smile skewed his face. "Hmm. You're a maid, Juliette. Can't I complain to you and have you fix this room up? Look at that bed. It's definitely missing *something*," he said with a laugh.

For the briefest of moments, Juliette let herself look

in Mr. Jameson's room—large and grand, one of the bigger ones in the house, it boasted an enormous, comfortable-looking bed of dark, polished wood with generous, soft-looking blankets. Somehow Mr. Jameson had already made the room look uniquely his, and for one stolen moment, Juliette let herself imagine what it would feel like to spend the night in this room, one long, glorious night of letting Mr. Jameson do what had kept them both up night after night imagining. *I won't sleep again until I've tasted every inch of you,* he had promised. And oh, how she wished . . .

Instead, she turned and ran down the long hallway, fighting feelings she didn't know how much longer she'd be able to control.

Thomas watched Juliette run down the hall, and he chuckled and closed the door to his room.

That woman . . . He didn't know what it was about her that had fascinated him since that very first day, but he sure as hell couldn't shake it.

*Don't do what you did to Georgina.*

He thought about the tears, the heartbroken face, the face of a woman he knew had loved him.

*Don't do it to another.*

His body, right at that moment, wasn't going to pay any attention to a warning. But it all depended on what Juliette wanted; the attraction was obviously mutual, and if she were willing, he was going to give in to a need that was so powerful he didn't even know how he was going to sleep that night.

# Chapter Nine

It was odd, Juliette felt, that there were so many unwritten rules in these grand households, yet they apparently were broken often enough. Last night as she had helped Sarah undress, Sarah had told her that another guest, Lord Faversham, was known for the very sort of thing Lord Cornelian had attempted, and that he had "ruined many a young maid."

The gentlemen didn't mind dallying with the serving girls, but otherwise they were not to be seen. A servant risked being dismissed immediately if he or she were seen by the master doing work like scrubbing or cleaning. Juliette wondered whether she and her fellow servants would be in danger of offending anyone's sensibilities at Hampton with so many guests entering and leaving their rooms at odd hours.

As she and Caroline and the other maids had struggled to get the after-breakfast, midday chores done without being seen by any of the guests, she had already spotted two guests in the hallway, and had nearly collided with a third as she had been carrying an armload of Miss Sarah's clothes toward the back stairs.

Now, she saw Caroline coming down the hallway carrying a full chamberpot, and although Juliette was dying to talk to her, she knew she would have to find a better time.

From farther down the hallway, she saw Brenna Banford emerge from her room; she could tell at a glance that her half-sister was preoccupied. Brenna's normally beautiful, almost lushly featured face was pinched with tension, and her usually rosy skin looked pale. She was walking quickly, her head down, and suddenly Juliette could see what was about to happen—because Brenna wasn't looking where she was going, and—

"Caroline!" Juliette called out.

It had been the wrong thing to do. She had thought if she could warn Caroline . . .

But Caroline had been so startled that she had jumped, and the chamberpot, full and suddenly off balance, had fallen to the floor, cracked, and spilled its embarrassing contents in an oozing, stinking, soupy mess on to the carpet.

Brenna Banford looked as if she was about to split at the seams. "I don't believe it—you *idiot!*" she shrieked. "I could kill you, you imbecilic beast! You don't even have intelligence enough to put one foot in front of the other, much less enough to be a lady's maid or any kind of maid at all!"

Caroline looked stunned, hesitating between starting to clean up and standing and facing Brenna Ban-

ford. "I'm sorry," she finally said. "I do apologize."
Even though, Juliette said to herself, it had been
Brenna's fault, since she had been the one who hadn't
been looking where she was going.

"Apologize all you like," Brenna roared. "I shall
still insist that you are dismissed immediately."

"Then you're a fool," Juliette heard herself say.

Brenna looked amazed and furious as she turned
from Caroline to Juliette. "How dare you speak to me
with such insolence?" she blazed. "You'll be out of a
job by day's end as well, I can assure you."

"And I can assure you that no servant in this household is going to lose her job because a guest wasn't
looking where she was walking and ran right into the
maid," Juliette said.

"We'll just have to see, won't we?" Brenna said.
"And in any case, my having been looking or not looking had nothing to do with your speaking so inso-
lently, did it? I realize you're rather new in your
position, but have you no idea that a maid isn't per-
mitted to speak to a guest unless she's asked a direct
question?"

*Have you no idea I'm your half-sister?* Juliette was
tempted—oh, so tempted—to ask.

But she knew she had to wait for the right moment.
That moment would definitely come, though, she
promised herself.

"We shall see which is stronger," Juliette said. "My
mistress's loyalty to me, or your desire to make a fool
of yourself. Now come, Caroline. Let's get something
to clean up this foul mess before another guest comes
out and faints dead away from the smell."

\* \* \*

"It was quite funny, actually, the way Brenna Banford's face looked when I mentioned the other guests fainting dead away."

Sarah shook her head. "Whatever am I going to do with you, my dear Juliette? I don't know how many times I'm going to be able to defend you from Mama. You do know that, do you not?"

"I do now," Juliette said.

"I *am* sorry," Sarah said, smoothing down her dress and taking a long look at herself in the mirror. "You know I would do everything and anything for you— but I've also told you that this week is one of those weeks to my mother. She wants everything to run perfectly smoothly. Tipped-over chamberpots, funny as they might be at the time, don't really fit into that category."

"And it *was* quite the fault of Brenna Banford," Juliette said. "She could as easily have knocked me over with *your* chamberpot in my hands."

"I'm simply saying," Sarah went on with a sigh, "I don't know that I can always guarantee to save your neck, Juliette. You have a lot of exposure here to an enormous number of guests from our circle of friends. If you *are* dismissed without a character at this point, I daresay it would be quite difficult for you to find another position."

*And then poor Harriet . . .*

She thought of her last factory job, one that she'd had in London. No matter how long and hard she had worked, she had barely made enough money for food and rent. Yes, she'd had a freedom she truly did miss, but working for the Whitehalls, she could save every farthing she made and give it to Harriet.

"Then I should tell you I'm seriously considering approaching Sir Roger," Juliette blurted out. Brenna had made her so angry that she had changed her mind about revealing her secret.

Sarah's face shifted, her beautiful features tensing in confusion. "That's a deeper issue," she said softly. "And we can't predict what Sir Roger's reaction will be. But it *is* about your heritage and your family, Juliette, and I would never dream of denying you the chance to pursue it. I suppose I'm just telling you that my mother will be pushed only so far; I know that." She turned and looked in the mirror at her backside. "Oh, dear. I do look quite ridiculous in this dress. Why is it that when the man *I'm* interested in pursuing is coming to visit, Mama insists on my wearing something that makes me look like a boudoir lamp, and when the man *she* wants me to marry is here, I can wear whatever I'd like?"

"Can't you go against her on this?" Juliette asked, trying to imagine Harriet dictating to her in such a way.

"I suppose at this point, dear Juliette, I'm trying to pick my battles wisely. I've already fought too many on your behalf." She smiled. "It's quite all right. I'll try to charm Andrew some other way, and hope that he can see past the five thousand layers of crinoline." She sighed as she sat down in front of the mirror. "Have you ever made love with a man?" she suddenly asked.

Juliette saw her face turn as red as a ripe tomato. "I—" she began.

Sarah grabbed her arm and led her to the bed, then sat down next to her. "Tell me!" she said. "I've had my adventures, but neither encounter came close to what I had hoped for. Yet you—I can tell by your face. You *must* tell me everything!"

Juliette was torn. Being kissed by Thomas Jameson was without question the most special, amazing thing that had ever happened to her. Every time she thought about it, she was gripped by pleasure and desire that were so strong, it was as if Mr. Jameson were kissing her right then and there.

And it wasn't just the physical feelings; for some reason, Mr. Jameson seemed to know her, and to want to know her more. She could pretend not to be interested, and she knew she should continue to do so, but the truth was that it felt wonderful to have this handsome, intelligent man so intrigued by her. *I won't sleep until I've tasted every inch of you,* she imagined him whispering, his breath hot against her ear.

And she felt a rush of desire so strong—

"Juliette," she heard Sarah say.

She looked at her mistress, who was smiling, her head tilted. "If you don't tell me this instant what is making you turn every shade of red in the universe, I promise *I* shall personally fire you from your position."

Juliette took a deep breath. "It's Mr. Jameson," she finally said.

She had thought Sarah would make some sort of joke about it, perhaps be amazed, but she looked quite serious. "Goodness knows you have more opportunities to make liaisons with Mr. Jameson here than you ever would back at Epping Place," she said quietly. "And I would never stand in the way of your happiness."

Juliette stared at her mistress. "From what I can see, Sarah, Mr. Jameson is a relentless flirt. I can't believe you're recommending that I . . ." Her voice trailed off as she let herself imagine, just for a moment, the feeling: Mr. Jameson laying her down on that huge, luxurious bed, kissing her neck, her shoulders, her lips . . .

"I know what I see on your face and in your eyes," Sarah said softly. "You're in the grip of something that's bigger than you are."

"As my mother was, and look what ended up happening to her. My situation is going to be odd enough, depending on what Sir Roger says; I don't think I need to muddy the waters any more than they'll already be muddied."

Sarah smiled mysteriously. "It's a short week and a vast house, Juliette, with landholdings that seem to go on forever. I know that if I can find a way to be with Andrew without a chaperone, I'll bloody well do it."

*And your life is as different from mine as day from night,* Juliette thought, but it was certainly a tempting idea.

*This is a test,* Juliette told herself as she walked toward the herb garden in the near darkness.

It was a beautiful night, and Juliette would have wanted to take a walk for no reason at all other than to smell the pungent herbs as the dew clung to them and released their scent into the crisp late-evening air. Most of the guests were playing various card games, and most of the servants were getting the rooms ready for the night. But Juliette had already readied Sarah's room. And now . . .

Would he come?

The garden was a place he had found her before, a place she had reason to visit every day. He was an intelligent man and a driven one. If he meant what he'd said . . .

*I won't sleep until I've tasted every inch of you—*
No.

She couldn't let herself be ruled by this absurdly powerful need.

But she was curious; maybe that was all it was.

Would Mr. Jameson pursue her here, or anywhere at all, or had he simply been teasing her?

She needed lavender and Oswego tea and mint and rosemary, and for these things, she had reason to be here. •

But her body was trembling, her breathing felt shallow, and her heart pounded as she thought that maybe, maybe this would be their meeting place.

*You're a fool, being seduced by thoughts you have no business thinking.*

And for Sarah to have egged her on . . .

She leaned over and began snipping at the rosemary, its heady scent making her heart beat faster. She lined up the dark green, fragrant stems, tied them loosely with string, and stuffed them into her muslin sack.

*You're a fool,* she told herself as she began snipping next at the lavender. *A hopeful, hopelessly romantic fool.*

She snipped away, inhaling the fragrance that had always reminded her of something from her childhood, though she didn't know what. She closed her eyes and inhaled deeply, once and then again.

When she opened her eyes, she was looking directly at Mr. Thomas Jameson.

She didn't know how long it took her to find her voice. She only knew that she was already thinking thoughts she shouldn't have been thinking as she took in that powerful frame, those strong, thickly muscled thighs, those eyes that made her lose her breath and her thoughts and her fears.

"How long have you been standing there?" she asked.

He smiled. "Long enough to see that you know what you're doing around plants. Did you grow up in this part of England?"

She laughed. "Not exactly. I grew up in London. We lived in the absolute opposite of the countryside, I think you could say: ten to a room or sometimes in the street, under tunnels. Once in the workhouse when my mum fell ill."

"How did you learn all of this, then?"

Juliette felt the color flood to her face. "My mother—well, my mother's friend taught me everything I know about sewing, but truthfully, I've made an awful lot up as I've gone along. I've read stacks of books and periodicals on herbs and cleaning and hair, but I have to admit I've made a lot of mistakes too."

"And you've been forgiven every time?" he asked softly, coming up in front of her. He reached out and tucked a lock of hair behind her ear, then tilted her head up toward his. "I had thought all these haughty noblewomen were extremely unforgiving."

"Oh, they are," she said, barely able to think with him standing so near. "But my mistress is different, Mr. Jameson."

His mouth curved up in a half smile that was surprisingly affectionate, yet also made her feel as if he was toying with her. "'Mr. Jameson'?" he laughed.

She had to smile. "I don't imagine you know all the rules of these vast, complicated households, Mr. Jameson. I could lose my job simply for the 'crime' of speaking to you without waiting for you to address me first. At the very least, I should call you 'Mr. Jameson.'"

He shook his head, his eyes dark and intense. "These rules," he scoffed. "You should come to America and see what it's like to live without all these strictures. A woman like you—you could become anything you wanted. What's your dream, Juliette? If you were a noblewoman rather than a maid—"

She thought of Sarah and how, in certain ways, her life was bound by as many rules as hers was. "That's the funny thing," she said. "My mistress has dreams as well, but because she's rich, she's supposed to be idle."

"I'm not interested in your mistress," he murmured, his hand burning against the small of her back. "I'm not interested in these women who can't even get dressed without the help of a servant. I'm interested in a woman who stepped forward to help a little girl she didn't even know; I'm interested in a woman who risked her job to save a young maid. Even if you *weren't* a beautiful young woman, those acts would have drawn me to you like a bear to honey." His hands wrapped around her waist, and he pulled her close against him. "But facts are facts, Miss Juliette—" He shook his head. "Miss Juliette what? I don't even know the last name of the woman I have in my arms," he said.

For a second, she couldn't think of her own name. She knew that Mr. Jameson's hands were holding her against him, that she could hardly catch her breath, that her heart was pounding and a river of need was warming the center of her body. But her name?

"Garrison," she finally answered, finding her voice.

"Juliette Garrison," he repeated. "I like it. Now tell me your dream."

She had to smile. No one had ever asked her before. "Oh, it's just—" She stopped, hesitating. "It's silly."

His eyes searched hers. "Some night—not tonight—I'll tell you more about when I was growing up. But tonight I'll tell you this: When I was five, my parents and I were on a ship bound for America—from England. I can still remember the smell of it—the sewage, the sweat. We were worse off than cattle. No food, there must have been inches, not feet, of space for each person. No lifeboats. Our ship was rammed by another ship in the middle of the night, just a stupid mistake." He paused, and in the moonlight, Juliette thought she could see a suggestion of what Thomas had looked like as a boy on that night. "Everyone said it was a miracle I survived. My parents and ninety percent of the others on board drowned. What would have been silly, I guess, would have been for me to dream something big at that time; I can't even say I was happy to be alive. I existed, period. But you—" He reached out and ran the back of his hand along her cheek. "You could be anything you want, anything you set your mind to. And I know a woman with a mind like yours has a dream."

She was glad it was dark enough that he wouldn't be able to see her cheeks flush. "Well," she began, "the main reason I've always lost my jobs is for being 'impudent, disrespectful, and far too opinionated,' according to one of my bosses. So I truly think—well, if I could have my way, I *would* have my own way: I'd own my own dress shop and do all my own designs, and if there was a shrewish, snobby customer who thought she could be rude to my employees, I'd cut her from my customer list as quick as you can say 'Get out of my shop.'" She began to laugh. "I'm sure

I'd end up losing loads of customers, but you asked for my dream, and that's it. I do love designing clothes, and I think I could be good at it."

"I can see it," he said, his eyes still searching hers. "Juliette Garrison Designs, a small but successful shop on the most fashionable street in London." He winked. "Or maybe in Boston. You really should go see America someday."

Juliette suddenly felt an overwhelming sense of vulnerability. Here she barely knew this man; he had made a casual comment to her, one he could as easily have made to a man, and she was already wondering if she could or should read any more into it than Mr. Jameson's actual words, or whether she should be disappointed—which she was—that he hadn't said, "You really should come to America someday—with me."

*Fool!* she berated herself silently.

She had never been drawn to anyone this breathlessly and unwillingly; even when she was only thinking about him, her body reacted as if he were touching her in ways she had never even dreamed of being touched.

Now, she could see he was smiling at her in a knowing, amused sort of way. "The thought of America seems to have taken away your power of speech," he said.

So now she truly did look a fool to him—a speechless, starry-eyed maid with a dream he thought silly. . . .

But she stopped her own thoughts—because for some reason, she believed that he didn't find her dream silly at all. And that was a new and amazing feeling, one she had never experienced before.

*It's nice, but it doesn't mean anything,* she warned herself. Thomas Jameson was probably equally encouraging to his local postman about *his* dreams and imaginings.

She forced herself to concentrate on putting at least one more coherent sentence together. "America *does* seem very appealing to me."

His gaze seemed to be almost burning into her, and she hoped he would speak because she certainly knew she couldn't; putting that one sentence together had used up all her powers of concentration.

"You'd have to get rid of what you're wearing," he said, taking hold of her blouse and giving it a tug.

She opened her mouth, intending to ask what he meant, but no words came out.

Thomas Jameson laughed. "Aren't these maid's clothes?"

"I—"

"In America, you'd just be Juliette Garrison," he said softly, drawing her tighter against him. "Not a maid, not Miss Whoever, just a woman—with a man who thinks you're amazing."

"You mustn't say that, Mr. Jameson."

He brushed his lips against hers. "Why not?" he murmured. "I told you I wouldn't have cared who you were when I first saw you, and I still don't. You're Juliette Garrison. I'm Thomas Jameson. Not 'Mr. Jameson,' ever again."

Mr. Jameson. That was what she had to call him to keep some distance between them, a vast gulf between the maid and the wealthy American shipbuilder. "Mr. Jameson," she said with a smile. "I think that just to irritate you, I shall persist in calling you Mr. Jameson."

"I think you won't," he whispered, his lips close enough to hers that she could feel the breath from each of his words on her mouth. His hands tightened around her waist, and she could feel his strong, powerful thighs against hers, warm and firm and persuasive.

"I think I will," she teased. "Mr. Jameson."

"Thomas," he murmured. "Or Tommy if you like that better."

"I told you I like Mr. Jameson. I can be very stubborn, you know."

"Oh, really? I can be very persuasive, you know."

He moved his hands slowly down over her buttocks, and it took her breath away. She felt his body, strong and hard, and she wanted to melt into him, wrap her legs around him and get as close as she could.

"I'm surprised you're not Mrs. Someone or Other," he murmured. "How on earth have you escaped marriage? In America you would have been snapped up in a heartbeat if you were willing."

"I've—" She hesitated. "I've been working my whole life, Mr. Jameson, and usually among women. And then in service, you're not generally supposed to have followers, nor marry."

"How lucky for me, then," he said softly, his gaze hypnotizing.

"Thomas," she heard herself whisper, because suddenly she wanted to know him so very much better.

He moaned and covered her lips with his again, drawing her into a kiss that was deep and long and mysterious because she felt so many new yearnings and needs; she felt weak with desire but strong with need, afraid of what she was feeling but wanting to give into it at the same time.

Thomas pulled back and looked into her eyes.

"I don't know anything about how your days and nights work," he said. "Can you meet me here tomorrow night?"

For a moment, words from her mother's diary sounded in her heart. *Diary, I know it's hard to believe* . . . Yet, she for one had never felt that "them upstairs," as Mrs. Winston always put it, were her "betters." Who was to say an American shipping-company owner couldn't be genuinely interested in her?

*But you know his type, and it doesn't matter whether they're rich or poor. Women fall at their feet, they use them and then throw them away.*

*Say no,* an inner voice warned.

*Don't fall into the trap men like him set for women.*

*Don't let your emotions and desires sweep away your intelligence.*

"I can try," she blurted out.

# Chapter Ten

It was too great a coincidence to believe, yet there it was, and Juliette could think of nothing but the sapphire necklace she had seen wrapped spectacularly around Brenna Banford's neck. It was odd, because earlier, as she had helped Sarah choose her jewelry for the evening, she had been wondering about what had happened to her mother's necklace.

*The necklace is gone from my room,* her mother had written, *and of course I can only think the worst—not that any of the other servants have taken it, because none even knew about it, and I know for a fact that none of them would do that to me.*

*No, the only person in the world who knew about it other than me is William, and possibly his mother. And that means that William, or more likely Lady Edith, came into my room and rooted around like a thief. One of them didn't want me to have the necklace after he decided that Hazel Crichton was to be his bride.*

What were the chances Brenna Banford would be wearing a sapphire necklace that exactly fit the description in her mother's diary—*eight sparkling sapphires with a group of tiny ones in the center cascading like a teardrop of blue?*

Now, she looked Brenna Banford's maid up and down from afar, trying to decide whether there was any point in asking her about her mistress's necklace. For one thing, she reasoned, what were the chances anyone would admit there was something out of the ordinary about its origins, even if it *were* the same necklace William had given her mother? Even if she learned the necklace had been stolen, what could she do about it?

Absolutely nothing, she knew.

Yet, she couldn't stop thinking about it—how the necklace glowed and shined on the pristine, perfect skin of a woman who hadn't worked for even a full minute of her life. Juliette couldn't stop imagining her mother when she had held it, a beautiful young woman whose heart hadn't yet been broken, who had still been full of hope and love. And she couldn't forget the words her mother had written about William Banford when he had finally proved himself to be, as Harriet had put it, no better than a piece of dirt. *I just wish I hadn't loved him so much, because he'll always have that in his heart, and I have the memory of a petty mama's boy who stole back a gift I truly did cherish."*

The necklace had disappeared only a couple of days

after William had given it to Kate. *William seemed surprised, but not all that surprised,* Kate had written, after she had told him about its theft.

And now, Juliette was nearly positive she had just seen it.

She looked over at Charlotte Traymor, Brenna Banford's maid, who at that point was peeking through the viewing area Hampton's servants traditionally made when balls were held at the house, a space in between the fabric-draped baluster of the upstairs landing through which the servants could watch the revelers below.

Miss Traymor, a woman of perhaps thirty, Juliette guessed, was standing next to Caroline as the two looked down through the crack. Juliette knew nothing about Miss Traymor beyond the fact that she had been quite kind to Caroline when she had finally made her way to Hampton, apologizing for her illness and thanking Caroline for filling in for her.

Now, Miss Traymor looked positively aglow as she watched the goings-on downstairs, her hands clasped together by her chest as if she were a child watching a procession of kings and queens.

As soon as Juliette moved into place next to her, she could see why Miss Traymor looked so elated. Brenna Banford looked like the belle of the ball at that moment, being swirled around the dance floor by the handsomest man in the room: Mr. Thomas Jameson.

Juliette felt the blood flow to her face in a hot rush.

Thomas—Mr. Jameson—seemed to be thoroughly enjoying himself, smiling and swirling Brenna Banford around the dance floor so masterfully that they looked as if they had been dancing together for years.

Juliette stared as Thomas's hand moved down

Brenna's back, and she remembered with a rush of humiliation how he had touched her the night before.

She was about to turn away—her questions could wait; what difference did it make whether she ever asked about the necklace or not? she asked herself.

But then she stopped.

She thought of what her mother had written, and how Charlotte Traymor was standing right here, and how she had always believed in taking a chance when such a perfect opportunity presented itself. Fate did matter, when you acknowledged its existence.

She turned and looked at Miss Traymor, almost sorry to interrupt the woman's obvious delight. "Your mistress looks quite lovely," she said, and was surprised to see Miss Traymor actually blush.

"Thank you," Miss Traymor said. "We agreed quite easily on what she should wear. And of course she wanted to wear the sapphire necklace tonight."

"Yes, I can see why; it's very beautiful." She paused, but only for a moment. "Is it a new piece of jewelry, if you don't mind my asking? It goes so perfectly with Miss Banford's gown."

Miss Traymor blushed again. "Thank you, since I did select the color of the gown on my own, in my mistress's absence. But actually, the necklace has been in the Banford family for quite some time, and has rather a dramatic history. Miss Banford's father apparently gave it to her mother when they became engaged. But soon after they were married, a young maid stole it."

The words, even though Juliette knew how untrue they were, nearly took her breath away. "Oh, really?" she managed to say, concentrating on trying to appear calm.

Miss Traymor nodded. "They say that this little maid had quite an obsession with William, Miss Banford's father. In any case, the necklace was found in the maid's room, the maid was turned over to the police, and all was well." She sighed. "And it certainly does suit my mistress and her perfect skin."

Juliette wanted to scream, to throttle Miss Traymor, to jump down through the ridiculous crack in the balusters and rip the necklace off Brenna Banford's perfect neck.

But she knew, for one thing, that Miss Traymor was only repeating what she had been told. And though Juliette didn't particularly want to admit it, probably Brenna Banford didn't even know the truth.

But Sir Roger might. And he and Brenna and Brenna's fiancé, Randall Banford, whether they were ready for it or not, would learn the truth before the week was out. Of that, Juliette was absolutely certain. She felt alone in the world, a fool for having given herself up to a passion that shouldn't ever have been part of her soul. But because she felt so completely alone, she felt closer to a past she had only just learned about, and closer to a mother she would never know. And for her mother, and to right at least some of the wrongs the Banfords had committed against her, she would take a stand that would probably change her life forever.

"You look quite pale, Miss Garrison," Miss Traymor was saying. "Would you like me to get you some cold water? It's the least I can do for you—well, I owe both of you—for having tolerated my mistress in my absence."

"Thank you, but I shall be fine," Juliette said. "I do believe I just need some air."

A few moments later, she had made her way outside, vaguely aware that she had crossed the paths of various guests who had wandered out into the fragrant night air, but not looking at anyone or even raising her eyes.

She was alone, with a memory that was going to burn in her throat and her heart and her veins unless she righted the wrong. She knew this, even if she lost her job. . . .

But if the Whitehalls dismissed her, how would she pay Harriet's share of the rent? At the moment Harriet needed her, and there was no way in the world Juliette could let her down.

Yet, Harriet had wanted her to pursue the truth. . . .

She thought about the night before, the intense desire and passion and pleasure she had felt, and she wondered if this was the exact path her mother had taken, either not knowing she was making a huge mistake, or knowing but not caring.

*I'm not interested in these women who can't get dressed without the help of a servant,* she remembered Mr. Jameson saying.

*What's your dream, Juliette? If you were a noblewoman rather than a maid.*

He should have asked what her dream would have been if she had been a noblewoman rather than a fool, she felt.

By the soft light of the moon, Juliette walked easily toward the stream Mrs. Winston had told her about.

Far from the hustle and bustle of the ball, the sound of the rushing water seemed magical and just what Juliette needed.

She had survived every trial of her life so far; she

would do what she felt she had to do now and live with the consequences.

And as for her heart—

"Juliette."

She turned.

How on earth—? She hadn't heard a sound, not a single footfall or intake of breath, not a snapped twig or a shifted pebble.

Yet here in the moonlight stood the man she least and most wanted to see, looking at her with a depth of feeling in his eyes that she had no desire to acknowledge.

"Tell me right now what someone said or did to you," Thomas demanded, coming up to her and trying to draw her into his arms.

She pushed him away. "I'm fine, and I didn't come out here to talk to you," she said in a hollow, thin voice that had already betrayed her.

"You're not fine," he said, moving so she had to face him. "And I want to know why."

"And why would that be?" she asked. "So you can share the information with your dance partner?"

He looked confused. "I've danced with half a dozen young ladies this evening," he said. "Which are you talking about?"

She shook her head. "It doesn't matter," she said. "I came out here to be alone, not to talk something to death. You can go back to your party and forget that you've seen me."

He took her by the shoulders and tilted her chin up. Face to face and eye to eye in the moonlight, Juliette couldn't, for a second, look away from this man she cared about far too much.

And then—damn!—she felt tears welling up in her eyes.

What a fool! She should have left when she'd seen him, even if she had simply turned and run without saying a word, like a deer in the night.

Now she was trapped in arms she didn't want to escape, her face inches from his, her heart too close to his in every way.

"Tell me what happened," he murmured. "I won't let you go until you do."

She sighed, her body telling her mind to trust this man who somehow already knew her so well. She knew, too, that he would certainly be true to his word. Until she told him, she would be imprisoned by these strong, muscular arms. . . .

"There's so much," she finally said, shaking her head. "For one thing, I'm not who I thought I was my whole life; my mother isn't who I thought she was," she began, and the look in Thomas's eyes made her go on and on until she had told him everything. "And I wouldn't have thought something like a necklace, of all things, could make me go all teary-eyed and angry at the same time, but it's made me feel crazy."

"And now you're planning something. I can tell from your eyes," he said, brushing the hair back from her face with his hand.

She tried to ignore the way even the simple touch of his hand made her feel. "I might have waited," she said. "I know I should wait until after this week, since this is such an important time for Lady Whitehall; and I probably *would* have waited. I always swore when I was growing up that I'd do whatever I had to not to be poor and to know where I was going to sleep each night. But when I heard what Brenna Banford told her maid about the necklace . . ." Her voice trailed off, and her heart began racing merely because

# GET UP TO 4 FREE BOOKS!

You can have the best romance delivered to your door for less than what you'd pay in a bookstore or online. Sign up for one of our book clubs today, and we'll send you **FREE\* BOOKS** just for trying it out...**with no obligation to buy, ever!**

## HISTORICAL ROMANCE BOOK CLUB

Travel from the Scottish Highlands to the American West, the decadent ballrooms of Regency England to Viking ships. Your shipments will include authors such as CONNIE MASON, CASSIE EDWARDS, LYNSAY SANDS, LEIGH GREENWOOD, and many, many more.

## LOVE SPELL BOOK CLUB

Bring a little magic into your life with the romances of Love Spell—fun contemporaries, paranormals, time-travels, futuristics, and more. Your shipments will include authors such as KATIE MACALISTER, SUSAN GRANT, NINA BANGS, SANDRA HILL, and more.

**As a book club member you also receive the following special benefits:**

- **30% OFF all orders through our website & telecenter!**
  (Plus, you still get 1 book FREE for every 5 books you buy!)
- **Exclusive access to special discounts!**
- **Convenient home delivery and 10 days to return any books you don't want to keep.**

**There is no minimum number of books to buy**, and you may cancel membership at any time. See back to sign up!

\*Please include $2.00 for shipping and handling.

# YES! ☐

Sign me up for the **Historical Romance Book Club** and send my THREE FREE BOOKS! If I choose to stay in the club, I will pay only $13.50* each month, a savings of $6.47!

# YES! ☐

Sign me up for the **Love Spell Book Club** and send my TWO FREE BOOKS! If I choose to stay in the club, I will pay only $8.50* each month, a savings of $5.48!

**NAME:** _____

**ADDRESS:** _____

_____

**TELEPHONE:** _____

**E-MAIL:** _____

☐ **I WANT TO PAY BY CREDIT CARD.**

☐ VISA   ☐ MasterCard.   ☐ DISCOVER

**ACCOUNT #:** _____

**EXPIRATION DATE:** _____

**SIGNATURE:** _____

Send this card along with $2.00 shipping & handling for each club you wish to join, to:

**Romance Book Clubs
1 Mechanic Street
Norwalk, CT 06850-3431**

Or fax (must include credit card information!) to: 610.995.9274. You can also sign up online at www.dorchesterpub.com.

*Plus $2.00 for shipping. Offer open to residents of the U.S. and Canada only. Canadian residents please call 1.800.481.9191 for pricing information.

If under 18, a parent or guardian must sign. Terms, prices and conditions subject to change. Subscription subject to acceptance. Dorchester Publishing reserves the right to reject any order or cancel any subscription.

JOIN NOW!

of the memory of the words. "I can't let that go; it's like a glove that's been thrown at my feet. I want a measure of justice for my mother."

He took a long, slow, deep breath, his eyes never leaving hers. "For some reason, I already know there's no use telling you not to do something when you've already made up your mind to go ahead," he said softly. "And I wouldn't be where I am today if I had listened to all or even any of the people who told me to wait or change my mind or go down a different road."

Juliette wanted to know everything about this man whose touch she already loved. "I wish I knew more about your life. I don't know anything about you except—" She stopped.

*—Except that you make me feel amazing.*

*—Except that you make me feel as if you truly do want to know all about me.*

*—Except that something in your past makes you understand so much about me that it's as if we've known each other our whole lives.*

"Except—" He paused and moved his hands from around her waist down over her hips, encircling her in a hot wave of desire. "Except that I still won't sleep—not a wink—until I've touched and kissed and caressed every inch of you?"

She opened her mouth and closed it, unable to speak.

Thomas Jameson evidently knew his power over her, because he closed his mouth over hers and drew her into a kiss that was smooth and deep and perfect.

His tongue entwined with hers, and she heard a sound come from deep in her throat—her own voice, a moan of desire mixed with pleasure and wonder. She had never dreamed a kiss could feel so good.

Thomas moved his lips down along her throat, and when Juliette felt his hand cup one of her breasts through the fabric of her blouse, her knees weakened, and she caught herself against him.

The feel of his shoulders, warm and muscled beneath his shirt, made her even more breathless, and when his fingers rubbed one of her nipples, she tightened her grip as if she were holding on for dear life. The warm waves of need suddenly pulsing between her legs had robbed her strength and replaced it with a desire that felt new and mysterious and wonderful.

Thomas's hands roved downwards again, over her buttocks, and she felt pleasure from both sides, from his hands, warm and persuasive, and his firm, insistent hips, a hard masculinity she had never experienced before.

In the moonlight, his eyes looked full of affection, heavy lidded with a desire she was sure matched her own. He kissed her again, and he moved a hand under her skirt, cupping it over one cheek of her buttocks, then circling it slowly, around and around. He trailed his hand around to the front, and as it circled Juliette's most private spot, she felt herself gasp, caught in a wave of need deeper than anything she had ever felt.

"Thomas," she whispered.

"Don't worry, darling," he murmured. "I won't hurt you. I'm just going to make you feel good."

He moved his hand inside the last bit of fabric that had separated him from her most intimate spot.

Juliette could hardly catch her breath. She felt a mixture of agony and pleasure as his palm stroked her. She grasped at Thomas's shoulders and breathed into the hair on his chest.

She trembled beneath the touch of his fingers as they probed her curls, and her breathing grew rough and ragged as an intense, urgent need gripped her.

"Thomas," she whispered, her voice hardly there. "I've never felt—"

She twisted beneath his touch, and moaned as he parted her lips and stroked her. "Thomas," she breathed.

He slid his fingers inside her and she felt a yearning so fierce, it was almost pain.

"Let yourself go, honey," he whispered, crushing her against him with his other hand.

The hot, moist urgency grew, and Juliette suddenly cried out, trembling beneath Thomas's expert, powerful touch. She bucked against him, crying out, biting at his shoulder as she exploded with pleasure.

She didn't know how much time passed before she could think consciously and rationally. She held on to him, breathing in his scent, feeling as if she were slowly, slowly coming back to earth.

So this was what all the fuss was about, she told herself. This was what made people do crazy things, and she completely understood why.

She had been so in the grip of her own fierce passion that she hadn't given more than a fleeting thought to this man who had given her so much pleasure. He was stroking her hair and kissing her softly, but he was breathing hard, and she could feel his need for her in every inch of his powerful frame.

She ran a hand along his thigh, then tentatively toward his center; she had felt his male desire for her nearly as fully as she had felt her own, and even though she didn't know what she was doing, she wanted to give him at least some of the pleasure he had given her.

But his hand gripped her wrist, and he laughed. "Not yet," he said. "Much as I want to, Juliette, you're not ready."

"But that was amazing," she said, meaning it. "I have no experience with this sort of thing." She hesitated. "But for some reason, I know I wouldn't have felt that way with anyone else."

His breathing suddenly grew faster and shallower, and he moved her hand off his body. "You have no idea what you do to me, Juliette."

*It must be what you do to me,* she thought, but she said nothing. She felt it was all too new, her feelings too raw, her body too absurdly responsive to his touch.

"Do you have to go back to the party?" she asked, nuzzling his chest.

"I really don't care if I never go back," he said softly, stroking her hair again. "But I *will* go back, for the same reason you should wait to approach Sir Roger until after you get back to London."

"Why is that?" she asked, loving the feel of his warm, muscled chest against her chin.

"Because as much as I'd like to scoop you into my arms and leave here tonight and spend the next year holed up with you on one of my yachts, I know I came here for a reason: to make money. And sometimes it involves dealing with people I'd definitely rather not be in the same room with."

"Who took care of you after your parents died? You were only five, you said?"

Thomas took a long, deep breath. "It was a tough time," he said. "I bounced around from family to family—someone always needed an extra hand."

"But you were five!"

He looked into her eyes. "Weren't you out on the streets working at that age?"

"Well, yes."

"So it was the same for me—I had to eat—only I didn't have a family to move around with. But when I was ten, a man named Mike McClintick took me in. I worked for the roof over my head and the food he gave me. I would have done anything for him."

He paused, and Juliette could tell he felt more emotional about this part of his life than any other.

"His youngest son died in an accident," Thomas went on. "His older brothers had egged him on, I guess you could say. They ran home, and when I got back, their parents kicked me out of the house. They blamed me for talking him into a dare."

"The brothers lied?"

"I wouldn't have expected anything else from them," he said. "I think Mike knew the truth, but it didn't matter: Their mother was half out of her mind with grief, and I was easier to blame than her own sons. And it was easier for Mike to put me out than to fight his wife."

"That's so awful," Juliette said.

"It's reality," Thomas said. "It's what people do every day just to keep going. What bothered me most was that Glenda, their mother, never knew the truth, but maybe she did, in her heart. And I had to move on; I didn't have a choice."

"So where did you go?"

"I stayed in the harbor, working for different shipbuilders. I loved the work—the ocean had gripped me even though it had taken my parents from me. And I never tried to be part of a family again. Those years taught me a lot about waiting for the right moment—

just the way I think you should wait for the right moment to approach Sir Roger, who seems like a wonderful man, by the way." He looked her up and down with a smile. "So even though when I saw you tonight, all I could think of was having a great time, now I have to get back to the reason I came to Hampton in the first place."

Juliette's throat closed. Was that all she was to him? A great time?

Oh, how she had been warned.

And oh, how she had fallen.

"What's wrong?" he asked softly, stroking her hair again.

She sat up, feeling as if she wouldn't be able to get a breath until she was far, far away from Thomas Jameson.

"I need to get back as well," she heard herself say softly, and she grabbed her clothes, dressed in a heartbeat, and took off into the now-dark night like a wounded deer.

She had been a fool. She had suspected as much from time to time, but now she knew for certain.

It wasn't too late, she told herself. For her heart it was, of that she was sure. She had fallen hard for Thomas.

But it wasn't too late; she would go on as she had lived before Thomas, even if she was a sadder and wiser woman.

# Chapter Eleven

Now that the moment had come, Juliette was amazed she had made the decision to approach Sir Roger. Looking back on her conversation with Sarah late the night before, she felt as if she had dreamed it rather than lived it. She could remember the fiery glint in Sarah's eyes, and Sarah's change of heart as she had said that if this was something Juliette wanted to do right away, Sarah would support her. Brenna had been simply beastly since she had arrived, Sarah had said, and maybe this whole thing would take her down a peg or two.

"And your mother?" Juliette had asked.

"My mother has been rather beastly as well, dear Juliette. I shall tell Sir Roger tomorrow morning that I must speak with him immediately. I would think eleven o'clock will do as the time, and it would work in terms of your chores, I believe, but of course I'll know more in the morning."

Now that moment had come, as Juliette waited outside the closed library doors, behind which Sarah and Sir Roger were talking. Sarah had promised that she would respect Juliette's request for discretion: She would tell Sir Roger only that Juliette had an important matter to discuss with him, and she would give her high opinion of Juliette's character as well.

Now, though, Juliette was beginning to get cold feet about her wish to break the news herself to Sir Roger. Why hadn't she agreed to let Sarah—a close family friend of the Banfords—be the bearer of what was sure to seem like bad news to the man?

*Because you've vowed to fight for your mother by yourself,* she answered from deep in her heart, and she knew that the words were true.

When Sarah opened the door and invited Juliette in, Juliette felt her knees turn to jelly: She had known Sarah long enough to feel confident about reading her expressions, and Sarah looked uncertain and nervous. She gave a nearly imperceptible shrug as Juliette walked in, then turned to Sir Roger. "Sir Roger, this is Juliette Garrison, my maid. Juliette, this is Sir Roger Banford."

Sir Roger didn't rise from his seat to offer his hand, nor had he risen when Juliette had entered the room.

*Surely not a good sign,* Juliette said to herself. But then again, she hadn't expected it to be easy. As far as Sir Roger knew, she was "just" a maid.

Still, he hadn't said a word.

"I'll leave you two in privacy," Sarah said. "And I shall be in the morning room if either of you would like to speak with me."

"Very well, Sarah," Sir Roger said in a surprisingly loud, rather commanding voice.

Sarah winked, again almost imperceptibly, at Juliette, and then left, shutting the door behind her.

Juliette forced herself to look at Sir Roger—she would be damned if she acted like a frightened scullery maid, yet she had found his voice extremely unsettling. And his refusal to address her!

"Since this is quite unusual," he suddenly said, his voice still booming, "I would suggest we dispense with formalities and proceed to the reason you've requested this meeting, Julie."

"Juliette," she corrected.

He raised a brow. "Juliette, then." He folded his hands. "Let's hear it, please, Juliette. I don't have much time."

So the moment had come, and the words she had planned so carefully during a nearly sleepless night had vanished from her mind. Her throat was as dry as parchment.

*Think of your mother,* she told herself.

*Think of the wrongs they did to her.*

*Realize you're alone in this world, that no one else will ever look out for you in any way.*

She thought of the photograph of her mother, of the beautiful young woman—really a girl more than a woman—laughing with her best friend, and Juliette imagined her as she had stood serving at dinner and heard the announcement that the love of her life was marrying another woman, and suddenly the words flowed. "My name is Juliette Garrison, Sir Roger, and until a few months ago, I thought that Harriet Garrison was my mother. But I recently learned that my mother died when I was an infant. She was a house parlor maid in London." Juliette paused; the answer to her next question would tell her all sorts of things about what sort of man Sir Roger was. "Does the name Kate Claypool mean anything to you, Sir Roger?"

If someone had asked her to place a wager about what Sir Roger's expression would be when she finished asking the question, she would have lost. She had been certain, given the man's overbearing, even rude, behavior that he would have pretended not to remember Kate Claypool—or, worse yet, he might truly not remember.

But clearly this man knew who Kate Claypool had been; the memory had made his face almost collapse in on itself for a moment.

Sir Roger opened his mouth, closed it, and opened it again, but when he finally spoke, it wasn't in the booming voice he had used earlier. "Kate Claypool was your mother?" he asked softly.

Juliette nodded.

"And I take it that you asked to meet with me because my son, William, was your father—?"

Juliette realized she had been holding her breath. Now she let it out, and said, "Yes. My—the woman I thought was my mother gave me my true mother's—" She stopped, realizing she had almost said too much. Just because Sir Roger had as much as admitted he was her grandfather didn't mean she could necessarily trust him. "Well, my mother had written down a few memories, and she apparently had wanted me to know who my true parents were."

"I see," Sir Roger said. He looked her up and down then, and pursed his lips. "You have my son's eyes," he said, with more emotion than she would have expected. "It's quite obvious, now that your origins are known." His lips pressed together in a thin line of pain. "And his mouth, I would wager, though your mother's mouth was similar as well."

For some reason, even though Sir Roger had already said he remembered her mother, Juliette was shocked that he remembered her so well.

As if reading her mind, Sir Roger gave her an intelligent and reassuring smile. "You look surprised, my dear, and I don't blame you. It isn't every house parlor maid who can be recalled twenty-some years after the fact." He sighed. "But I can honestly say that your mother was an unforgettable woman." He shook his head, reaching for his pipe. "I can also honestly say that I'm glad to have found you."

She had never heard any member of the aristocracy—except for Sarah, of course—talk this way, and she was amazed. Here the Banfords had done everything they could to drive her mother away from their family, and Sir Roger was saying that he was glad to have found her!

"My beloved wife," he went on, his old, booming voice beginning to take over again, "died ten years ago. She would *not* have been happy with this morning's events." He stood up. "But this is a day I never thought I'd see, and one I always hoped for. The way we handled what happened between William and your mother has always been one of my deepest regrets." He held out his hand to shake hers, then held out his arms and drew Juliette into a hug. "I'm old enough and successful enough, Juliette, to do what I wish when I wish, and where I wish. I daresay there are various people in this world who won't welcome my feelings, but my word is the last word in my banking ventures and in my family, and I don't permit arguments. As soon as I return to London, I shall meet with my solicitor."

Juliette didn't know what to say. Sir Roger was so welcoming and so kind. And of course, she could just imagine whom he was talking about as far as arguments! "I don't know what to say," she replied honestly. "I hope you do realize my aim wasn't a visit to your solicitor. I merely—"

"Hush," he cut in. "Now don't do that beautiful, spirited mother of yours a disservice. Fortune is an issue in each and every person's life; to deny that is to be disingenuous. Now go and be well and enjoy your last few days in service without destroying Lady Whitehall's week, if you will. You won't be receiving any money from me at the moment, Juliette, but you realize it will be quite inappropriate to continue as a maid."

She nodded. She had come to the same realization herself, except that honestly, if she wasn't going to continue in service, then what was she going to do? She was responsible for two people at that moment— herself and her beloved Harriet. And surely if she had to pay for food and housing for herself, there wouldn't be enough to cover Harriet.

"Perhaps we might wait to let the news out until I secure another position—?"

He smiled. "I'm hardly going to announce the news in the London *Times,* my dear. But you might indeed have to face some unpleasant consequences of the public's knowing your heritage. As I myself will, but you won't see me losing one second of sleep over it. Life is far too short to worry about what others think of you, Juliette, and the sooner you learn that lesson, the better off you'll be. I only wish my other grand-daughter could learn it."

Once again, Juliette was so surprised by her grand-father's words that she didn't know what to say.

"Thank you," she finally said. "I can't tell you how happy I am that I asked to meet with you. I never ex-pected . . ." Her voice trailed off.

To her surprise, Sir Roger winked. "You'll find soon enough, my dear, that like downstairs, things upstairs are not always what they seem. But do ready yourself for unhappiness from unexpected directions. I imagine you and I will be the only two people in the world who are pleased by this little reunion."

Sir Roger gave her a grandfatherly peck on the cheek before he left the room, and for a moment, Juli-ette just stood there, touching her cheek where he had kissed her. It was an odd feeling, being kissed by a man who was her flesh and blood, and she realized that even if nothing else at all ever came from this "re-union," as her grandfather had put it, the kiss had suddenly become enough. And she knew that most of all, it had been a message to her mother that she was still remembered, admired, and loved.

"Grandfather," she said aloud, wondering how it would feel to actually say the word to her grandfa-ther's face.

"I did it, Mother," she said softly. "And you've been fondly remembered—not reviled at all—this whole time."

She took a deep breath and realized she felt con-tented and satisfied in an odd new way, in a way she hadn't anticipated. It had nothing to do with being partially a member of the aristocracy, or even of hav-ing been accepted, apparently wholeheartedly, by Sir

Roger. She felt that now her mother's soul could finally begin to rest in peace; of course, not all the wrongs against her could possibly be righted, but she had begun the process, like turning over one small pebble at a time in a great, long road.

"Promise to keep a secret?" Caroline asked as she and Juliette dusted the windowsills of the dining room. They were late with their cleaning, and even though Rachel and the Hampton maids were helping with all the chores, there was still much to be done. Every carpet downstairs had to be swept this morning with a hard whisk brush, and it was taking much longer than Caroline and Juliette had anticipated.

"I need your advice," Caroline went on, "and I need you to tell me the truth."

"What is it?" Juliette asked. She couldn't read her best friend's expression at all; she just knew from the flush on Caroline's beautiful, pale skin that something had happened.

Caroline took a deep breath. "You know—of course—that Martin said we couldn't see each other, that Lady Foxcroft had forbidden him to have any relations with anyone outside the household."

"Yes, yes, of course," Juliette said.

"Well, Martin is thinking of leaving. He said Lord Wootten is about to buy a motorcar and that he was consulting with Martin quite a bit about it, and one thing led to another, and Martin is fairly certain Lord Wootten will offer him a position if he wants—as chauffeur, and he's thinking of asking if they'd take me on as a maid to Lady Wootten."

Juliette tried to picture Lord and Lady Wootten, but the truth was that she had been so enmeshed—

engulfed, if she told the truth—in her own affairs that she had taken less notice of the Whitehalls' guests than she would have under normal circumstances. From what she could remember, though, Lord and Lady Wootten were an attractive couple, perhaps in their mid- to late fifties. She remembered that Lord Wootten was a favorite of Mrs. Winston's, who always liked to make his special apple-crumb dessert, and Lady Wootten had laughed in rather an engaging way the other night during the ball.

"It sounds like a wonderful opportunity," she said, "although I can't say I know the Wootens at all. But would you like me to ask Sarah about them?"

Caroline's face flushed a deeper red. "Would you? Rather on the sly, if you know what I mean? Lady Foxcroft will have Martin's head if she senses that he's even considering a change, and then he'll be sacked without a guarantee of anything at all from the Woottens."

"I can imagine," Juliette said, thinking about how she had seen Lady Foxcroft eyeing Martin on the first day of hunt week as if he were her personal property, and hers alone.

"Can you imagine—well, of course you can—how nice it would be for me to be a lady's maid instead of house parlor maid? Apparently Lady Wootten was impressed that I was able to step into position when Miss Traymor was ill. And the fact that Lord Wootten said that to Martin! Can you imagine Brenna Banford going out of her way to pay a servant a compliment?"

Brenna Banford, my half-sister, Juliette thought, and she smiled.

"What is it?" Caroline asked.

"Now will *you* promise to keep a secret?"

"Of course. Tell!" Caroline said, standing up and looking quickly at the clock. "But tell me quickly so I don't get sacked before any of these wonderful things can happen."

"I met with Sir Roger," Juliette said. "Just this very morning."

Caroline's hand flew to her mouth. "And?"

"And, amazingly enough, he was quite friendly. Even happy. Apparently he had been quite fond of my mother. It was only his wife, apparently, who disliked her so much."

"That is so wonderful," Caroline said, hugging Juliette. "I'm so happy for you. And so happy you actually did what you had said you would."

Juliette sighed. "I didn't truly know I would until Miss Traymor said the necklace had been stolen by a scullery maid. It made me so mad. And now—well, I don't truly know what will happen now."

The chime on the front hall clock sounded, and Juliette and Caroline both jumped.

"Oh, dear," Caroline cried out. "They'll all be streaming in any moment now, if they're true to form. Have we been slower than usual this morning? Lady Whitehall will have our hides!"

"I don't know," Juliette said. "We still haven't even finished sweeping! I still have those piles of dust to gather up!"

Caroline looked around the dining room, surveying the scene with an eye Juliette knew was ten times more experienced than her own when it came to cleaning houses. "Quick, sweep them behind those tables," Caroline said.

"Are you sure?" Juliette asked. "That seems like

154

the type of thing Lady Whitehall would suddenly inspect for."

"*I* don't know!" Caroline cried, sounding genuinely nervous. "I guess you might be right. All right, let's sweep them up and get out as fast as we can."

The two women worked so quickly Juliette felt they would have been a blur to anyone who saw them. They finished sweeping and gathered their brooms, pans, and cloths, and headed out the door of the dining room as quickly as they could.

But it was too late. They were suddenly face to face with a whole crowd of guests who had come in from the outside, and Lady Whitehall, whom Juliette hadn't ever pictured as the outdoors type, was at the head of the group.

She gave Juliette and Caroline, who were both so laden with cleaning equipment that Juliette wondered if their faces could even be seen, a death glare.

With a barely audible "Harumph," she stormed past them.

Juliette followed Caroline's lead—Caroline was heading as quickly as she could for the back stairs. But Caroline dropped one of her dustpans, and it fell with a clatter, echoing through the front hallway like a Chinese gong. And Juliette, who had been following Caroline so closely she could nearly touch her, bumped into her and toppled over her back when Caroline bent over to pick up her pan.

Juliette felt a firm hand grip the upper part of her arm, and though she had been half-expecting Lady Whitehall to fire her and Caroline on the spot, she couldn't imagine her mistress having even one-hundredth that much strength in her grip.

She turned and found herself face to face with Thomas.

Out of the corner of her eye, she could see that a big group of people was still milling about in the front hall, but at that moment, all she was thinking about was Thomas, and how she wished she had been anywhere in the world other than in the front hall when he had come in.

"I need to talk to you," he said. His eyes seemed to be darker than usual, fired with passion, but she didn't want to let herself believe it.

"Lady Whitehall is right there," she said, as Caroline opened the door to the back stairs and began to head down.

"Meet me later, then."

It was too much. He was holding her arm as if he owned her, and she wanted him to and hated her own response. He was looking into her eyes as if he needed her, and she loved it and hated it at the same time. He was breathing hard, and she was breathing hard, and she wished they were the only two people in the room so that she could truly tell him how she felt. And then he would take her in his arms. . . .

*No.*

"I don't think you would have grabbed me like this if I were Miss Whitehall," Juliette said, feeling as if her voice were going to erupt out of her chest, she was so angry and churned up.

"I'd grab you no matter who you were, and you know that," Thomas said.

"That's what you'd like to think," Juliette answered. "You're no better than these Englishmen you love to mock."

"The hell—" he muttered.

"I'm quite surprised the Whitehalls are so liberal with their servants," Juliette heard someone say, and she looked up to see Brenna passing by with her fiancé, Randall. "Imagine your mother's maid simply hanging about like that for all the world to see."

"That one we just passed is quite lovely though," Randall murmured.

Juliette couldn't hear Brenna's reply, but from the tone of her voice, she could tell the other woman hadn't been happy with Randall's comment.

"We're not done," Thomas said, his voice hoarse with emotion.

He stormed off, and Juliette finally made her way down the stairs, happy she had made—she thought—some sort of point to Thomas. If he thought he could simply "have a great time" with her and be done with it, he was quite mistaken.

Yet she couldn't help wishing it had all been different—either that she had never met him, or that he felt the way she wanted him to feel.

*You're falling into your mother's footsteps even though you never knew her.*

She wished Harriet were there to talk with, but it was probably better she wasn't at Hampton to witness what Juliette knew she would refer to as "foolishness." At least without Harriet, she could pretend she wasn't being completely crazy.

# Chapter Twelve

Thomas had thought he had been learning the end bits of the worst news about his company in the cables that had come over the past few days, but now he realized he had been wrong. His newest schooner, the *Jessamine,* captained by his best man and with Hank on board for the *Jessamine*'s maiden voyage, was missing or seriously off course; it had been bound to dock in Lisbon two days earlier, but now . . . no one knew where she was.

And according to his assistant, Mark Wharton, some of the men on the building crew had discovered that various materials used in the *Jessamine*'s construction had been different—and cheaper—than what the designs had called for. Cyrus Compton, it turned out, had taken more than money; he had cut costs in all kinds of places Thomas had never even guessed at.

And now, six men were missing at sea, along with important cargo and Thomas's reputation. But all that really mattered to Thomas was finding the men alive.

Petey Pennington, the kid Thomas paid to bring him cables from the post office day or night, had waited at Hampton to see if Thomas wanted to send a reply, but Thomas had sent him back to town. He needed time to think about what to say—what *could* he say? His whole business was unraveling, and all he could think was that he should never have taken on Cyrus Compton as his partner.

He had sworn to be a loner when he was ten years old, and he had gone against his own rules.

It was the same as when he had gone against his own rules with Georgina; he had ignored his own instincts and warnings just because they'd had a good time together. When he looked back, he could count dozens of times she had sent him signals he had completely ignored—"when we're old and gray," she had said more than once; "when we travel the world and you're wealthy and famous"; "when we look back on this day"; and on and on, signals that were now ridiculously clear to him.

He could remember the tears streaming down her face, later on, when she had said completely sincerely, "But we talked so much about the future!"

And he'd had nothing to say that wouldn't have hurt her. He had been a lunkhead and he had told her as much, but all she had wanted was him.

He didn't want to make the same mistake with Juliette, yet he found it impossible to stay away from her. She was innocent, inexperienced, vulnerable. She needed a man who could offer her a secure future, someone who wasn't afraid to make a commitment to a woman.

For a second, he wondered why the thought of Juliette with another man sent a shot of rage through him—but he chalked it up to what he knew to be true: When they were together, they were like a house on fire. Could he be the kind of man she needed? Could he risk giving his heart again?

He thought about the *Jessamine* again and wrote out a cable for Enid and Mark Wharton. He would return to London as soon as his money-raising here at Hampton was done—these people in England were definitely his best prospects for new funds at the moment.

And he'd make sure he didn't lead Juliette on in any way. Something was bothering her, he knew; he'd find out what, and then he'd be sure he didn't make the same mistakes with Juliette he had made with Georgina. No need to hurt any more people than he had already hurt.

"I'm quite proud of you, you know," Sarah said as Juliette combed out her hair. They had gotten so used to speaking to each other in the mirror, looking at each other's reflections rather than at each other. But now, Sarah turned to face Juliette. "It took quite a bit of nerve to approach Sir Roger, but you did it."

She opened an ivory box on top of her dressing table and handed Juliette a small silver butterfly pin, a pin Juliette had always loved for its delicate attention to detail.

"I want you to have this," Sarah said.

"Thank you," Juliette said. "But you don't have to give me anything. You've given me enough just by speaking to—" She paused. She would have to get used to saying the word, she knew. "My grandfather," she finally finished.

Sarah smiled. "How strange to hear you say that. Stranger for you, of course. I can't imagine what it would have felt like to grow up without being surrounded by family and friends."

"I did have family," Juliette said. "My mum—Harriet—and Grace just happened not to be related to me by blood, but I didn't know that at the time. And we had deep friendships with other families in similar circumstances to ours."

"I didn't mean that you were completely alone," Sarah said. "I guess I just can't imagine growing up thinking I was one person and then finding out I was someone else entirely."

Juliette said nothing, thinking about what Sarah had said but not wanting to continually contradict her. But the fact was that she *was* the same person; and she hadn't been seeking a change. What would be different was how the world would see her.

"I can't even begin to imagine how Brenna will react," Sarah said, adjusting her corset. "Except that it will be quite badly. She doesn't even like to lose at whist. In fact she hates to lose at anything. She'll probably make a complete fool of herself."

"Well, I don't think she'll make a fool of herself here at Hampton," Juliette said. "Sir Roger—my grandfather said he would contact his solicitor about me, so I imagine that's something that will wait until everyone returns to London."

Sarah was smiling. "Do you know she tried to rant at me this afternoon—yet again—about what she referred to as our 'servant problem'? 'That one insolent maid is a scandal just waiting to happen,' she said, and she went on to tell me that you and Mr. Jameson had been in a most compromising position in the front hall this afternoon. And in the meantime, she's spent every free moment trying to do the very same thing, while she's engaged to her cousin Randall!"

Juliette felt her face flush. "I do apologize about this afternoon. There *were* quite a few people about, returning from the hunt. Thomas—Mr. Jameson—doesn't give one whit about what people might think. I hope your mother didn't have a fit over it."

Sarah raised a brow. "She's getting close, Juliette. This week hasn't gone the way she had wanted it to go." She paused. "I'm glad she didn't see Lady Foxcroft in the compromising position I saw her in this afternoon."

"Lady Foxcroft?"

Sarah's eyes shone. "I know you can keep a secret, so I don't have to tell you not to breathe a word. But do you know that handsome footman they have? He has that dark mustache and those rather striking cheekbones."

"Martin," Juliette said.

"That sounds right. Well, I suppose you would know. In any case, I went out early this evening toward the Critchfield Road—my father always used to take me walking at that time of evening, and it's something I won't give up simply because I might lack a chaperone. In any case, I saw a carriage, one I recognized as Lady and Lord Foxcroft's. It was rather off to the side of the road, where one might pull over and not ever be seen; one *wouldn't* be seen by passing carriages, in fact. But I was walking." She smiled.

"And Martin and Lady Foxcroft were in a *very* compromising position indeed."

Juliette stared. Martin and Lady Foxcroft? Out here at Hampton? She had known that Lady Foxcroft had taken a fancy to Martin, just by the way she had looked at him, but that they had actually made love!

*Oh, poor Caroline,* she thought—especially now that Martin had painted the possibility of a different and exciting future together.

"Are you quite certain?" she asked Sarah. "I mean, could you possibly have mistaken something quite innocent for what you call a very compromising position?"

Sarah's face turned scarlet, and Juliette realized she had never before seen her mistress blush. "I'm quite certain," she said softly. "Juliette, the man was on top of Lady Foxcroft, and his hand was under her skirt. *And* he was kissing her. *And* she was making sounds that would make a seaman blush. I think if a herd of elephants had thundered past, they wouldn't have even noticed. It looked like quite a passionate moment for both of them."

And Martin had practically proposed to poor Caroline!

Had Lady Foxcroft somehow realized Martin was thinking of leaving, or had these "passionate moments" been going on all along behind Caroline's back?

"Are you all right?" Sarah asked. "You look quite shaken, Juliette."

"I'm fine," Juliette said, shaking her head. "It's just that sometimes I feel completely disillusioned about these relationships between men and women."

Sarah smiled. "Including yours with Mr. Jameson?

Brenna was absolutely fuming with envy over you and Mr. Jameson. I do believe she'd even forget her reputation and future for a chance at the man."

Juliette glanced at the clock and said nothing. This was around the time she had met Thomas on other nights, but she had no intention of wandering out into the darkness again, whether she needed something or not. The truth was that she did need a bit more rosemary to make up Sarah's hair rinse for the next day, but she could make do with sage in its place. "If you don't need me for anything else, Sarah," she said, "I'll go downstairs."

Sarah was eyeing her mischievously. "Don't tell me you're meeting him!" she whispered.

Juliette shook her head, her body wishing that Sarah were right.

But she wouldn't chase after Thomas; she wouldn't put herself in such a vulnerable position again. Every time she thought about what had happened between them, she felt weak in the knees—but wasn't that more of a reason not to meet Thomas than to meet him? If he were looking to have a "great time" with someone, she had the feeling just about anyone would do.

Sarah sighed dramatically. "You disappoint me, Jules. But of course, take your leave. And sleep well. Tomorrow is a busy day, and you'll have to be on your toes every moment."

Juliette nodded and went down the back stairs for a cup of tea. Her body felt unsettled, and she cursed it— it was as if it didn't matter that she felt hurt and furious and determined not to be with Thomas, as if her brain had no power at all over her heart or her body.

She was heading down the stairs toward the landing on the entry floor when she stopped.

Thomas was standing there gazing up at her, leaning against the wall with his arms crossed, looking as casual and unsurprised as if he'd had an appointment to meet her.

"I'll walk with you out to the herb garden," he said.

"I'm not going to the herb garden," she snapped, reluctantly reaching the landing.

"Why not?"

"Isn't that my business?"

"I want to know," he said.

She laughed, and she was glad he was standing close to her, because she laughed right in his face. "Well, isn't that nice? You want to know, so I have to tell you?"

He not only wasn't laughing, he wasn't even smiling. In fact, he looked furious and oddly impassioned. "What I meant was that I want to know if it's because of me."

She couldn't tell him the truth. "Mr. Jameson. If I needed to go to the herb garden, I would go, whether I thought I would run into you or not. I can't imagine what it's like thinking that the whole world and everyone's actions revolve around oneself. I—"

He pulled her to him and lowered his mouth to hers.

Part of her wanted to protest, but it was only, unfortunately, a small part, and powerless against the wave of desire and pleasure and need that swept through her.

She opened her mouth and opened her soul and wished that she was doing neither, but oh, what a pull he had on both.

"Come to my room with me," he murmured, his lips and breath hot against hers.

She almost laughed. "Your room?" she squeaked.

"Why not?" he asked, holding her hotly against his hips. "Tell me you don't want to," he whispered.

She could have tried to tell him, if she had been able to find her voice. But even if she had been able to speak, or even to catch her breath, her body would have given away a truth that was obvious: Her nipples were tight against her blouse; she knew that her pulse was pounding at the base of her throat; and where she could feel the pressure of his masculine need, she was certain he could feel the heat pulsing from her as well.

"Come with me," he urged, his voice husky.

She remembered—she knew she would never, ever be able to forget—the intense pleasure he had given her and how much she had wanted to give it back to him. She remembered crying out as his commanding fingers had coaxed her to ecstasy. And she remembered—for too brief a moment—why she had vowed she wouldn't go off with him again.

"You've been in so many of these rooms as a maid, Juliette. Now come as my woman. I want to stretch you out on that bed and look at you, and run my lips along every inch of your beautiful skin."

Hmm.

*Just once.*

It was a crazy idea, one that would surely get her fired on the spot if she were discovered.

But when had she ever been concerned with following all the rules?

"Let me go first," she whispered.

He shook his head, a gleam in his eye. "Take my hand," he said.

"No. If we're going to do this, I don't want to get caught before we even reach your room. You go up your normal way, up the other stairs. And I'll meet you."

His eyes burned into hers. "You won't change your mind—" he warned. "Because if you're thinking of it—"

"I won't change my mind," she murmured, and she brushed her lips against his. She didn't know what it was that was making her so bold, but she knew that part of her was trying to be sure she *didn't* change her mind. "Go. I'll meet you."

He turned away, then turned back and covered her mouth with his. "I'll see you up there in half a minute," he whispered.

"I promise," Juliette said, and she watched as Thomas slipped out the door to the front entry hall.

She had no idea if anyone was on the other side, but she wasn't worried. No one would dream of asking Thomas why he was on the back stairs, and if they did, he would laugh in their face and proceed upstairs.

She was the one who would have to be careful. Two of the Hampton maids were responsible for most of the guests' rooms, tending the fires and hauling coal and water upstairs, and at this time of night, it would have been highly unusual for any maid to be slipping surreptitiously into a guest's room.

She ran up the stairs, opened the door to the second-floor landing, peeked out, then walked down the hallway as if she belonged there. She knocked lightly on Thomas's door, just in case anyone was watching, and then opened it, stepped inside, and shut it.

She didn't know why, but being in the room as a guest rather than as a maid just about took her breath away. She looked around at the beautifully polished armoire, the gleaming china, the shining glass of the barrister's bookcase. Then she looked at the bed, seeing burnished wood and fine linen sheets she could have put on the bed herself, and she imagined struggling with cleaning the room, then hurrying out before Thomas arrived.

Only now, the door opened, and Thomas took her in his arms. His breathing was already ragged, his nostrils flared, his breath hot against her lips.

He reached out and pulled her apron off with fingers she saw were actually trembling. He unbuttoned her dress quickly, then slid it down over her shoulders.

His eyes were heavy lidded, dark with desire, stormy with a passion she knew matched her own. "From the moment I first saw you," he murmured. "From that first moment, this is what I've wanted."

He lowered his lips to hers, then dragged them along her neck, while his warm, strong hands splayed over her waist, then down along her buttocks, pulling her close.

She gasped when she felt his arousal, felt herself melting and needing him in a way she knew was new and deep and powerful.

He unbuttoned her chemise, then edged it off with his teeth and stood back to gaze down at her, hunger in his eyes. In her wildest imaginings, she wouldn't have dreamed she would be able to stand before him so brazenly, but she knew he thought she was beautiful. He lowered his lips to one of her breasts and drew her nipple into his mouth, stroking and flicking it with his tongue. He trailed his lips down her stomach, and she ran her fingers through his hair as a primitive yearning heated her insides.

He knelt in front of her and slid the last bits of soft fabric she was wearing down off her skin, and the heat of his hands on her buttocks deepened her desire.

Nuzzling her stomach with his lips and then the tip of his tongue, Thomas moved downward. Juliette cried out, half disbelieving what he was doing as his tongue probed between her curls. He stroked her and silkily entered her with his fingers, possessing her more deeply. He coaxed her, his touch tender but commanding, his tongue unrelenting, urgent, searing her with a mix of pleasure and agony.

"Thomas," she whimpered, her knees buckling. She trembled as he stroked her, cried out as her desire and need spiraled into an explosion of exquisite pleasure.

She was only half aware, still in a whirlwind of feeling as Thomas scooped her up and laid her on the bed. She watched as he tore off his clothes, his gaze never leaving hers.

"I can't believe we have this big, beautiful bed and I couldn't even wait to get you on it," he murmured as he braced himself over her.

She ran her hands over the thick muscles of his chest, his hard shoulders, arms that were taut with muscle. Through the fine sprays of hair on his chest she found his nipples, and she played with them as he had with hers. She felt oddly bold and completely comfortable with Thomas, yet she had no knowledge of what might feel good to him.

"Does this feel good?" she asked as his nipples grew taut and peaked beneath her touch.

He groaned. "You have no idea," he said.

He was obviously aroused, his need hard and urgent against her, and she tentatively reached down. As she wrapped her fingers around his thick shaft, Thomas gave another groan of pleasure that was intoxicating to hear. Juliette loved thinking she had the same power over him that he had over her.

"I want to do this right," Thomas said, his lips wet against her ear. "Are you sure you're ready?"

Juliette thought of all the protests she had meant to make, all the reasons not even to have met Thomas, much less make love with him.

But this was a passion that was too deep to resist. She was in love with the man, whether she wanted to be or not.

"I'm sure," she whispered as his fingers coaxed her again. Gently, he moved between her legs, and Juliette cried out as he began to enter her. It seemed impossible that he would fit, even ready and yielding as she was.

"It's going to hurt a little at first, but I'll make it up to you," he whispered as he moved inside her gently. She felt one sharp pain, and Thomas stopped for a moment, kissing her cheeks and her forehead and her lips, showering her with kisses. Then he began moving again, slowly going deeper and deeper, his strokes possessive, powerful. Juliette felt as if he fit her perfectly, his chest against her breasts, his rough cheek against her smooth one, his urgent, hard flesh sliding in and out of her. And she felt something new, as if with every thrust, Thomas was taking deeper and deeper possession of her very soul. She reached a place she now knew well, felt such deep pleasure there was no turning back, and she cried out. His thrusts suddenly felt fiercer, move desperate, and with a moan, he exploded inside her. As he slowed, still clenching her hair, his heart pounding against her chest, she realized they were both drenched in sweat, breathing raggedly, connected deeply.

He felt her let out a breath against his chest and wished he could say the words he knew she wanted to hear: *I love you.* His emotions were so confused, he didn't know how he felt. The one thing he did know was that he couldn't make any new commitments until his life was straightened out.

This interlude with Juliette had been heaven, an escape from the seeming hopelessness of his situation. Try as he might, he couldn't deny himself the comfort of her arms.

He got out of bed and walked over to the window. It would be morning before he knew it, time to get back to reality—lost men, a lost ship, a lost business.

He saw a flicker of light and then another flicker beyond the trees toward the Critchfield Road and then a set of carriage lights turning in toward the estate.

Petey Pennington with a cable.

It had to be.

Thomas leaned down and kissed Juliette. "I have to go," he murmured.

*I feel different,* Juliette said to herself the next morning, and she wished it weren't true. She wished she didn't love Thomas; she wished she had had a stronger will; she wished she had never walked into the sweet shop on that day that now felt so long ago.

Though she wasn't late to the kitchen, Mrs. Winston looked up sharply the moment she entered. "Well, my goodness gracious me," Mrs. Winston cried out, dusting loose flour off her hands into a large bowl. "Look what the cat dragged in with the early-morning mouse." She looked Juliette up and down. "You look different," she said, peering at her more closely.

Juliette felt herself flush and turned away. She would heat Sarah's water and bring it upstairs before Mrs. Winston could guess at anything.

She hurried upstairs, and found Sarah already awake, stretching as Juliette entered the room.

She looked Juliette up and down. "You look different. Have you done something to your hair?"

*I made love all night with the man of my dreams,* Juliette thought, *like a fool and against all my promises to myself.* "I just threw it back because it's in need of a wash," she semi-lied.

The door flew open.

Lady Whitehall, her face as pale as the pure-white pitcher Juliette had just picked up, had flung open the door.

She looked tall and regal, as usual, but frightened as well. Her mouth opened, but no sound came out.

"Mama?" Sarah said, standing up and walking over to her. "Mama, are you all right?"

It amazed Juliette that there was so little physical contact in families like the Whitehalls: Sarah didn't hug her mother or draw her into her arms, or even touch her face.

"Sir Roger is dead," she said.

Sir Roger. Grandfather. The grandfather she hadn't yet been able to call "Grandfather."

"What? What happened?" Sarah asked. "Are you sure? Was it his heart?"

Lady Whitehall looked pained and angry. "The poor man was apparently stabbed while he slept. His footman found him a few minutes ago when he went in to help him with his morning dressing. Your father is sending Grant to bring in the Sommerfield police." She paused, and Juliette could see that Lady White-hall was nearly in a state of shock. "Oh, dear," she murmured. "Imagine something like this happening right here at Hampton."

# Chapter Thirteen

As Petey Pennington waited, Thomas wrote the last of the morning's cables, and as he wrote, he wondered how much worse his luck was going to get.

No word had come to his company in Boston from Hank or any of the crew members, and no one had cabled in news of any out-of-the-ordinary ship sightings.

Thomas felt powerless and furious, yet he knew the most logical thing to do was to stay put and continue raising money.

*You were made for the sea and to build ships. You're not meant to be with these people.*

He felt torn, but he knew Hank would want him to stay put. *No money, no more ships,* he could imagine Hank saying. *Go and squeeze every last shilling out of each and every one of them, Tommy.*

He gave Petey a generous tip for having come to

Hampton twice in one morning, cleaned himself up, and headed downstairs.

As soon as he walked in to the dining room, he could tell that something was wrong. It was too early for breakfast to be served—these people lived like kings and queens, eating breakfast at 10:00 or 10:30 or even later.

But Mr. Blake, the Whitehalls' butler, barely greeted him, and the maids hurrying around looked shocked and panicked.

A man he had never seen before appeared at the entrance to the dining room, followed by Lord Whitehall.

"I'll need to question all the guests this morning," the man was saying to Lord Whitehall.

"You must be joking," Lord Whitehall said.

Thomas had the feeling Lord Whitehall was so preoccupied that he hadn't even seen him standing there.

"Hardly," the man replied. "I can interview the servants at my leisure. But once your guests get wind of this . . . development, they'll be leaving for London in droves."

Lord Whitehall jumped when he spotted Thomas. "Ah. Mr. Jameson. I hadn't realized . . ." He paused. "Thomas Jameson, this is Inspector Albert Hannigan, Coroner of Sommerfield County. Inspector Hannigan, Thomas Jameson. Mr. Jameson has come from America for a brief visit." He paused, and Thomas could tell that whatever he was about to say was causing him great emotional pain; he looked twenty years older than he had the day before, his face ravaged by grief. "I'm afraid there's been a death—Sir Roger, by another man's hand. Inspector Hannigan has come to determine the circumstances surrounding the death."

Thomas was amazed and deeply saddened. Sir Roger had been murdered? Of all the people he had met since arriving in England, Sir Roger had been his favorite by far, except for Juliette. He couldn't believe that here at Hampton, in this hushed, proper atmosphere, someone had murdered a man. "How did it happen?" he asked. "And when?"

Mr. Hannigan glanced at Lord Whitehall. "From what I've been able to determine, Sir Roger was stabbed between late evening—apparently he was in the drawing room until 9:30—and quite early this morning."

"All the more reason it couldn't possibly have been one of our guests," Lord Whitehall cried out. "What guest of mine would be inclined to stab someone in the chest while he slept?"

"This is a hunt week, is it not?" the inspector asked.

Lord Whitehall's face reddened. "It's hardly the same," he sputtered. "Now, for goodness' sake, let's move into the morning room. There will be scandal enough without all the world listening to our speculations. Poor Lady Whitehall is lying down with a cool cloth on her head, and I daresay some of the ladies will faint when they hear the news."

"Next of kin?" Inspector Hannigan asked. "Is there a widow? Children?"

"Sir Roger's wife and son predeceased him," Lord Whitehall answered. "His only relations—and they're here at Hampton this week—are his granddaughter, Brenna, and her fiancé and cousin, Randall Banford."

"I see," the inspector said. "Well, as I said, I shall need to speak with each of your guests. And the servants. And of course I shall need Sir Roger's room to remain out of the reach of everyone, both guests and servants alike."

It was obvious to Thomas that Lord Whitehall wasn't used to being given orders or even suggestions: His face was strained and rigid with anger and indignation, and his breathing had become rapid and shallow.

"Is there something you haven't yet told me, Lord Whitehall?" Inspector Hannigan asked. "Because if there isn't, I'd like to proceed. If indeed you have a house full of guests, it's going to take me quite some time—"

"But what can anyone say?" Lord Whitehall asked, sounding, Thomas felt, like a child. "Everyone was no doubt sleeping except for the . . . the culprit, I suppose you could say. And he can quite easily say he was sleeping as well."

It was hard for Thomas to read Inspector Hannigan's expression, but it almost looked as if he was half smiling, or about to laugh at the absurdity of Lord Whitehall's reaction. "It's quite clear to me, Lord Whitehall, that you are understandably unfamiliar with our investigational methods. But the fact of the matter is that you must cooperate with me in any way I say. At minimum, that will require you to summon your guests to whatever room you'd like to gather them in, so that I may speak with each one—in turn— about what happened."

He turned to Thomas then. "Mr. Jameson, I understand you're a guest here, and you're now privy to certain information nobody else knows. Please—both of you—reveal nothing to anyone else except that there is an investigation into a matter of grave urgency. You'll let me proceed then, the way I'd like.

Now, the next of kin, Miss Banford and Mr. Randall Banford. They've been informed?"

Lord Whitehall's face reddened. "Not yet, Inspector. They're both quite late risers, and since I believe my wife is still indisposed . . ."

Inspector Hannigan nodded. "Just as well. If you'll have Lady Whitehall summon Miss Banford, and if you'll summon Mr. Banford, then we can inform them of their relative's death and proceed with the questioning."

Lord Whitehall's face had stayed red, and now he was shaking his head. "I must object to your choice of words, Inspector Hannigan. I understand the need to question my guests and staff. But I implore you to realize—these are all upstanding members of the aristocracy—"

Inspector Hannigan gave Lord Whitehall a look that was dark enough and annoyed enough to make him stop speaking in mid-sentence.

"And I repeat, a murder has been committed here—in *your* house. I will proceed with your cooperation or without it, but I can assure you that everything will proceed more smoothly—and appear more proper—if you cooperate as enthusiastically as you possibly can, Lord Whitehall."

Thomas studied Lord Whitehall's face—his shifting emotions were easy to read, as anger softened to acceptance and then flared up again—and he wondered whether Lord Whitehall's resistance to the investigation stemmed from the usual aristocratic resistance to any kind of inquiry that seemed too personal, or whether he felt he had something to hide.

And Thomas thought about Juliette and how she would fare under questioning. She was a quick thinker and a confident speaker, but if the story came out about her relationship to Sir Roger, how would the police react?

"It truly isn't necessary," Sarah was saying to Juliette. "I think there are enough maids helping, Juliette. Not unless you *want* to go in there."

"I don't mind," Juliette said. She needed something to take her heart out of this well of sadness. How odd it was that she had only just met Sir Roger, and now . . . She couldn't let herself get caught up in regret over what might have been—she knew she should be glad Sir Roger had welcomed her into his life, and she *was* glad. But if only she had met him earlier; and if only someone hadn't hated him enough to kill him.

"If you're sure, then," Sarah said. "I do think it would be a help. People are feeling quite agitated, and I believe that with more servants present, they might be more reserved."

"As I said," Juliette said, "I don't mind at all."

Sarah looked into her eyes. "I *am* sorry. About your grandfather. It's a pity you never were able to know him. He was everything that his granddaughter— well, his other one—isn't."

Juliette nodded and left the room. A lump had formed in her throat, and she was suddenly near tears.

She hadn't known her grandfather at all. She didn't know what he liked to eat for breakfast or what his favorite food was or his favorite books. Yet, she had known him a bit: She had seen genuine affection in his eyes, heard true regret in his voice, shared her feelings with him without reserve.

And now he was gone, but she would still have those memories, and the memory of the smell of his pipe tobacco and shaving lotion and tweed jacket. She had known her grandfather just a tiny bit, but a tiny bit, she knew, was better than not having known him at all.

When she walked into the dining room, she could immediately see what Sarah had meant. Apparently after a guest was questioned, he or she was free to go back to his or her room. The ones who remained knew only that something serious had happened. What little conversation there was seemed hushed and tense, and nerves were obviously beginning to fray.

"This is quite over the top," Juliette heard Lady Phoebe Vandermeer say to another woman. "Olivia must be absolutely dying of embarrassment."

"I can't imagine how she'll ever recover socially from this . . . this abomination," her friend answered. "But then again, we still don't know exactly what has happened. It's evidently quite serious."

Juliette was just beginning to take the raspberry teacakes around when she felt someone at her side. It was Sarah, looking pale and nervous. "Inspector Hannigan says he'd like to see you immediately," she said softly.

"Me?"

Sarah's face colored, and she looked nervous. "I don't know what Brenna has told him, but you'd better tell the whole truth as far as your relationship with Sir Roger is concerned; that's the only reason I can think of that he wants to see you before speaking with the rest of the guests."

"Very well," Juliette said, setting down her tray.

A few moments later, she entered the library, which

had apparently become the official interview room at Hampton. Juliette knew she shouldn't be nervous—she hadn't done anything wrong. But she couldn't help feeling ill at ease when she looked at the inspector as she approached him. He was dark haired, with sharp, ferret-like features and a gray-streaked, short-shaven beard, and he was eyeing her as if he was surprised she had agreed to speak with him.

"Are you Juliette Garrison?" he asked, his voice loud and sounding annoyed.

"I am," she said.

He gestured to a chair at the end of the desk. "My name is Inspector Hannigan. I'm the coroner for Sommerfield County. I believe you already know there's been a death in the household."

She felt the tears burn behind her eyes. "Yes," she said, her voice quavery. *My grandfather,* "Sir Roger Banford has been murdered."

He nodded. "And you were given this information by whom?" he asked.

"By Lady Whitehall," she answered. "I was in her daughter's room at the time. I'm maid to Miss Sarah Whitehall."

"I see. And when you were told of Sir Roger's death, was the news a complete surprise?"

She stared. "Yes," she answered. "Quite."

He nodded, then reached under the desk and held up a corkscrew. "Does this look familiar?" he asked.

She looked at it more closely. "I believe it's the corkscrew for the wine cellar downstairs," she answered. "But I couldn't be certain of it; I've never looked at it that carefully."

Had that been the murder weapon? she wondered. Or perhaps found with her grandfather's body?

Inspector Hannigan was nodding. "But it could conceivably belong downstairs."

"Conceivably, yes," she answered.

"And this," he said, holding up a carving knife. "Does this look familiar?"

Juliette shrugged. "Again, I can't be certain, Inspector Hannigan. We've only been here at Hampton for a few days," she said. "It could be from downstairs, but I really don't know for certain."

He nodded, put the knife back, and held up a pair of scissors.

Juliette's heart skipped a beat. They looked exactly like her large sewing scissors. In fact, if she weren't mistaken, they *were* her scissors, the ones Harriet had given her for her twelfth birthday in a magnificent sewing kit she still used today.

"Do these scissors look familiar?" he asked.

"They're mine, I believe," she said. "Or they look just like mine. I could tell you for certain if you let me see them, because there's a small nick—"

She stopped. Not that she had anything to hide, but she probably would do well not to go out of her way to say they were hers.

But the damage had clearly been done. "I see," Inspector Hannigan said, holding up the scissors to indicate the nick.

He looked at Juliette for a long time before he spoke. "Were you acquainted in any way at all with the deceased? I believe you said you were Miss Sarah Whitehall's personal maid."

"That's correct," Juliette said. "But I was actually— recently—acquainted with Sir Roger—" She paused, knowing that what she was going to say would sound strange and possibly untrue to someone else's ears.

Inspector Hannigan tilted his head, apparently ready to hear what Juliette had to say. He was obviously poised to begin writing again, and something in his expression made Juliette feel he had already known that she and her grandfather had spoken. "I wasn't going to say anything about it until Grand— Sir Roger told me it was the right time, but the fact is that he was my grandfather, something I didn't know until quite recently."

"I beg your pardon," Mr. Hannigan said. "Your grandfather—?"

"His son, William, who died a few years after I was born, was my father. My mother was a maid in their house."

"I see," Mr. Hannigan said, writing rapidly. "And is there any proof of your claim, Miss Garrison?"

She felt her face flush with anger. She had never set out to "claim" anything other than the truth—that much and no more. "It isn't a claim," she cried out, her voice more strident than she had meant it to be. "It's the truth, and it isn't something I was looking to find out, either. My mother wrote a diary all about it."

Inspector Hannigan looked doubtful. "Have you ever heard the term 'fiction,' Miss Garrison?"

Fury caught at her throat but luckily not at her voice. "Have you ever heard the words 'true story,' Inspector? As I told you: I never set out to claim anything. I was quite happy in my position as maid to Miss Sarah Whitehall, and I remain quite happy in it."

"But yet you apparently confronted Sir Roger here at Hampton—"

"I never confronted anyone here at Hampton," she retorted, her heart pounding. "I can't imagine where you've gotten your information, Inspector, but I can assure you that I never *confronted* Sir Roger about anything."

"So you're stating that you didn't discuss your idea that he was your grandfather?"

*Idea!* It was all Juliette could do to hold her tongue. Yet she knew that she was most certainly irritating Inspector Hannigan. "I did discuss the issue with him, yes. I didn't confront him, nor did I ask him to do anything about the fact that I am—was—his granddaughter."

He nodded. "May I say that I'm quite relieved to hear you state that you did discuss the matter with Sir Roger, since I can tell you that he made extensive notes about it already. Now, you've stated that you didn't ask Sir Roger to 'do anything' about your claim. Can you tell me, then, what precipitated that—shall we say exchange of information?"

"Do you mean why did I tell him he was my grandfather?" she asked, beginning to hate the inspector. If he were the man who was supposedly going to catch the person who had killed her grandfather in cold blood, she could see that his death would never be avenged.

"Yes," the inspector said. "You confronted him when, exactly?"

"Yesterday," she answered. "Although as I said—"

"Yes, yes," he said impatiently. "It wasn't a confrontation," he repeated in a skeptical voice. "What I'm saying is that there was a gap of time between your apparently learning of your possible heritage and your raising the issue with Sir Roger. Why the delay?"

Juliette was beginning to feel as if she had been speaking a foreign language to this man since she had walked into the library. "As I said, I hadn't planned on necessarily ever saying anything. Then when I found out that Sir Roger would be a guest here at Hampton, it seemed like a natural opportunity."

Surprisingly, Inspector Hannigan smiled, but Juliette saw that it was a mean, mirthless smile that stretched his already thin lips even more thinly across his bony face. "I see. A natural opportunity." He looked into her eyes with a surprising directness. "Do you understand, Juliette, the situation you've presented me with? I would assume that you understand how the facts look: You decided to tell Sir Roger he was your grandfather, either because you simply wanted to or because it was in fact true; you did so; he apparently made various legal provisions for you, and in fact cabled his solicitor; then he was murdered. And, just to make matters nice and neat, your scissors were the murder weapon."

Juliette felt the blood rush to her face once more and wished she had better control over that annoying habit: Obviously Inspector Hannigan had already decided that she was guilty of murder, based on his set of "facts."

And now, she even *looked* guilty!

It suddenly occurred to her what she could say in her defense, depending on the time of her grandfather's death: She had been with Thomas, a thought that even now made her knees weak.

"Is there something else you'd like to tell me?" the inspector asked her.

She tried to analyze her situation the way Harriet had always taught her to think things through: *On the one hand, if I sweep the steps all along Merrick Street, I might collect enough for a meal even if I catch cold. But on the other hand, if I try to stay warm, then we shall surely have not a bite to eat for ourselves tonight.*

*If I tell him the truth about what I was doing last night, I shall surely lose my job and my reputation, and Harriet will be put out of her flat when I can't pay for her share.*

*But if I don't tell the truth, I shall be in danger of being accused of murder. And if I'm convicted, the sentence will surely be death.*

Yet, she hadn't been accused. Even now, Inspector Hannigan seemed to be waiting for her to tell him something else. "I do believe that if I had intended to commit a murder, Inspector Hannigan, I would have been smart enough to choose a weapon that couldn't so easily be traced back to me," she said. "And even though it may be difficult for you to believe, since I knew my grandfather for such a short time, I happen to have loved him. Killing him is the last thing I would have ever done."

The inspector was looking thoughtful, which Juliette hoped was a good sign. "You've made some points I won't be able to ignore, Miss Garrison; I'll grant you that. But understand the position I'm in, and the facts as the public will see them. You'd be well advised to stay here in Hampton or back in London, and to go no farther until this matter is resolved."

"I have no intention of fleeing, Inspector, because I have no reason to flee. I've answered all your questions truthfully, and I'll be here to answer any more you might have in the future."

Inspector Hannigan looked at her carefully. "Very well, Miss Garrison. Then that will be all for now."

*Tell him,* an inner voice suddenly said.

But he had let her go. And surely her argument had

been an excellent one: Why, if she were to commit a murder, would she use a weapon that could be traced right back to her?

There was a true murderer in the house. And when Inspector Hannigan was finished with the investigation, if she were lucky, the truth would come out.

# Chapter Fourteen

Mrs. Winston had gone into high gear, and woe betide anyone who got in her way. "If you can't keep up with the pace, girls, get out now," she called. "The guests are on edge, the Whitehalls are on edge, and we don't need anyone curdling a guest's tea with milk and lemon, or spilling the tiniest crumb or drop! Is that understood?"

"Yes, Mrs. Winston," came a collective murmur from around the huge center table, which was covered with trays laden with tea cakes and shortbreads that Mrs. Winston had expertly put together during the past hour.

"Mrs. Winston is in her glory," Caroline said under her breath, "which I suppose is a good thing. She's distracted, in any event."

Juliette nodded, feeling extremely distracted herself. Had she done the right thing, she wondered, by not telling Inspector Hannigan the truth? From the talk she had heard in the kitchen during the past half hour, it seemed that there were several possible suspects in the case: Despite Lord Whitehall's assertion that none of the guests could be involved in any way, apparently Sir Roger had lent money through unofficial channels to several people in London, some of whom were here at Hampton. Yet, she wondered, did what Inspector Hannigan perceive as her personal stake in Sir Roger's longevity count for more?

"Are you all right?" Caroline asked softly. "You look so pale, Juliette."

"I shall be fine," Juliette answered. "As long as the truth comes out, somehow. Apparently the killer used my scissors."

Caroline looked stunned. "How do you know?"

"The inspector told me. He called me in for questioning."

"But surely he can't suspect *you*—"

"I'm on his list," Juliette answered. "But you say there are others, right?"

Caroline nodded. "Martin said that Lady Foxcroft told him several men right here in this house would have benefited quite handily by Sir Roger's death."

Juliette looked into Caroline's eyes. She knew that as a friend, she had to tell Caroline what she had heard about Martin and Lady Foxcroft. "It sounds as if Lady Foxcroft speaks quite freely with Martin."

Caroline's cheeks darkened. "I agree. Very few people in their circle have the sort of relationship you and Miss Sarah have. There are several things Martin has told me—conversations he's shared with Lady

Foxcroft—that make me nervous about what Lady Foxcroft's intentions are. That's why I hope he jumps ship as soon as he can to work for Lord Wootten."

"Actually," Juliette began, "Sarah told me—"

"Caroline!" Mrs. Winston called out, clapping her hands. "If I have to call your name again, you'll live to regret it. Now come help poor Rachel here with these dishes before she breaks Lady Whitehall's favorite teaware."

"Promise you'll tell me later?" Caroline whispered.

Juliette nodded, knowing that no matter how difficult it was going to be to tell Caroline what she had heard, she owed it to her best friend to let her know what Sarah had seen.

A few minutes later, she walked into the dining room, carrying a tray of berry tarts and lemon cakes.

At the far end of the room she saw Inspector Hannigan chatting with Lord Whitehall. Lord Whitehall looked upset, as if he had aged ten years, and he kept turning back to Inspector Hannigan, speaking, then turning to face his guests, who were for the most part seated, then turning back yet again to speak with the inspector. It was the first time Juliette had ever felt that he looked unsure of himself, and she could imagine why. Apart from his grief over the death of his good friend, he would have to face the greatest scandal of his life—and even worse, Juliette was sure, the sharp wrath and deep disappointment of Lady Whitehall.

"Ladies and gentlemen," he began, and immediately the buzz of voices was hushed, as suddenly as if a lid on a jar had been closed over a chirping cluster of crickets. "My profound apologies for the inconveniences of this morning. And of course, my deepest sympathies to the family of Sir Roger Banford. By now, all of you know what transpired here at Hampton last night, and I'm quite certain you will all forgive the great inconveniences of the day in the interest of justice. I believe Inspector Hannigan has all the information he needs from you at this point, and we should like to thank you for your understanding. In light of Sir Roger's untimely passing, we will cease our hunt week early in order to attend Sir Roger's funeral. But please follow whatever plans suit you. Our staff will be here to serve you until the final guests have taken their leave."

Out of the corner of her eye, Juliette saw Thomas stride in just as a few people had stood up and begun to leave. He walked straight up to Lord Whitehall and began speaking with him, then turned and briefly spoke with Inspector Hannigan.

But the inspector had already begun to walk away from Lord Whitehall. Indeed, Juliette felt, as she looked up from the tray she was holding, it looked as if the inspector was heading straight toward her.

She went back to doing what she was doing—it was absurd that he would continue to think she'd had anything to do with her grandfather's death—didn't everybody know at this point that quite a few people in the gathered group of guests had had something to gain from Sir Roger's death?

A moment later, she felt someone at her side. It was Inspector Hannigan, looking quite grave and formal. "Miss Garrison," he said, as if the weight of the universe were hanging from her name.

Right away, she knew she wasn't going to like what he was going to say, but she tried to keep her expression and voice neutral. "Yes, Inspector Hannigan?"

"I trust I don't have to reiterate the need for your

continued presence either here at Hampton or at 48 Epping Place. You are still a suspect in the murder of Sir Roger Banford."

"Are you out of your head?" came a voice that, though anger had changed it, Juliette would have recognized and responded to even in her sleep.

Inspector Hannigan jumped back from Thomas. "I beg your pardon, Mr. Jameson. This is police business—"

"And I can save you hours of wasted time and effort by telling you that Juliette is innocent," Thomas said.

"Is that right?" Inspector Hannigan replied, his voice suggesting Thomas was facing an uphill battle.

"Did you not determine that Lord Whitehall was murdered last night, sometime between nine-thirty and the early morning?"

"I did make that determination, sir. Yes."

"Then Miss Garrison couldn't have had anything whatsoever to do with Sir Roger's death."

Juliette realized she had stopped breathing. A small crowd of people who had been heading for the door in order to begin getting ready to leave Hampton had slowly come to a stop to eavesdrop.

"And why is that?" Inspector Hannigan asked.

"Because she was with me," Thomas said, with a passion that apparently surprised many of the onlookers as much as it surprised Juliette: She heard several gasps from behind where she stood.

She felt the blood rush to her cheeks and she longed to run from the room, but she knew it was important to stand her ground.

"Good Lord," she heard a woman say off to her right, "the chit just lost her job in the space of one unthinking moment."

# Chapter Fifteen

"I've never been as disgusted with my family as I am at this moment," Sarah said, flinging herself on her bed like a child. "My mother doesn't even want to *begin* to listen to reason. She wants you out before the day is done."

"I'll find work," Juliette said. "I need to find it right away, Sarah, because of my mum's rent. But I'll find something somehow."

Sarah shook her head. "I know you will, Jules; you're so talented." She smiled. "Probably in three months' time I'll be walking down Regent Street and will see 'Designs by Juliette Garrison' in the window or some such thing." She laughed. "I'm actually thinking of myself and wondering how I'll ever find anyone remotely as good as you."

Juliette had to smile. Here she had nearly been charged with murder, and no doubt was still officially under suspicion, and Sarah was more worried about keeping her on as her personal maid. Not that Sarah wasn't a wonderful person—Juliette knew she would miss Sarah enormously, that she was definitely one in a million as far as employers went.

Juliette winked. "Face the fact that you won't and move on." Her smile faded, though, as she thought of what had happened, and how her grandfather had died.

"What about Mr. Jameson?" Sarah asked, sitting back up and smoothing down her hair. "He did say he intended to marry you."

"He says all sorts of things," Juliette said. "That's how he got where he is today—he told me he never worries about what anyone else thinks—ever." She shrugged. "He got me out of a difficult situation, and I suppose I have to be grateful for that."

Sarah was looking at her carefully. "And you think that's all he was doing?"

Juliette sighed. What was the truth? That when she imagined Thomas's words as real, she loved the idea in every way: It would mean that he loved her, that every night she would be able to fall asleep against his strong, warm chest, that every morning she would be able to breathe his manly scent, that whenever they wanted, they would be able to give each other pleasure and laughter and love.

But she knew that his words had just been words, a gallant act designed to save a woman he knew was innocent of a terrible crime.

"What Thomas did is Thomas to a *T*," she said, sighing again. "It was true that we spent the night together—"

Sarah's eyes widened, and she was grinning. "I

knew it!" she said. "You looked as guilty as a fox this morning. But where? In his bed?"

Juliette nodded. "Can you imagine? It was a miracle no one saw me go in."

"You scoundrel! I can't begin to tell you how envious I am of you."

"Don't be. Now I'm . . . well, it doesn't bother me that I'm a so-called fallen woman—I've never truly thought I'd take another job in service if this one ended. I don't for a moment think I'd ever find another mistress like you, and I do miss my freedom. But Thomas doesn't mean anything other than to save my neck."

"So you say," Sarah said. "But imagine if he did mean it!"

"I have," Juliette said. "But I'm more of a realist than that. I don't want to lead myself on. It's just as well that your mother's ordered me off the property. I don't think I could bear to talk to Thomas just now. I don't need him to explain that he didn't really mean a word he said."

Sarah was shaking her head. "I don't want to sound like my mother, nor to diminish what happened to your grandfather. But aside from the truly horrible fact that he was murdered, I still can't believe that it happened here at Hampton."

"I know," Juliette said. "Do you have any ideas who it might have been?"

Sarah sighed. "I know that Inspector Hannigan is interested in a couple of Papa's friends who apparently borrowed money from Sir Roger outside normal banking channels, and I suppose the thinking is that they stood to benefit by his death. The most obvious people, to me, are Brenna and Randall, even though it's impossible for me to actually imagine, but Inspector Hannigan has already ruled them out."

"But why?" Juliette asked.

"It's probably a function of class, for one thing," Sarah said, "wrong-headed as that may be. You're the only one who has no money to speak of, whereas Randall and Brenna are already quite well off. And apparently both Randall and Brenna summoned their servants at various times in the night, giving them alibis. The police are looking at you as 'the maid who would be a mistress,' I think."

"Don't they know I've been taking care of myself my whole life? I know how to look out for myself better than Brenna does!"

"Not in their view," Sarah stated. "Brenna has money; you don't; and if Sir Roger provided for his heirs, his children and his children's children, in his will, which he apparently did, then you would receive the greatest benefit from his death. But there *are* other suspects, to be sure, Juliette. I know that Lord Cornelian was in quite a hurry to leave Hampton before Inspector Hannigan could speak with him; and there are certainly other men—and perhaps women as well—who owed money to Sir Roger."

Juliette sighed. "Well, I suppose I'd better get my things packed if I'm to catch the carriage to London."

"Oh, they'll bloody well wait if they have to," Sarah sputtered. "I still can't believe how my mother's acting—it's as if she can't get you off the property soon enough. 'It's three scandals at the very least, Sarah,'" she said in an uncannily good imitation of Lady Whitehall's voice. "'Juliette's questionable lineage, Juliette's extremely scandalous behavior with Mr.

Thomas Jameson under our very own roof, and the accusation of murder. I can't say I simply won't have her in our household, because she is indeed here, obviously, but the sooner she can leave, the better for everyone concerned.' "

"Your mother is a product of her upbringing, Sarah. There isn't another woman in this house who would have acted any different. Now I'd better pull my things together," she began, but she felt suddenly quite choked up saying goodbye to Sarah, even though they had promised to keep in touch.

Saying good-bye to her friends in the kitchen was more difficult than she had anticipated—and she still hadn't told Caroline about Martin. But Caroline had promised to visit her at Harriet's on her day off, and they gave each other teary hugs.

Mrs. Winston wrapped her in a bear hug that nearly broke her ribs. "Now, I can't tell you to stay out of trouble, dearie, because you're already in it up to your eyeballs, but you speak up for yourself and watch your back. *We* know you didn't do anything wrong, but we have to make sure the world knows it as far as Sir Roger's unfortunate passing goes."

"Thank you," Juliette said, hugging her back.

Mr. Blake was more formal, of course, in his good-bye, but he did kiss Juliette's hand, and she could see true affection in his eyes as he spoke. "Your stay with us was all too brief, Juliette. I do wish you well." He paused, looking as if he couldn't decide whether to say his next words or not. Finally, he spoke. "You'll be in an unusual, dare I say awkward, position in society when you leave Epping Place and our company— belonging neither upstairs nor down. I trust you'll conduct yourself according to the highest standards nevertheless; if you do so, you'll never have cause for regret."

"Of course," Juliette answered, realizing that even though Mr. Blake's stuffy formality had annoyed her while she was working at Epping Place, she would in fact miss him.

She didn't want to say a formal goodbye to Lord or Lady Whitehall. Apparently Lady Whitehall was still confined to her bedroom, not having recovered from the shame and shock of the night's events, and Lord Whitehall was probably still talking with Inspector Hannigan.

She left, carrying her bag, by the servants' entrance, and began to look for the carriage Mr. Blake had arranged for her.

There were several lined up along the curved driveway in front of the entrance to the house—Juliette imagined most guests were eager to leave before they were dragged any deeper into what they no doubt viewed as a horrid mess.

She began to feel uncomfortable as she realized several of the carriages already had passengers, and many of those passengers were staring at her—the maid who had been accused of murder, the maid who had spent the night with the American, the maid who "claimed" to be part of the Banford family.

Well, she would be away from these people soon enough, and she would never look back. Her highest hope, assuming she wasn't arrested on the accusation of murder, was to find a job working for a dressmaker; the hard part, she knew, would be to find a position that paid her enough to support Harriet and herself. If she had to work in a factory, that would do as well, again as long as she could afford to live and eat.

She saw Hodgson, the Whitehalls' coachman, waving her ahead and realized she was supposed to go in the Whitehalls' own carriage. But as she picked up her pace and began hurrying along, she heard her name called by a female voice she didn't recognize.

She turned and was surprised to see Brenna Banford walking up to her. The voice that had called out had sounded strange and tight, as if the person had just drunk a potion of bitter alum, and Brenna's face looked pinched and angry.

Truthfully, Juliette was amazed Brenna would even want to exchange words with her in front of all these carriages and onlookers, but she supposed that much had changed since the death of Sir Roger Banford.

"I want you to realize something," Brenna said, coming up so close to Juliette that it almost seemed as if she were under some sort of spell. She looked as pale as a ghost.

Juliette simply looked at Brenna. She no longer had to try to act proper for Sarah's sake, nor to follow any rules at all. Yet, she felt that all she might have wanted to say days earlier—how Brenna had no right to speak to anyone the way she had spoken to Caroline, how she was certainly no better than Caroline and in fact much less knowledgeable and skilled—had been made insignificant because of their grandfather's death. What was important was that a wonderful man was now dead; it didn't matter that Brenna needed to change her attitudes about people and the world around her.

"Are you leaving Hampton?" Brenna asked.

"Isn't that rather obvious?" Juliette replied, setting her bags down.

Brenna looked into her eyes for a long time before

speaking. "I understand it was your scissors that killed my grandfather."

"Our grandfather, do you mean? Yes, that's what Inspector Hannigan concluded."

"Do you think someone was trying to make it look as if you committed the crime?"

"I really don't know," Juliette answered, wondering where Brenna was headed with the conversation. "If that's what someone was thinking, I don't think they thought it through all that well; if I *had* wanted to commit a murder, I certainly wouldn't have left such a calling card."

Brenna nodded slowly. "I see your point." She was silent then, and it looked as if she didn't know how to say her next words. "I want you to know that I think you believe what you've said about my grandfather. Apparently Sarah has seen the famous diary, and I know that it does exist. But that doesn't prove anything in it is true. When I was eight, I told everyone at my boarding school that I had a friend named Glinda back in London, and her parents took me to France and Italy on every school vacation. But it wasn't true—not in the slightest."

"That's all very well," Juliette said, her heart beginning to race. "But that has nothing to do with me or my mother or the father we both shared. Does it?"

"That remains to be seen," Brenna said, raising a brow. "I want you to know that while I don't think you could have killed my grandfather, I do think you're guilty of trying to be part of a family that isn't yours. Whether your mother wrote the diary to get attention, or to engage in a fantasy to take her away from the drudgery of her daily life—"

"Get away from me this instant," Juliette said.

"I beg your pardon?"

"If you don't want me to knock you to the ground with this valise, I suggest you move away, and move away quickly."

"You heard the lady, Brenna. Now move." Coming around from behind Juliette, Thomas reached down to pick up the valise. "You're upsetting my fiancée."

"Your fiancée, Thomas Jameson? Don't tell me you think the world is going to believe your declaration is anything other than an attempt to save this poor girl from facing murder charges."

"I don't care *what* the world believes," Thomas said, in a voice Juliette loved because it was so obviously drenched with contempt. "I don't care what *anybody* believes. Any country where people find it impossible to believe a nobleman, shipping magnate, or member of the so-called aristocracy would fall in love with a maid isn't a country I intend to spend a minute more time in than I have to, Miss Banford."

Brenna Banford's face was nearly purple now. "And you think anyone here at Hampton is going to invest in those bloody ships of yours if that's the way you feel about our country?"

"If they don't, it's their loss, not mine." He turned to Juliette and held out his arm. "Are you ready to turn your back on being a servant for the rest of your life?"

Juliette took his arm and smiled. She loved that he was rubbing Brenna's nose in their relationship and her changed circumstances.

She took one long, last look at Hampton, then turned back to Brenna. "Don't think that anyone else is going to share your opinion, Brenna. Do you know that if you had been more open-minded and generous in your thinking, I probably never would have even brought up the question of my connection to your grandfather? Now, though, you're guaranteed a good, long fight for your inheritance. And let me tell you something else: For the first eight years of my life, the nicest place I lived—the *nicest,* mind you—was in a room with six other people. So you tell me: Which one of us do you think will be the tougher, stronger fighter?" She forced a smile. "Enjoy the rest of your stay at Hampton. Let's be off, Thomas. I'm already sick of the sight of this place."

Juliette could tell from the barely suppressed smile on Thomas's face that he liked what she had said. And the way he was squeezing her arm as he hefted her valise under his other one made her feel wonderful.

But could she dare to hope?

Thomas helped her into the carriage, then settled in next to her as the vehicle pulled out with a lurch.

"That half-sister of yours probably won't sleep for a month," Thomas said, smiling. "She's probably furious, thinking of all she could have said to you but didn't."

"I would imagine," Juliette said. "It felt quite wonderful saying those things to her. And it made me start to look forward to being out of service again." For a moment, her stomach clenched as her body reacted to too many memories of life out of service. On too many nights, she had gone to sleep hungry and cold and wet from the London rains; too many days she had worked all day for nearly nothing, and she couldn't shake the physical feeling of insecurity and fear that had come from so many years of deprivation.

"What's wrong?" Thomas asked.

She shook her head. "It's just . . . old fears, I suppose you could say, about not having a roof over my head or knowing where I'll be sleeping each night. I know I can find a position somewhere, doing something, and I should be able to pay my mum's—Harriet's—share of the rent as soon as I find a position, but my old fears are hard to get rid of. I went into service because security meant that much to me. Now I know I'll never be a servant again, and I'm glad, but there's still a part of me that's a knot of fear; I just can't shake it."

"You'll be fine," Thomas said. "I know it as surely as I know my own name, Juliette."

Juliette knew Thomas meant what he was saying, but he seemed distracted, as if he were thinking about something else.

And she wondered whether he was thinking of the very public proposal he had made to her. She knew—deep in her heart—that Thomas had made the announcement only to save her from further suspicion.

But what if—?

"I want to tell you that I have to leave England for a while," he suddenly said.

Juliette nodded, wishing she didn't feel as if the world were crumbling. Thomas had never promised her anything—never. And she had known that the proposal hadn't been a real one. *She* was the one who had decided to risk her heart the night before.

"What about your investors here?" she asked, her voice hollow. "Wasn't that the purpose of your coming to England?"

"It was," he said, "although I don't know if I actually have any investors at this point."

"Because of what happened at Hampton," she said.

"Because that's the way things work," he said. "If

we could all control everything we wanted to control, everyone would be rich. It hasn't been the best of weeks for me, Juliette, and probably what's happened here at Hampton is the least of my worries. I have a schooner, a new one with all my best men on it, missing at sea, and my partner has disappeared with the company's accounts."

She stared. Here she had thought they had shared so much; yet, apparently some very important things had happened to Thomas, and he hadn't even hinted about them before that moment. "When did all this happen?" she asked.

"Mostly after we arrived here at Hampton. That's what all the cables have been about."

Juliette was stunned. "I can't believe you didn't tell me."

She couldn't read the look in his eyes. "I told you I'm a loner, Juliette; I always will be. Now, I'll be leaving tomorrow, if everything goes the way I want. But I will be back. And there's something important I need you to know."

"Yes?"

She tried not to let her heart lift at the sound of his voice, the warm affection she was sure she saw in his eyes.

"Everyone here who knows you—everyone—must think that my proposal to you was real. Do you understand?"

She nodded, trying to control her emotions.

She understood what he hadn't said.

*Do you understand that my proposal was only for show? Do you understand that I don't love you? Do you understand that I never will?*

"I understand," she said, forcing a smile. "Do you

know how long you'll be away?" she asked, her voice still hollow and uncertain.

He shook his head, pursing his lips, and she was surprised to see his face take on a rather complicated look. "I couldn't begin to guess," he said in a voice that didn't invite further questions.

Thomas could hear more than he wanted to in her voice, and he could tell just by the look in her eyes that she wanted to hear how he felt about her, that he was coming back for her.

He thought of the night they had spent together, and he thought a man would have to be crazy not to want to come back to that.

But she wanted more, just the way Georgina had wanted more. And more, he couldn't give—or wouldn't give, he wasn't sure which.

He felt he understood Juliette better than he had ever understood anyone, and he knew what she wanted. For her, as spirited and fearless and smart as she was, security still meant everything; all those years without a roof over her head, without knowing where her next meal was coming from had taken their toll.

What did he have to offer her? He had been a wealthy man. Now, there was a chance he was a man with nothing but a set of past accomplishments.

Sure, he had been knocked back before and had scrambled up again, but there wasn't a chance in the world that he was going to drag her down with him.

He looked into Juliette's eyes before he spoke, and he wanted to tell her the truth. This was Juliette, the woman who had told him her dreams and her secrets. But he owed her something other than the truth this time; he owed it to her to point her in the right direction, which was away from him—far away from him—except as far as the public was concerned.

"I've probably lost everything I have," he said. "I don't know what's going to happen. All I know is that while I'm gone, you'll have to tell people I had to take care of my business, which is the truth. And when I come back, you have to tell people we're still planning to be married—which is a lie, but no one except you and I will know it."

"Of course," she said quietly.

He could see the hurt in her eyes, and he wanted to take her in his arms.

But he held himself back, and when he saw her trying to keep herself together, to arrange her mouth into a semi-smile, to take a deep breath against the hurt, he sat back and acted as if what he had said didn't bother him in the least.

# Chapter Sixteen

"You can't be leaving," Rachel said the next day, tears streaming down her face.

Juliette was touched by how upset the young kitchen maid seemed to be, but she knew that all the attention she had paid to Rachel had meant a lot, coming from an "upper servant."

"Now we'll have some snotty, snooty lady's maid who won't even lower herself to sit with us for a meal," Rachel went on, rubbing her eyes. "And I won't get no more hand-me-downs—"

"*Any more* hand-me-downs, Rachel."

Rachel smiled through her tears. "See? That's what I mean. How'm I destined to learn proper English without you here anymore, Miss Juliette?"

"I'll come visit," Juliette said. "I promise."

"But you'll be married and a proper English lady!"

Juliette thought of the promise she had made to

Thomas—not the promise to love him forever, as she would have liked to say in a marriage ceremony, merely the promise to pretend. "I can still visit," she said. "And I promise I will, Rachel."

She said goodbye to the rest of the servants, most of whom had already returned to London, and carried her bags to the omnibus, remembering that day that felt so long ago when she had first met Thomas. If she had been smarter, she would have given a completely false name that first day, and Thomas never would have found her—

*He's a determined man,* an inner voice said, *and an intelligent man. He would have found you anyway.*

If she had been smarter, she told herself, she never would have let him kiss her.

*He's a determined man,* an inner voice said. *He would have found a way to convince you.*

If she had been smarter, she told herself, she never would have shared her most private thoughts, nor listened to his—though apparently, he hadn't shared as much as she had thought.

*He's a determined man. He knew there was a way to convince you.*

But for what purpose had it all been? she wondered. Merely to make love with her, when so many other women clearly would have been willing? To have some fun with a British servant in order to see what it felt like?

She was certain she knew Thomas Jameson better than that. When he could have had so many others, he had chosen her for a reason.

But clearly not for the reason she had hoped.

The bus was crowded and smelled of bodies and

sweat and old food, and Juliette was glad to emerge from it forty minutes later at East Hanford Street.

As she walked up the stairs a few minutes later to Harriet's rooms, she felt a sudden, deep sense of dread: Was her mum all right? Had the infection spread and done more damage? Had she been hauled off to the poor ward and dumped?

Juliette knocked on the door, then opened it and listened.

Silence.

Utter and complete silence, the dead quiet of a house that was filled with commotion at night, but whose occupants were all out working.

"Mum?" Juliette called out, setting down her bags.

Her stomach twisted and soured. If Harriet had passed away—

"Juliette?" came a thin, weak voice from the back.

In a moment, Juliette was holding her mum in her arms, trying not to think of how thin and bony she felt, how she was as light as a piece of cloth. "Thank God," she whispered, tears streaming down her face. She buried her face in Harriet's hair and stroked the back of her head the way Harriet had done to her so many years earlier. "Thank God," she whispered again, realizing how deeply she had missed the woman she had always thought of as her mother.

Harriet was looking at her through narrowed eyes. "'Tis neither a Sunday nor a Tuesday, dear, so what are you doing here? Ye lost yer job again, did you?"

Juliette felt her cheeks flush. "Yet again. I lost it for more reasons than all the other times combined. And the police are apparently interested in my whereabouts as well." Suddenly she realized that nearly everywhere she looked, clothes and bedding and dishes were piled into boxes. "You're moving?" she asked.

Harriet sighed. "Surely not because we want to. But we've fallen so far behind . . ." Her voice trailed off. "The landlord hasn't been bad; for a landlord, he's been one in a million. But enough is enough, he said. Polly and Alice lost their jobs along with all those other workers at the sheet warehouse, and with me not working, he doesn't see the possibility of us even making up what we owe him." She narrowed her eyes as she looked Juliette up and down. "So tell me what happened. Lady Whitehall accused you of thievery?"

"It's even more serious than that, I'm afraid. My grandfather—Sir Roger Banford—was murdered during the night—"

Harriet's hand flew to her mouth. "God in heaven. How—?"

"Somebody stabbed him during the night at Hampton—hunt week at the Whitehalls' estate."

"And the police suspect *you*? That's the death penalty you'd be looking at."

"I know that," Juliette said.

"Of course you do, dearie. I'm thinking out loud because my heart is in my mouth for fear of what could happen. You have no means of defending yourself, no way to stop the police if they have their minds set on saying it's you who did the deed."

Juliette realized she was embarrassed to tell Harriet what had followed, how Thomas had stepped forward to defend her, how the alibi he had given her was in fact the truth.

*This is your mum,* an inner voice said, *the only mum you've ever truly known. You can tell her anything.*

And she knew that this was true, that there was no one in the world she was closer to than Harriet.

"There's something that happened, though, that changed the police's view of things," she said softly. "I met a man, an American. It's not going to change my future, because . . . well, he's already gone back to America—I think. But I did fall in love with him. It was a mistake, I wish I hadn't, but he's so wonderful in every way—"

"Why did he leave?" Harriet asked, her voice fierce. "Why would he leave now, when you're in trouble? Who is this man?"

"He's a businessman—the owner of a ship-building company. He had to go—"

"When you're facing death?" Harriet blazed. "I don't begin to understand someone like that, child. I wouldn't even want to."

"He isn't like that, Harriet. Really."

"Then why did he have to leave? What was so important?"

Juliette felt her face color. Harriet was wrong; she knew it in her heart. "He might have lost everything," Juliette said. "One of his ships is lost at sea."

Harriet looked unconvinced and dissatisfied. "Your whole life, dearie, I've seen your mother in your eyes and heard her in your voice and seen her in your smile. I don't want to see her tears come pouring from your eyes; I don't want to see her face twisted in grief. How is it that even though you didn't know your mother for more than a few heartbeats of precious time, you're walking down the same path she walked?"

"But I'm not," Juliette said. "Thomas Jameson is an American—"

"Aye, that is true," Harriet said thoughtfully. "They

do tend to follow their own rules." She shook her head. "I just wish, what with all the troubles you seem to have, that you didn't have troubles of the heart as well. Now, you said your American changed things for you. How do you mean?"

Juliette had wondered whether she would be embarrassed by what she was about to say. And she did indeed feel her cheeks heat as she spoke her next words. "Well, Thomas announced to the police—actually, it ended up being virtually to the entire household—that I couldn't have killed my grandfather because I was with him, with Thomas, when the murder occurred."

Harriet looked enraged. "He did no such thing!" she cried. "Tell me he did no such thing!"

"He did," Juliette said. "He did because he felt he had to, Harriet. I was facing a charge of murder."

"And now—oh, good Lord, girl, you put your dear mother to shame as far as having a talent for getting yourself into trouble."

"I hadn't planned on looking for another job in service, anyway," Juliette said, wanting to shift the focus of the conversation. "For all the troubles and lack of money and certainty, I always enjoyed the freedom I had sewing, when I had money for the rent."

"The 'when' is a big 'if' these days, you know," Harriet cut in. "And that was what you always said, wasn't it? That you wanted the security that came with service?"

"Well, I don't have much choice in the matter now, do I? And at least it appears that Thomas did shift suspicion off me."

Harriet was scowling. "It isn't enough," she growled. "Men and their unthinking behavior. If you ask me, we'd all be a world better off without a one of them. Now you're thrown in with more than a hundred skilled factory seamstresses who're looking for work, when you should—" She stopped and looked at Juliette long and hard. "Did you introduce yourself to Sir Roger?"

"I did," Juliette said. "I hadn't thought I ever would; I really hadn't thought I would do it at Hampton. I'm not sure I would have ended up ever doing it, except that Brenna, my half-sister, was so beastly. Do you know she was wearing a necklace I'm quite sure was my mother's, and her maid told me that a servant girl had stolen it from Brenna's mother? That pushed me over the edge. And you know Sarah, torn between that small part of her that can't help being a proper lady and the much larger part that enjoys stirring things up. She's friendly with Brenna Banford, but she can't stand how she puts on all those airs, so she was truly looking forward to Brenna's horror over learning a maid is actually her half-sister."

Harriet shook her head. "Enough about Brenna Banford. How did Sir Roger react to your announcement?"

Juliette was surprised to feel tears stinging her eyes. "He was happy to meet me," she said. "He could have denied the truth, since I have no real proof that he's my grandfather, or he could have been what I had expected, which was hostile and unfriendly and angry, but he was actually happy. And relieved that I had found him. The most amazing part of all was how well he remembered my mother."

For a moment, Harriet was smiling. But her smile quickly faded. "We have to prove that you are indeed Sir Roger's granddaughter," she said in a strong, steely voice Juliette could remember well. "Sir Roger might have been all lovey-dovey, Juliette, but his heirs, Brenna Banford and whoever else there might be, certainly won't take kindly to sharing their money with the likes of you."

"Well, Sir Roger certainly believed me," she said. "He even said how much my eyes are like my mother's. Do you think that's true?"

Harriet shot her a look of annoyance. "I have more important things to worry about, dear, than whether your eyes resemble your mother's—which they do, by the way, very strongly." She sighed. "You're very much like William as well, except that he ended up proving to be a piece of rubbish." She put her lips together in a tight, thin line. "I do remember that Kate said she had left a pile of letters from William back at the Banford house. He wrote them from India. He was very much in love with her at the time, and she told me he was delighted at the idea of being a father. 'We can get started right away on the enormous family I've always wanted,' he wrote to her. I can remember questioning the truth when he added, 'the rest of the world be damned.'"

"Are you sure she didn't take them with her?" Juliette asked. "She seemed to be quite good about details—her diary and all; I wouldn't have thought she would leave letters behind—and important ones at that."

"But they weren't important at that point," Harriet said. "She had forgotten them, initially, in her wish to get away from the house. And then, when she remembered them, she realized it didn't matter because she would have burned them in any case. 'I hope somebody finds them and has them published in the *Times*,' I can remember Kate saying." Harriet shook her head. "It *was* a sad thing, though—a terrible thing, really. Not so much because William was any great loss—she knew that he wasn't—but because the affair robbed her of faith and trust. She felt a fool for having believed him, and who could blame her for that?" Harriet reached out and ran the back of her hand along Juliette's cheek. "I guess that's one reason I hate to think of you walking down the same path."

Juliette shook her head. She didn't really disagree with Harriet, but she didn't want a river of sympathy to flow in her direction. "I'm not," she said. "Really. And I thought you wanted to concentrate on my proving I'm Sir Roger's granddaughter."

Harriet looked surprised. "You're right, dear. And we have no time to lose. I truly doubt that the letters are still there, but I remember exactly where your mum said they were. The only trick will be getting into the Banford household. When is the funeral going to be?"

"Sarah said it would be tomorrow," Juliette answered. "And I had been planning on going, whether Brenna and her fiancé like it or not."

"That sounds like a good decision," Harriet said. "When you go to the house, you can look for the letters and get out of there before anyone is the wiser. It's a long chance, dear, but I think it's the only hope you have."

Juliette knew that Harriet was correct in trying to think about practical things; that had always been one of her great strengths and the reason they had survived on the streets when others had perished.

But Juliette knew she had probably already lost what was most important to her, and what she had never really had in the first place: the chance to be with Thomas, the chance to dream that the words he had spoken to her hadn't been lies.

# Chapter Seventeen

Juliette adjusted the rather heavy black bombazine skirt part of her dress and cleared her throat. She didn't feel odd in the expensive, cast-off mourning dress Harriet had salvaged from one of her room-mates; she was accustomed, after all, to wearing Sarah's much finer cast-off clothing on her days off.

But she was uncomfortable even imagining what her next words were going to be as she stood looking up at 24 Glendynn Place.

She had never entered the front door of a house as a guest, she realized. Why now, she wondered, now that she knew she had a right to enter the upstairs en-trance, did she suddenly feel uncomfortable, when before, thinking of herself as "only" a maid, she had never felt the clear distinction nearly everyone else in London felt so sharply?

For one thing, she supposed, she had never attended a funeral for a member of the aristocracy. The ones she had attended had all been extremely emotional events that had cost more money than the deceaseds' families had been able to afford, but everyone knew that to be buried by the parish was a disgrace; better to use every penny one had or borrow if one could. Harriet had always secretly felt that one never knew what happened to the bodies of those poor souls the parish looked out for; Lord knew there were medical schools aplenty waiting for the cadavers, laws or no laws.

But for the wealthy, Juliette knew, funerals were an entirely different matter. Sarah had told her it would begin at ten o'clock, that the procession would lead to the church, and that after the burial, mourners would gather back at the house. Juliette had seen funeral processions of the wealthy many times in various neighborhoods in London, and she had expected to see a velvet-draped coach, many carriages, and of course mourners outside the house.

Yet, the street in front of 24 Glendynn Place was virtually empty.

Had Sarah given her the wrong address?

She took a deep breath, walked up the stairs, and rang the bell. She would find out soon enough.

After almost a minute, the door was opened by a butler who could have been Mr. Blake's brother: gray-haired and bespectacled, he was looking down his nose at her as if he knew how uncomfortable she felt. But that couldn't possibly be true, she told herself.

"Good morning," he said in a voice Juliette felt already contained a question.

"Good morning," she said, stepping into the foyer.

"My name is Juliette Garrison. I've come for Sir Roger's funeral."

The butler looked at her for an uncomfortably long time. Before he spoke, he removed his glasses. "Sir Roger's funeral took place yesterday, Miss Garrison," he said.

Juliette felt as if she had been slapped. Yesterday? She had missed her own grandfather's funeral?

"If you'd like to leave your card," the butler said.

Her card. Juliette was about to say that she would call at another time when the door to the morning room opened.

Brenna Banford stepped out, followed by her cousin Randall. "What on earth—" Brenna began.

"Miss Garrison," Randall cut in, moving toward Juliette. "It's good to finally meet you. Why don't you come in? Would you care for a cup of tea?"

Brenna looked furious, and she wasn't moving back into the morning room. "Randall, are you out of your mind?" she cried out.

"Calm yourself," Randall said in a voice Juliette imagined would be appealing to women of all backgrounds. He was a handsome man, with fine, even features, and his voice was low and smooth and kind. His light brown hair was combed straight back from his forehead, and something about his whole manner was extremely gentle. "Do forgive my fiancée," he said to Juliette. "It's been a trying several days, as you know. Merton, bring in some tea."

"Very well, sir," Mr. Merton said and shut the door quietly.

Juliette looked around the beautiful room, letting herself imagine for a few moments what it might have been like to grow up in this house as Brenna had.

"It *is* a lovely room," Randall said, as if reading Juliette's mind. "Sir Roger always appreciated the finer things. Unlike so many people I've known with large, well-stocked libraries, Sir Roger had actually read every book in this room."

"Good Lord, Randall, are you honestly going to pretend that this girl wasn't horribly rude to me at Hampton?"

Randall Banford closed his eyes for a moment, making Juliette think Brenna's voice had been a source of irritation to him for a long time. When he opened them, he was looking at Juliette rather than at Brenna. "You will forgive Brenna, won't you? She's been understandably upset these past few days." He paused. "As have we all. But she appears to have forgotten her manners. Won't you sit down, Miss Garrison?"

"No, she will not sit down!" Brenna cried. "And you will not call her 'Miss Garrison,' Randall. This has gone far enough, and *I* shall end it if you won't." She looked into Juliette's eyes. "Is there a reason you came today, other than to continue your absurd little playacting?"

Juliette almost felt like thanking Brenna for her behavior: Every time doubt began clouding her motivations, Brenna said something so annoying and condescending and infuriating that all Juliette's resolve came rushing back.

Now, she looked at Randall rather than at Brenna; two could play at Brenna's little game if necessary. "I had thought today was Sir Roger's funeral," she said. "I truly regret I missed it."

Randall looked sincerely sympathetic. "That's a shame; I'm sorry you did as well. We moved it up a day at the suggestion of the minister, for a variety of reasons. But I'm sorry you couldn't attend."

Juliette didn't know what to say. Randall seemed as sincere as Brenna seemed hostile, and his friendliness somehow made Juliette feel weaker. She looked around the room, at the fine, leatherbound books that ranged from floor to ceiling in intricately crafted shelves; at the richly colored Oriental rug that nearly covered the beautifully polished wooden floor; and she felt her grandfather's presence as clearly as if he were standing next to her.

She felt like crying over the fact that she had missed his burial. The ceremony in the church was something she didn't mind having missed, but it would have meant a lot to her to have seen the coffin lowered into the earth. . . .

"I do believe you need something stronger than tea, Miss Garrison," Randall said gently, as the butler brought in a tray.

Randall quickly poured something into a glass and handed it to Juliette. "Please. Sit down and drink; you'll feel far calmer in a moment."

Juliette took a sip. The liquid was warm and sweet and tasted expensive.

"I believe I've seen everything now," Brenna said, shaking her head. She looked at her fiancé. "And I believe you've forgotten who Juliette Garrison is."

Randall laughed. "I haven't forgotten. She believes she was Sir Roger's granddaughter, and I understand why. Just because we disagree with her doesn't mean we should throw her out of the house."

Brenna took a long, tortured breath. "If you think you can dictate your wishes to me, Randall, you had better think again." She reached out and took Juliette's glass from her. "I don't permit servants to drink," she said. "Now please leave the house at once."

"Brenna Banford!" Randall cried out. His voice was actually shaking with anger. "We haven't yet married, you know; and we don't *have* to get married."

Brenna looked even angrier than when Caroline had dropped the chamberpot at Hampton. She ignored Randall and fixed her eyes on Juliette. "I'm asking you nicely and civilly to leave this house, Juliette. You have nothing to gain by continuing your visit here, and perhaps a good deal to lose. I'm quite ready to have Merton summon the police."

Juliette wanted to avoid that. Even though she was innocent and had done nothing more than attempt to attend her grandfather's funeral, the police might take a dim view of her having to be thrown out of the house. It would also make it impossible for her to come back to search for the letters.

"Don't be absurd," she said to Brenna in her most aristocratic voice. "I'll save you from making a fool of yourself in front of the police, Brenna. You seem to forget that I came to pay my respects to our grandfather, not to see you; I have no more desire to prolong this visit than you do."

Juliette looked up and smiled at Randall, who did seem quite nice. Her head spun and her stomach still burned from what he had given her—brandy, she was fairly sure—but when he steadied her with a hand at her elbow, she immediately felt better. "Thank you, Mr. Banford," she said. "I can find my own way out."

"Don't be silly," he said, and he walked her out to the front door. "You'll have to forgive Brenna for her—well, her childish behavior. Brenna certainly isn't willing to share any of her inheritance with you—she doesn't see the need for it. But I wanted you to know that if things work out for me the way I'd like, I might be able to give you a token payment as a—well, as an acknowledgment that you believe you're right in what you say."

Juliette didn't know how to respond. Here she had come to a funeral and found out she had missed it, and she knew she had missed the chance—for that day, at least—to search for the letters.

She was desperate enough for money it would be crazy to refuse whatever token Randall was offering; yet she knew she would refuse it, because it sounded as if she was being offered some sort of consolation prize.

Did Brenna and Randall truly think she would simply turn and walk away because they didn't want to accept the truth?

*You weren't expecting any money to begin with.*

But that was before Brenna had shown her true feelings. Now, the money, if Juliette received any, would be a way of righting the wrongs committed against her mother.

"I'm not a charity case," Juliette said, for some reason suddenly remembering the social-welfare project she had supposedly been conducting when she had saved the little girl at the confectioner's shop from the police.

"I didn't mean to imply you were," Randall said, sounding surprised.

"Then why on earth would you offer me money?" she asked, quickly lowering her voice when the butler reached the foyer. "Either you think I'm Sir Roger's granddaughter or you don't."

Suddenly Randall's whole face was transformed. "You're beating a dead horse here, Miss Garrison; I can promise you that. No one is going to believe you, and the matter is now officially closed for all intents and purposes. The more you press the issue of money that might be due you, the more interested the police will be in your activities. Of that I can assure you. Merton, please show Miss Garrison the door."

"Very good, sir," the butler said, but only after a moment's hesitation. It was a pause Juliette was fairly sure Randall hadn't even noticed; but to her servant's ears, it had been as clear as a bell with her name written on it.

"You've got to get back to that house," Harriet said. "If the letters aren't there, then we'll know it. But if they are, you can act. From the way you describe Randall Banford, I believe I know his type all too well: kind but smooth, and smooth means selfish when the mood strikes. If there's money to be had and he spends it all in a month, where'll you be then, dearie?"

"There may not be any money," Juliette said. "For all we know, Sir Roger was as in debt as half these other supposedly wealthy men are."

"I thought word was that he had lent money to several of the guests at Hampton," Harriet cut in.

"True," Juliette agreed, "but we don't know how many could actually pay him back, or what he spent on gambling or hobbies or Brenna or—or whomever or whatever. What matters more to me is proving Brenna wrong. I still can't believe she took the glass from my hand like that."

Harriet gave her a dark look. "It's one of the reasons I'd rather be near starving and on my own, dear, than in service. That girl needs a good comeuppance.

But right now, we'd better get searching for a new roof over our heads or we'll be sorry indeed when the winter sets in."

"You're in no shape to go pounding the pavement," Juliette scolded. "Let me go out on my own."

Harriet was looking at her carefully. "I feel you've lost the street smarts you used to have, dear. You don't even know the neighborhoods to search in."

"I'll start right here," Juliette said. "I'll walk and walk and keep on walking until I find a place to let."

Harriet shook her head. "I can't say I'm comfortable with the idea, dear, but I suppose I'm in no shape to go myself. So you'll have to do it. But look over your shoulder and don't be walking where you don't feel comfortable. It's a rough and hungry world out there, and not a thing like what you've been used to."

"I'll be careful," Juliette said, glad she had a safe place to leave her mother's diary, along with the beautiful pin Sarah had given her and all her other worldly goods. She could remember hauling satchels that had felt as big as elephants around the streets when she had been five and six years old. Even though she and Harriet and Harriet's friends had to get out by the next day, she knew that having a small bit of time was better than having nothing at all.

She kissed Harriet goodbye, wrapped the shawl that had once been Sarah's around her shoulders, and set off in search of someplace—anyplace—that would provide a roof over their heads.

Juliette had walked for miles before she saw the first "To Let" sign. It was in the first-story window of a soot-blackened building that had surely seen better days: Many of the windows were cracked, and most were so dirty that curtains would have been an unnecessary luxury. The few that did have coverings had "curtains" made of torn sheets and old, soiled towels, and Juliette couldn't help thinking about the countless hours the maids at Epping Place had spent cleaning the windows until they had sparkled and shone.

She knocked on the door, thinking that it would take the owner of the house some time to answer. Judging by the condition of the building, she was picturing an old, decrepit woman who could hardly move or fend for herself.

But the door was immediately whipped open by a middle-aged man who was anything but decrepit. He looked as if he could be a dockworker, obviously strong and alert and able-bodied. "Good evening," he said. "What can I do for you, milady?"

"Good evening," she said. "I've come to see about the rooms to let."

He raised a brow. "A lady like you?"

Juliette realized that her mourning clothes were rather fine looking, and she was carrying a purse that had belonged to Sarah. "I work in the needle trades with my aunt and some friends," she said. "We need a place to live, and we're clean and quiet and able to pay on time."

He nodded slowly. "Sounds like a decent enough prospect," he said. "D'you want to see the place?"

"If I may," she said, looking past him. The building looked dark and dirty inside, and it smelled of old onions and rotten meat.

"Ladies before gents," he said, holding out his arm.

Juliette could hardly see, but what she could discern looked truly squalid. Heaps of what looked like garbage and old clothes were strewn about in the corners of the large room, and she could feel a cool, strong draft blowing right at her from a broken window. She knew that she and the others could clean the place in a day's time, but would it be worth it?

"It feels rather chilly in here," she said.

When she turned back, the man was shaking his head and chuckling. "'Rather chilly,'" he mimicked in what Juliette felt was a rude voice. "You *are* quite the proper young lady now, aren't you?" he said. "And you say you work in the needle trades?"

"I've been a lady's maid for the past year," she said, feeling she didn't particularly want to discuss her background with this man. But she didn't actually know how much information one had to give to a landlord, and she wished she had asked Harriet more questions.

"And you were given the sack, I take it."

"No, not at all," she said. "I wanted to spend time with my aunt."

"And I'm a monkey's uncle," he said, moving toward her. "I can imagine in one of those strait-laced houses, a ripe young thing like you must have driven the men right over the edge. Is that how it happened?"

*Get out of this place,* an inner voice said.

Juliette felt as if her tongue was caught in her throat. "Not at all," she said, but her voice had come out like a frightened child's.

He reached out and grabbed her by the arm. "Don't do yourself a disservice, missy. Those upper-crust men with their upper-crust wives must have been wild for you."

She wrenched her arm away and ran toward the door. She tripped over something—some old, soft pile of something she hadn't seen—and caught herself against a doorjamb, but not before she had fallen headfirst against it.

The pain made her feel as if she were going to pass out.

*Keep your wits about you and think,* she told herself. *You knew more about surviving on the streets when you were five years old than you do now.*

"Listen to me," the man said, catching her by the shoulders and spinning her around to face him.

Now that she was close, she smelled liquor on his breath and the sour, acrid stench of old sweat and unwashed clothes. She began to wonder if he even owned the house. Perhaps he was just a tenant, pretending to rent it out to lure unsuspecting women. . . .

"Now, don't be in such a hurry," he said in a voice he probably thought was smooth and seductive. "One of the great things about owning a house is that I can make it possible for women who might be down on their luck or out of a job to have a spot of breathing room until they're back on their feet."

She was close to the front door, but was she close enough to make an escape without him grabbing at her and catching her again?

He was watching her carefully, and she knew she had better respond than look as if she were desperately considering making a run for it. "I'll be sure to tell my friends," she said. "In fact, since they're right outside, maybe they can come in and see the place themselves. They were eating, so they didn't want to come in until they'd finished."

The man smiled. "No, they weren't. Do you take me for a fool? I believe you intend to live with your friends, but I can promise you that they're not outside right now."

"Yes, they are," she said, feeling as if her heart had

stopped in her chest. The man obviously knew the truth, and he was walking toward her.

If she made a run for the door and he caught her, she would have to fight him off.

Did she have a chance of distracting him?

"Now, why would I lie?" she asked, her voice shaking.

*Do something he isn't expecting.*

*But what?*

*Do something other than just stand there!*

She looked past him, her heart pounding, and she imagined a bunch of rats streaming out from a crack in the wall—

—And then she screamed.

The man jumped, and she raced for the door, tore it open, and ran.

She ran along the sidewalk until her lungs hurt and the soles of her feet felt as if they had been paddled.

And then she turned, praying he hadn't followed.

There were all sorts of people milling about, most moving quite quickly, and everyone appeared to be walking purposefully.

Juliette tried to get her bearings—she wasn't even certain where she was anymore, only that she was in a bustling section of the East End. From what she could see, she had successfully escaped that horrible man.

She felt like a fool, like an innocent who hadn't ever spent a day or a night on the London streets.

I'm neither upstairs nor downstairs, she said to herself, watching people hurry past her in the evening rush home. All these people had probably been doing whatever sort of work they had done that day for nearly their whole lives. They knew they belonged to the working class, and they knew how to operate well within their own world.

But now, it seemed that she belonged to neither world.

*You'll simply have to learn your street skills one by one again,* she said to herself. *Service softened you quickly, but you can get your edge back.*

She looked around again to try to figure out where she was—at the corner the sign said Tipton Street, so she could simply walk that nearly all the way back.

She didn't know what she was going to tell Harriet. She couldn't expect Harriet to come out and pound the pavement with her. She supposed the answer was simply not to charge into any house that happened to be for rent unless she felt that the owner seemed halfway decent.

But it was already getting dark. What if she started early in the morning tomorrow and *still* didn't find a place by nightfall?

She walked quickly past a butcher shop and two vacant, rundown shop fronts. She was waiting at the corner for an omnibus to cross when a newspaper in the window of a small, cluttered shop window caught her eye.

She walked close enough to see it clearly, and then she read the words: "Police still seeking banker's slayer." Underneath was a grainy-looking photograph of a woman, and beneath it, a caption: "Lady's maid Juliette Garrison has not been ruled out in sensational case."

# Chapter Eighteen

Thomas didn't think he would be able to breathe until he actually laid his eyes on Hank and the crew.

When he had heard the news, he had been about to sail for Morocco, having first heard that the *Jessamine* had been spotted headed for shore. But now here he was in Normandy after Hank had cabled Boston that he and his crew had all arrived safely in lifeboats.

Thomas walked past the dock workers in the half light of early morning, and he said a silent prayer. *Let no one have lost his life. No one.*

And in return, what would he give?

*Anything,* he thought.

He had started from nothing and built an empire, and he would try to do it again if he could. But if he couldn't, at least if all his men had survived . . .

He reached the dock and saw the battered lifeboats

that had saved his men, and he felt a lump in his throat.

A minute later, he was patting Hank on the back, and as he looked around, he could see that every crew member had made it.

"One part luck and ninety-nine parts skill is what you have to thank for our being here," Hank said with a wink. "But it's not myself I'm talking about. 'Tis each and every man who stands before you had to scramble for safety, and we actually saved a good bit of the cargo."

"You'll all receive the biggest bonuses I can afford," Thomas said, looking from man to man. "Each and every one of you. Now tell me what the hell happened," he said to Hank.

As he listened to Hank's tale—from the horrific sound of the larger ship plowing into theirs, to the miraculous boarding of the lifeboats—he was so flooded with relief that every man had survived, he was nearly in tears. The sea had already claimed three of the people most dear to him. If anything had happened to Hank or the crew, he would never have forgiven himself.

And even though he longed to return to England— to Juliette—he knew his obligations to his men must come first. He had a business to rebuild, people whose lives depended on him. He couldn't let them down or let them suffer because of his mistakes.

"I would need verifiable experience to even consider you," Miss Loretta Glover was saying, looking down at Juliette above her lorgnette.

Juliette had known this would be necessary; dressmakers' shops had the highest-level sewing positions available in London, and nearly all the women employed in them had served apprenticeships of several years.

Juliette was ready with a lie, but she didn't know if she'd be able to say it well or not. "All my experience has been in America, actually. I only just returned this week."

"I see," Miss Glover said, sounding unimpressed. "And is there a reason I would hire you before promoting one of the girls who has worked here for five or six years? Or a London girl whose experience I can easily check?"

"I've been told I'm one of the best seamstresses around," Juliette said. "I can cut and fit and make patterns, and in America I made dresses from start to finish. I had quite a large following of clients and had been planning to open my own shop."

"Then why didn't you?" Miss Glover demanded.

Juliette suddenly realized that Miss Glover reminded her of a younger version of Lady Whitehall, with the same sharp blue eyes and fine, patrician features. "I had to travel here with my fiancé," Juliette blurted, wondering why she hadn't planned her answers better. "And as you know, it costs rather a lot to start up a business."

Miss Glover was looking at her carefully. "And is there a reason for me to think you aren't planning on stealing my best clients away from me?"

Juliette smiled what she hoped was a winning but sincere-looking smile. "I hope to be good enough to steal your clients away. But my fiancé and I are planning to return to America in a year or so."

Miss Glover was obviously considering the possibility of hiring her. "You do realize you would need to demonstrate your skills before I even consider hiring you for a position; there are girls who have worked here without pay for years who wouldn't be happy to see you begin with no apprenticeship whatsoever."

Juliette knew it was a reasonable request, but the fact was that she was desperate for money. One of her mother's friends had found new rooms for them and they needed rent money. Although the prospect of a long-term future here at Miss Glover's was appealing, she couldn't afford to work without pay. "I understand why you need to see the quality of my work, Miss Glover. But I should think that after a day's work, you would be able to tell if I meet your standards. And if I do, then I'll expect to be paid for that day."

Miss Glover laughed. "You must be joking. A trial is a trial."

"And if my work pleases you, it's work that should be paid for."

"I do believe your visit to America damaged your judgment, Juliette. But if you're so confident about your work, I suppose that's a good sign. If I hire you, I'll pay you for the trial period. But the period will be three days."

"Three days?"

Miss Glover looked even more imperious than before as she glared at Juliette from above her lorgnette. "You may take the offer or leave it, Juliette. As it stands, I'm being far more generous with you than I've ever been. But something tells me that any girl who would march in here and begin making demands might indeed be worth my taking a bit of a chance on."

"Thank you, Miss Glover," Juliette heard herself say before she had even given herself time to consider the offer. Three days without pay was a crazy idea and one she could ill afford. But then again, since the sheet warehouse had burned down, London was filled with skilled seamstresses who would probably end up doing slop work, hand-sewing in dark alleys by shared candlelight or in equally dark houses, simply because there wasn't enough work to go around; so she had no guarantee that she would find another job within three days if she looked elsewhere. "You won't be disappointed in my work, Miss Glover; I promise you that."

Miss Glover looked at her carefully. "I hope for both our sakes that you're right. Now, what did you say your last name is, Juliette?"

"Maywood," Juliette answered.

She had started a new job on a firm foundation of lies; pretty much the only thing she had said that was true was that she was a good seamstress. But the last thing she needed was to have Miss Glover connect her name with the Whitehalls, and she could tell from the newspaper article she had read that the murder of her grandfather was the talk of the town.

"Very well, Juliette Maywood," Miss Glover said. "Welcome to Miss Glover's Designs. I hope that you've told me the truth about yourself, and that our association will be long and productive."

*I've told the truth,* Juliette said silently, *with just a few unimportant untruths thrown in.*

Juliette was late getting back to the house, and she had expected to find all the boxes and bags already stacked outside on the street and the women preparing to move them.

But surprisingly, she saw nothing outside the house

except a young woman pushing a pram and two children playing with a ball and string. She had been excited about telling everyone the news of her job, and of course most excited about telling Harriet, but now, she began to wonder: Was she so late that they had already packed everything up and gone to whatever house Polly had found? And would the landlord tell her where they had gone?

She opened the door, and the first things she saw were all the boxes and bags still piled in a heap. The first thing she heard was wailing, a long, low cry of sorrow. And the first thing she knew was that something bad had happened.

She dropped her bag and forgot her good news as she ran into the front room.

There lay Harriet, stretched out on the bed, her arms folded across her chest. Pennies lay on top of her closed eyes, and her arms were folded across her chest.

Polly, Harriet's closest friend in the world, sat at the head of the bed, sobbing, her shoulders shaking.

"What happened?" Juliette cried, running to the bed. She knelt down and laid her cheek against Harriet's. Her skin felt as smooth and soft as it had all those years before, when Juliette had loved her as a mother. Except that now, it was already cold, the life already gone. . . .

"She seemed so much better," Polly said, shaking her head. "How could this have happened? I had come in to tell her it was time to move our boxes and bags and whatnot, and she stood up. Then she grabbed her chest, and she fell over and was—" She began sobbing again, and Juliette hugged her. She looked down at Harriet, wishing she could have had just one more talk with her, just to tell her that even if she hadn't been her mother by blood, she had been the best mother Juliette ever could have hoped to have.

"And the parish will have to bury her," Polly sobbed. "We gave all we had over to the new landlord this afternoon. Unless you have something, Juliette."

"I won't have anything for days," Juliette said. "But we can't let the parish bury her. *You* know that was something Harriet always considered the greatest shame. Who's keeping watch?"

"I am," Polly said. She explained the three other women were going to start moving boxes as soon as morning came. "The landlord was nice enough to say we could stay until we get our affairs taken care of. And of course we have to pay the extra days' rent when we have the money. Normally he's the devil in the flesh, but when he heard what had happened— well, I guess everyone has their weak points, and I think he's afraid—you know," she said, glancing down at Harriet.

"I'll go to Sarah," Juliette said. "She'll lend us the money, and if she won't, I know Caroline and the others would each chip in. Even if I have to make some sort of a scene in front of Lord and Lady Whitehall, I'll do what I must."

An hour later, Juliette was knocking on the servants' entrance at 48 Epping Place, still not truly believing Harriet was gone. In a way, she felt it was good she'd had to travel on the omnibus and do all that walking, because it had stopped her from thinking about the fact that Harriet was gone. She knew that if she had been the one keeping watch, she would have sat there crying her eyes out, wishing she had told Harriet how much she had meant to her, wishing she had told her just one last time how much she loved her.

Now, she knocked at the old, familiar door, and she waited. It was late, and she knew everyone would wonder who could be knocking at this unexpected hour.

The door opened, and Mrs. Winston's hand flew to her mouth. "Juliette!" she murmured, and she wrapped her arms around her in a hug Juliette felt was that much more heartfelt since Mrs. Winston no longer had to deal with her "headstrong bullheadedness." "Come in, come in, before you catch your death out there in that chill wind. Mr. Blake, look who the wind blew in," she called as she hustled Juliette inside. "We've been worried sick reading the articles about you, and worried sick over how we'd be able to find you, what with the police still so interested."

"There was more than one article?" Juliette asked as Rachel jumped up from her silver sorting and gave her a hug.

"Oh, I'd say three, in the various papers. Always mentioning 'other suspects,' of course, but they seem to love to put your drawing in the paper, I suppose a pretty face being able to sell more papers than a gnarl-faced gambler."

"You mustn't run from the police," Rachel said, nearly in tears. "We know you're innocent, Juliette, but people do love to talk."

"I'm not running," Juliette said. "I had to find a place to live, and now I have, only—" She stopped, suddenly overcome with sadness about Harriet. "My Harriet died, just this morning."

Mrs. Winston looked crushed. "No! What happened?"

"It must have been her heart," Juliette said. Seeing the sympathy in Mr. Blake's eyes unleashed the tears in her own, and she wiped at her eyes as she spoke. "She had recovered from the coughing and the fevers, but something else—apparently she grasped at her chest, and she fell, and that was it, and now I've come because we have no money to bury her, and the worst thing for her would be if the parish did—"

"Come, come, dear," Mrs. Winston said, pulling Juliette into her arms. "Between all of us downstairs we should be able to lend you the money; we know you're good for it."

"Thank you, Mrs. Winston," Juliette said. "And thank you, everyone. Truly, I don't know what I would do without your friendship. But I was also thinking of asking Sarah to help me if she could. We want to have the funeral tomorrow at the church in Barrett Place. Do you know if she's upstairs?"

Mrs. Winston exchanged a significant look with Mr. Blake. "I don't want to be one to gossip, Juliette," she said quietly, and she shot a look at Rachel, who had completely stopped working. "Back to your organizing, Rachel, and the same goes for everyone else in this room; we're not getting wages to sit around for idle gossip now, are we?"

"Yes, Mrs. Winston," Rachel said, hurrying to start her silver sorting again.

A few moments later, Mrs. Winston leaned in close to Juliette's ear. "The first thing we heard was that Sarah had asked her mum if Caroline could be her maid; she felt Caroline had given it a good try with that Banford girl, and she wanted to give her a boost. It's Caroline's half-day off today, but she already started this morning." She looked around to make sure no one was listening. "So it seems Lady Olivia gave in on that point, even though she wasn't too happy about losing Caroline's services for the general household. But evidently that wasn't enough. Caroline said Miss Sarah went quite—well, agitated when she realized she didn't know where she could find you. 'Because of *your* turning Juliette out of the house, you've made her look guilty,' she said to her mother yesterday. 'And I don't know how to contact a dear friend.' Well, you can imagine Lady Whitehall wasn't swayed toward taking you back in; I don't think there's a man or woman who walks the face of this earth who could change Lady Whitehall's mind once it is made up. Apparently this morning, Miss Sarah asked Caroline to pack a bag for her, then changed her mind and said she'd pack it herself. She walked out the front door by herself, and no one has seen her since. Lady Whitehall is frantic, although Lord Whitehall says he's quite sure Sarah's fine, that she's simply been driven to run off because Lady Whitehall is so rigid with her."

"And Caroline doesn't know where she is?" Juliette asked.

"If she does, she isn't saying; and Lord knows she wouldn't dare to keep a secret like that from me."

Juliette almost smiled; she knew that there were indeed few secrets at 48 Epping place, and she was quite sure that Mrs. Winston's version of the conversations that had supposedly been conducted "privately" were perfectly accurate.

She had the feeling she knew what had happened: Sarah had probably run off with Andrew, frustrated by all the strictures in her life and by the loss of her friend and maid.

"When you see Sarah, please tell her what happened to Harriet," Juliette said.

"She'll want to know where you're staying, dear, and for that matter, so will we. This business of reading about you as if you're some sort of killer on the run isn't my cup of tea, I can assure you."

Juliette took a pen and paper from Mrs. Winston's desk and wrote down the street name Polly had given her. "I don't know whether this is correct or not," Juliette said, "and I don't know if we'll truly end up there or not; I feel as if I don't know anything at all. But I got a job at Miss Glover's Designs in Regent Street, and I believe I *will* be able to hold on to that."

She had thought Mrs. Winston would look happy for her, but the news brought a frown to the old woman's face. "Now listen to me, dear, as you never listened any of the other times we spoke. You sew and you look pretty and you keep your mouth closed, do you understand me? Jobs like that are as difficult to come by as a shiny piece of gold in a mud puddle, and I don't want to hear in a fortnight's time that you lost it because of an argument or a disagreement or an offense taken when none was meant. Do you understand me? The same goes for any dealings you might have with your landlord: The place is fine, you'll pay your rent, and life will continue. Agreed?"

"But what if it isn't fine?" Juliette asked. "What if there's a problem with the rooms or with the job? Are you telling me I shouldn't speak up?"

Mrs. Winston put her strong, work-worn hands on Juliette's shoulders. "Yes, dear, that's exactly what I'm telling you. If you had kept your mouth shut all these years instead of pointing out every flaw and imperfection you see, you would be the queen of England by now."

"And you would be the queen of exaggeration," Juliette said.

"See? There you go again." She smiled and hugged Juliette. "But truly, dear, make me a promise that you'll hold your tongue. You'll go so much further in this world."

"All right, but I need *you* to make me a promise," Juliette said. "If Thomas Jameson comes looking for me, which I'm sure he will, tell him you don't know where I'm living—"

"But the police—"

"He said we were together that night, and that's true. No one can say it isn't. Beyond that, our pretending to be engaged really isn't going to help. And for the sake . . ." Her voice trailed off. How could she still feel wounded and vulnerable when the pain of losing Harriet was so great as well? Yet just thinking about never seeing Thomas again made her want to cry. "For the sake of my heart, Mrs. Winston, it's important that I not see him."

Understanding brightened Mrs. Winston's eyes. "Very well then, dear. I promise."

# Chapter Nineteen

Miss Glover looked at the seam for what felt like a full day, going over it from top to bottom, then bottom to top, her eyebrows so high on her forehead that Juliette wondered if they would ever lower into their normal position again.

She handed it back to Juliette, and Juliette didn't know if she was imagining a half hidden smile on that long, dour face or not. "You may proceed," she said, and walked out.

Alice Knowlton, a rosy-cheeked young girl who looked more as if she belonged on a farm than in a dark London dress shop, smiled. "Now I've seen everything, and I'm only nineteen years old."

"What do you mean?" Juliette asked.

"That's a very high compliment in Miss Glover's book, and she never gives compliments until someone has been here—well, in my case, I apprenticed for four years, and she finally told me I had done a good job at the very end. Never once before." She leaned over so she could take a better look at Juliette's stitching. "You *are* rather good, though. Where did you apprentice?"

Juliette hesitated. She didn't particularly want to lie to the young girl, but then again, she knew she had better stay consistent with her story. "I was in America."

Alice Knowlton's face lit up. "America!" she said with a sigh. "I would love to go. Or even to Australia."

Juliette smiled. "Anywhere but here?"

"It just seems that there's so much freedom in those countries, so many different choices one can make. Do tell me everything about it."

Juliette looked around. Although some of the other women were talking nonstop, Juliette didn't want to take a chance. She had no intention of losing her job over a silly mistake. "We can talk later," she said quietly. "I'm going to go back to my stitching."

Alice looked disappointed, but she shrugged and went back to her own work, stitching a hem on one of the most beautiful gowns Juliette had ever seen.

"Has anybody seen the man Miss Grace Covington is going to marry?" another young woman, Marion Aplet, asked. "I think he's the handsomest man I've ever seen in my life. I was thinking if we make her wedding dress too tight, he might become available for one of us!"

Over giggles from the others, Alice murmured, "Marion is the dreamer of our group.

"What about Mr. Westfall?" another young woman asked. "He's positively dreamy."

"But he's probably the devil to live with," another

woman said. "He's come out against every one of Balfour's proposals. If he had his way in Parliament, England would be a dictatorship, and he would be the dictator."

How different these women were from the ones she'd most recently been working with.

"I saw his picture in the paper just yesterday," Alice Knowlton said. "He was quite handsome, although I think whoever took it didn't do him justice. His eyes positively bore into you when he looks at you."

"And what are you doing staring googly-eyed at him in the front room when you're supposed to be back here sewing?" demanded Emily Brownell, a woman Juliette didn't care for.

"A girl can dream," Alice said, and turned with a flounce back toward Juliette.

"What about the murder at Hampton, in Sommerfield County?" Marion said after a brief silence. "The *Illustrated Weekly* had almost a whole page about it."

"Men like that often lead mysterious lives," Alice said. "The paper says he lent money to all kinds of people, so you don't know what sort of gutter creature might have done it."

"But it was out at the estate, wasn't it?" Marion asked. "So it was probably one of the guests. Some upper-cruster they'll never catch."

Juliette looked down at the seam she was sewing and tried not to listen to the conversation.

*Don't let your cheeks turn,* she told herself. *Because if they do, everyone will notice, and then . . .*

"Would you look at those cheeks!" Emily Brownell called out. "I haven't seen anyone—" She stopped, and narrowed her eyes at Juliette, looking at her for too long. "What did you say your name is?" she asked, her voice sharp and suspicious.

"Juliette Maywood," Juliette answered as confidently as she could.

Emily Brownell was still staring at her—quite rudely, Juliette felt, for someone who probably prided herself on her good manners.

"Juliette Maywood?" she repeated. "It wouldn't by any chance really be Juliette Garrison, now would it? You look exactly like the picture in the *Illustrated Weekly*, and now here you are as red as a tomato, with the same first name—"

"Why don't you mind your own business?" Alice called out, setting her sewing down for a moment. "Just because you're as jealous as a green monster that Juliette is such a fine seamstress doesn't mean you have to make every nasty accusation that comes into your head!"

Emily Brownell's disdainful, fatigued expression made Juliette feel that she and Alice had been clashing for a long time, probably over the most minor of issues. "I know what I've seen," she said wearily.

To tell or not to tell? Juliette wondered. If she could know that Miss Glover would believe her, she would have taken the chance of revealing who she was. She *was* innocent, after all, and none of the noblewomen who frequented the shop needed to know the details about the personal lives of the women in the back room.

But there was a reason she had lied, she knew: People tended not to want to keep a murder suspect in their employ. And now that she *had* lied, why would she reveal the truth unless it was absolutely necessary?

"Things are not always what they seem," Juliette said quietly. "Surprisingly enough, you're not the first person who's told me about the resemblance and the coincidence with the names. I haven't seen every newspaper picture, but I've been told that the resemblance is rather strong."

Emily Brownell looked angry, her lips compressed in a tight, thin line and small red blotches appearing at her cheekbones. "Yes, well, we'll just have to see about 'coincidences and resemblances,' won't we?"

"Oh, don't mind her one bit," Alice said loudly. "None of us let Emily's 'resemblance' to a very annoying person bother us in the slightest. Isn't that right, ladies?"

Among mutters of "a body should mind her own business" and "I don't like to pry where I'm not wanted," all the women went back to work.

Juliette wondered how much longer she would be able to keep her identity hidden; and if it *were* revealed, would she lose her job before she had a chance to defend herself?

Miss Glover swept into the room in a cloud of perfume and looked around. It was nearly ten o'clock, and Juliette imagined all the other women felt as ravenously hungry and thirsty as she did. But she knew that one of the requirements of working in a shop like Miss Glover's was that the seamstresses and stitchers and cutters either had to work extremely long hours or sometimes the opposite, no hours at all when business wasn't good.

Now, Miss Glover walked past each woman and checked to see how far she had gotten on her garment. Apparently she never let one woman go home before the others, because she didn't want to encourage what she called "hurried sloppiness." Juliette knew that everyone desperately wanted to go home, but would they be allowed to?

"Very well," Miss Glover said with a sigh, evidently quite well aware of how hungry they all were. "You may leave."

Each woman carefully smoothed out whatever she was working on and then hung up the garment. Juliette wasn't one of the ones to rush out; she knew that for some of the women, every moment counted. They were hurrying home to kiss their children goodnight, or to see their husbands. She would let them rush out, then walk back to her own empty rooms. Her heart would break yet again when she saw that Harriet was dead and gone.

She gathered her purse and cloak and walked out into the night, drawing her cloak around her shoulders against cold air that suddenly chilled her to the bone.

As she walked—quickly, because, even though she didn't have any money in her purse, a thief wouldn't know that; it was too late to be out by herself—she thought about what had happened today with Emily Brownell, and how it was virtually inevitable that Miss Glover would find out her identity.

It was the morning of the funeral, and Juliette felt her heart break one more time as she looked at her beloved Harriet. When she had found out Harriet wasn't her mother, she had loved her all the more for all those years of love and sacrifice, all those years Harriet had worried more about Juliette's and Grace's well-being than about her own.

*At least she's not in pain anymore,* Juliette said to

herself, and she knew this was a good thing. But what if she had been able to find rooms the day before? Surely the stress of all their worries had led to Harriet's death as much as anything had.

It was a small group of mourners by the grave, and Juliette couldn't help wondering what her grandfather's funeral had been like. Though there were not many mourners, she knew that each woman had loved Harriet deeply, and she hoped Harriet could feel all that love now, as her body was being lowered into the deep, cool earth.

As the minister began to speak, Juliette saw that Polly had begun to cry, and soon her own tears were flowing. Why had Harriet died now, just when they were starting a new part of their lives? Why now, when Harriet had actually seemed to enjoy plotting and planning how they would right some of the wrongs that had been perpetrated against her mother?

Juliette wiped at her tears as the minister finished speaking, then followed Polly and the rest of the women as each threw a clump of dirt on top of the coffin.

She had thought she was the last person in the small line of people, but she felt someone behind her.

She kept walking, then looked back.

Thomas was tossing in a small clump of dirt. He seemed to be saying a silent prayer, looking down into the hole. Then he looked into Juliette's eyes as if he had known she was watching him. "I'm sorry," he mouthed, and she felt a new flood of tears begin.

What on earth was Thomas doing here?

Why hadn't he gone to America?

Juliette felt his arm, warm and strong, around her

as she walked away, and he stopped and pulled her into a gentle embrace.

"I'm sorry about Harriet," he said softly.

"How did you know?"

"Mrs. Winston," he said. "She said she wasn't going to tell me where you were living, but she wanted me to know about Harriet." His eyes were searching hers, and she could see that he seemed not to know how to say what he wanted to say. "You can't just drop off the face of the earth like that, Juliette," he finally said.

"I thought you were going to America."

"I was. But my men ended up landing safely in Normandy." He reached up and wiped a tear from her cheek with his thumb. "Don't you remember what we're supposed to be doing?" he asked. "I'm supposed to be your betrothed, or whatever they call it here. How do you think it will look to the police if I don't even know where you are?"

"I don't care," she blurted.

"What do you mean, you don't care? You'd *better* care if you don't want to end up convicted of something you didn't do." He wiped another tear from her lower lashes. "You're hurting right now, and I wish I could make that better for you. I wish I had met Harriet, and I wish she were still here. I can't change any of those things, but I *can* help save you from being convicted of murder. Don't pretend you can do it yourself, Juliette."

"I'm not pretending," she said. "I just don't want—" She stopped.

*I just don't want to look at you and feel so drawn to you.*

*I just don't want to look at you and wish we were more than a lie.*

251

*I just don't want to need you so much.*

"What are you doing for the rest of the day?" Thomas asked.

"We have to move our things into our new rooms," she said, wishing she didn't feel so close to tears.

"I'll help you," he said. "My friend, Gregory Chiswold, has given me his carriage for a few days. That should make things easier for you."

Two hours later, Juliette was glad she hadn't fought Thomas on the issue of his helping her and her friends move. They had successfully transferred all their things to the new rooms, and then Thomas had bought everyone a meal at a nearby pub as his memorial gift to Harriet.

"Don't let *that* one get away," Polly whispered as the other women began leaving.

Juliette half-smiled. "Then you don't share Harriet's opinion," she said. "Harriet didn't want me to fall for Thomas."

"Then I can guarantee you Harriet didn't meet Thomas, did she—?"

"I told her all about him," Juliette said. "But it's a moot point, in any case. Thomas has made it quite clear we don't have a future together except in the eyes of the public and the police. I'm only telling you the truth because I know you wouldn't divulge it to anyone."

"Dearie, haven't you seen the way he looks at you?"

*Don't believe her,* Juliette told herself.

"And the way *you* look at *him*," Polly went on.

Thomas came back from saying goodbye to the other women, and Polly kissed Juliette on the cheek. "You think about what I've said, dear, whether you want to or not. And by the time you come back to our rooms, they will be as clean as a whistle."

"I'm coming with you," Juliette said.

A glint lit Polly's eyes. "Not quite yet, dear. I believe Mr. Jameson has some business with you first." She blew Juliette a kiss as she walked off.

She tried not to look at Thomas as they walked together, his arm linked in hers, but she couldn't help it: He was just so handsome, somehow even more so than she had remembered.

They stopped in front of a carriage, and Thomas helped her in. A few moments later, Thomas reached out and touched her cheek with the back of his hand. "I'm not going to mouth some platitude about how Harriet is in a better place," he suddenly said. "It stinks that she died; I wanted to know the woman who raised you. And she would have liked seeing you in your new job, not as a servant—"

"There's nothing wrong—"

"I didn't say there was anything wrong with being a servant," Thomas said. "At least, there's nothing wrong with the people who are servants. But it is a crazy system, Juliette; you have to admit that. I only wish Harriet was going to be able to see you enjoying your new life. And I wish I had known the woman who raised an amazing young girl who turned into an amazing young woman."

Juliette fought tears. Why did it matter to Thomas that he had never met Harriet when he was so obviously not going to be a part of Juliette's life in the future?

"Don't fight your tears," Thomas said, pulling her into his arms.

"I'm not fighting the tears," she murmured against his shoulder. "I'm fighting you."

"I just wanted to be here for you," he whispered, stroking her hair. "Just let me do that much for you."

The carriage pulled to a stop, and Thomas helped Juliette out into the street in front of a grand-looking house that reminded her a lot of Epping Place. Thomas linked his arm with hers and led her up the stairs, then opened the door.

"This is my friend's home, where I've been staying. He's out of town for a few days."

It was a beautiful house, the entryway furniture decorated in unusually vibrant maroons and purple-reds, and for a moment, Juliette pulled herself out of her grief over Harriet and let herself appreciate the beauty of the house's furnishings.

Thomas opened the door to the morning room and motioned for Juliette to enter. "This is what I wanted to give you," he said, and he held up the mourning dress she had made for Sarah when she had first begun working at Epping Place. Sarah had been horrified when Lady Whitehall had asked Juliette to demonstrate her skills on what Sarah had called such a "horribly morbid project," and she had told Juliette afterward that she didn't want to offend her, but would hide the dress behind all her others to ward off bad luck.

"Where did you get that?" she asked.

"Mrs. Winston wanted you to have it."

Juliette almost laughed. "And she didn't feel the need to ask Sarah about it?"

"Apparently Sarah's off on her own somewhere, though it's supposed to be a deep, dark secret—of course. But Mrs. Winston said Sarah would want you to have it, and I'm sure she's right."

He set it down on the *recamier* and pulled Juliette into his arms. "I've missed you," he said.

\* \* \*

He could see the sadness in her eyes, the tears right below the surface, and he knew Juliette's heart was broken over the loss of Harriet. He knew how much she had loved the woman who had raised her as her own, and he wanted to make it better for her somehow.

"At least she saw you were on your way," he said, stroking her hair. "She knew you had approached Sir Roger, right?"

Juliette nodded unhappily. "She *was* happy about that," she finally said. "I don't think she was too surprised he was glad to finally meet me. I guess his wife was the one who hated the idea of my mother and William being together."

"Your grandfather was a wonderful man," Thomas said. "I liked him enormously."

Juliette was half smiling. "It's nice to hear someone say 'your grandfather' like that."

He looked into her eyes and saw so much feeling—but not enough hope, he felt. "It will all turn out the way it's meant to," he said.

"No, it won't," she murmured, tears beginning to brim at her eyes. "We're just together because you're protecting me—"

"No, we're not," he whispered, brushing his lips against hers.

He drew her into a kiss that felt like the deepest kiss of his life. Juliette tasted so sweet, and her lips were so soft. . . .

He needed to possess her. He drew back and looked down at her tear-stained face and he knew this without feeling the words; he felt a yearning that was beyond physical, beyond language or logical thought.

He sealed his mouth over hers again, and when he

heard a feathery moan come from deep in her throat, he felt his need uncoil into hard, primitive desire.

His fingers shook as he began to undress her.

She reached for him, for his shirt, for his pants, and he let her this time; he could see passion in the languid, hungry look in her eyes, a need he knew matched his own.

As he slid her clothes down over her soft, smooth skin, he could feel his heart knocking in his chest. He opened her chemise and ran his fingers over the silk of her breasts, and he lingered at her nipples with his thumbs. He was desperate for her, but he was going to take his time.

He could see desire in Juliette's eyes as she ran her fingers along his chest and the flat hardness of his stomach. He held his breath for a second, trying to catch himself.

She bent and ran her lips along his chest, catching a nipple in her teeth and twirling her tongue around its edges, then trailing over to the other side.

She ran her hands lower, teasing his thighs, hungrily circling in his curls, then gently, tentatively touching his engorged length.

He held her and thought he was going to lose his mind from wanting her so much. Her touch was searing and steady but agony as well. He wanted to be inside her; this was what they were both so desperate for. He scooped her into his arms and carried her upstairs.

When she wrapped her arms around his neck, he felt an odd, new intimacy he had never experienced in his life, and he questioned it. Why did a move so simple, even innocent, feel so important?

* * *

Juliette clung to Thomas as he carried her to a bedroom, and she half wished he hadn't taken the time to take her upstairs. She could feel all her vulnerability beginning to creep in at the edges, her love for this man, her desire for him, a need that was beyond reason.

Thomas laid her down on the bed and brought his mouth down on hers. She wrapped her arms around his back and gratefully succumbed once again to his touch. This was the easy part, letting her body respond to this amazing man without questions about the future or the past, and she gave in to the pleasure as Thomas began trailing his lips between her breasts and down her stomach.

With an experienced hand, he teased around her curls and traced feathery circles along her thighs and above her mound. He tormented her with his palm, and she moved beneath his commanding touch, her need burning. She ran her hands over the strong, muscled expanse of his back and over his firm buttocks, and then she touched his male desire again, amazed at how strong his need for her was.

"Not yet," he whispered. "I want to be inside you."

"I'm ready," she gasped.

His fingers found the sensitive nub at the center of her curls, and she trembled beneath his touch. "I need you," she whispered. "Thomas—"

Gently, he moved his desire-slicked fingers inside her, his thumb still coaxing her most sensitive flesh, and Juliette reached for him.

He moved on top of her and, bracing himself above so he was gazing down at her, he parted her legs with his. She couldn't believe she was lying naked beneath this man who truly was magnificent, this man who had sparked something mysteriously primitive and deep in her even when he had just looked at her on that long-ago day in the sweet shop.

She could feel his insistent hardness against her folds, and he moved and drove it in just a bit. She felt her body yield moistly to his and she spread her legs wider as he deepened his thrusts.

His strokes were deep, fierce, tender. She felt possessed by him, but she felt her power as well; he needed her as much as she needed him, and she could tell with every move of his engorged need. Her desire began to shift to sweet agony and pleasure, and then she clenched around him, raking his back as she cried out, digging into his shoulders with her teeth and going over the edge into bliss.

He deepened his thrusts, unrelenting as he drove into her with an urgency she had never felt before. "Juliette," he cried out, and he spasmed, pouring into her with hot, breathless pleasure.

Juliette breathed in Thomas's scent and closed her eyes. She couldn't honestly say she wished she had never met him; she wouldn't have traded her time with him for anything, even to save herself from the heartbreak of what she knew was coming.

But she half wished she had been smarter, or that she had figured out some way to protect her heart.

What was it Harriet had said? That although she hadn't known her mother for more than a few precious heartbeats of time, she was walking down the same path her mother had taken.

*Harriet didn't know Thomas,* an inner voice said.

But *she* did, and she knew what was possible and what wasn't. What was possible was the chance to love him a little longer, until he went back to America. What was possible was the chance to feel the exquisite desire and pleasure that burned beyond anything she had ever imagined. What was possible was to pretend, if only for a tiny bit longer, that she and Thomas weren't simply pretending to be engaged.

But that was all, and fool that she was, even she wasn't foolish enough to think she could hope for any more.

An image of Harriet came into her heart and her mind then, the memory of Harriet looking into her eyes, holding her cheek and telling her not to follow her mother's path.

Tears burned behind Juliette's eyes, then brimmed over. How could she have been so untrue to her Harriet, that on the very day they had laid her to rest, she had made wild, passionate love?

She felt Thomas's hand stroke the back of her head slowly and steadily. "It'll do you some good to cry, Juliette," he said softly.

At these words, tears began to pour out of her eyes, and Juliette melted into Thomas's arms, her guilt feeling like a cold, wet, black cloak over her heart. "I can't believe we made love on the day we laid Harriet to rest," she said.

"It's the most natural thing in the world," he said gently, still stroking her hair. "It's affirming life, doing something wonderful—"

He stopped, suddenly oddly aware of the silkiness of Juliette's hair, the softness of her breath against his skin, the beat of her heart against his chest.

*This is what you want.*

"I just—" She hesitated, and in the subtle movement of her ribs, he could feel the tears that had just stopped were about to begin again. "I just don't think I can do this anymore."

Her voice, even though it had been quiet, rang in his heart like a loud bell.

*Say the right thing.*

"What do you mean?" he asked instead.

"It's just—I guess when something like this happens, when someone you love dies or anything else major happens in your life, it's natural to take a step back and look at everything. And I can't do this anymore, pretending we're engaged. . . ."

*Say the right thing.*

He could hear the uncertainty in her voice, and the love, and the deep feelings that would have been obvious just by her lovemaking alone.

*Say the right thing.*

He stroked her hair and thought about how differently he felt about Juliette, how even from the first day . . .

*Say the right thing.*

But he was meant to be a loner. And now, he was a *poor* loner on top of everything else.

And so he stroked her hair again and said words he knew she wouldn't want to hear. "We have to keep it up until you're not a suspect in any way, Juliette. That's all there is to it."

# Chapter Twenty

It wouldn't do to arrive at ten o'clock at night at the Banford household; of that, Juliette was certain. And she was desperately hoping Thomas wouldn't come to meet her after work tonight; for a man as intelligent as he obviously was, he just couldn't seem to understand that she was torn, needing to see him but needing also to protect her heart.

So, for both of these reasons, Juliette was hoping that Miss Glover would release them early that night. But it didn't look as if that were about to happen. Miss Glover was walking up and down the rows of seamstresses, looking not happy at all as she examined each woman's work.

"Is there something I've failed to communicate to all of you about this group of dresses?" she called in a voice that sounded even more imperious and exasperated than usual.

Of course she didn't expect any of the women to answer her, and they didn't.

"The vast majority of these gowns must be ready in exactly seven days. That means five, because I'm assuming some of you will have performed work that has to be fixed once these ladies come in and try on their dresses." She walked down the row, shaking her head. "I see some of you are much further along than others, but—" She sighed, then shook her head again. "I suppose tonight will be the night you may all go home to do whatever you have to do for the rest of the week—cooking, shopping, seeing your families. The rest of the nights are going to be long, late, and difficult—you might not be able to leave at all—so I suggest you take advantage of tonight." She gazed down at the dress Alice Knowlton had been sewing and looked as uncertain as Juliette had ever seen her look. "I hope I'm not making a mistake. Now go before I change my mind."

Juliette hung up her gown and hurried out with the other women. If tonight was going to be the only night she would be able to leave Miss Glover's at a decent hour, then tonight would have to be the night for going to the Banford house.

She wished it could have been another evening, though. She knew she looked disheveled and tired; the amazing afternoon with Thomas yesterday had taken its toll in a sleepless, anxiety-filled night, and her face showed it.

But she didn't have a choice. Gathering herself together, she set out, and half an hour later was standing in the area outside 24 Glendynn Place, knocking quietly at the servants' entrance.

She heard voices raised behind the door, and she

could understand why her knock had provoked discussion: It was too late for a tradesman to call, so no doubt anyone in the kitchen or scullery would be curious about who was visiting.

A woman who looked as if she was the cook or housekeeper opened the door and gave Juliette a long, neutral look. Probably in her late fifties or early sixties, she reminded Juliette of Mrs. Winston with her lined, handsome face and gray hair mostly hidden by a cap. "May I help you?"

"Yes. May I come in, please?"

Out of the corner of her eye, she saw all the people seated at the table—they must have been having their dinner—turn their heads to stare at her.

"Yes, of course," the woman said.

The butler Juliette had seen the other day, Mr. Merton, came in from the other room and gave Juliette a long, careful look. "May we help you?" he asked.

Juliette was more nervous than she had expected to be. At Epping Place she had felt so comfortable below stairs, surrounded by friends and people who had seemed like family.

But she didn't know these people at all. And her request was going to be outlandish, completely outside of everyone's daily experiences.

Her best hope, she had the feeling, was going to be in the older staff members. If they had been here when her mother had—

But that was twenty-four years ago.

She looked at the butler and housekeeper. She was certain Mr. Merton knew something, based on his reaction to her the other day. "Would it be possible to speak with you in private?" she asked softly, not wanting to be rude to the other staff members. But she didn't know them at all; if one took it into his or her head to go and tell Brenna Banford—

Yet she didn't know how the butler and house-keeper would react, either.

*You have to take a chance,* she told herself. Because truly, it was her only hope. If she could find her mother's letters . . .

The curious glint that had been in Mr. Merton's eyes the other day was back, and Juliette felt more hopeful as she followed the couple into a small room that was obviously the upper servants' sitting room.

"Thank you for inviting me in," she began after the three had sat down. "My name is Juliette Garrison. My mother was Kate Claypool. She worked here—"

"Oh, my dear," the woman said, holding her chest as if she were about to faint. She looked at the butler. "You were right, Mr. Merton. Oh, my dear," she said again, looking at Juliette and shaking her head. "You are the picture of your mother, dear, in every way. And of your father as well."

The butler was smiling. "That she is, Mrs. Glenfield, as I said."

Juliette was so relieved, she felt like hugging Mrs. Glenfield and Mr. Merton. "Then you were both here when my mother worked for the Banfords?"

"That we were," Mrs. Glenfield said as she stood up. She poured three cups of tea as she went on. "I was head house parlor maid and quite close with your mum. Well, not her best friend in the world—she had her outside friend, Harriet Garrison. But in the household, well, we were all quite close at the time. And Mr. Merton—George here, you were what back then? Footman, weren't you?"

"Indeed I was." He looked expectantly at Juliette, and she knew it was time to explain why she had come.

"Of course I don't need to tell you all that has happened; you probably know from reading the papers and all the talk in this house that I've been accused of the most terrible crime."

Mrs. Glenfield stuck her nose up in the air. "We know the source of those accusations," she said haughtily.

"Mrs. Glenfield," the butler chided.

"You don't need to hush me, George. You know there isn't a chance in the world that girl will come down here. She'd rather go out on the street in her knickers than set foot in servants' quarters; you know that as well as I do."

"But the others," the butler said softly. "You must keep your voice down."

Mrs. Glenfield looked skeptical. "None of us knows what's to happen, Juliette, except that we'll all want to be finding other positions. We're just staying on until Sir Roger's affairs are settled out of respect for what a fine man he was."

"Everyone is going to leave?" Juliette asked, glancing over at the table. It was obvious that the three young women and one man still seated at the table were trying to pretend they weren't eavesdropping, but they weren't doing a very good job of it.

"I can't imagine who would want to stay on," Mrs. Glenfield said. "That Randall fellow, Miss Brenna's fiancé, is quite nice most of the time, but her plain and simple nastiness takes the cake every day of the week."

"I can imagine," Juliette said.

Mrs. Glenfield was smiling at her. "You truly are

the picture of both your parents. No wonder Sir Roger was happy to meet you."

"How did you know he was?"

"Albert over there. Apparently Sir Roger told him all about it and was quite overcome with emotion. Sir Roger always was his own man, Juliette, never one to follow convention if it didn't fit in with his thinking. He was quite fond of your mother, and always thought highly of her intelligence."

"Then what happened?" Juliette asked, feeling anger edge sadness out of her heart for a moment.

"Lady Edith won, that's what happened. As independent a thinker as Sir Roger was, Lady Edith ruled the roost. And in the end, he probably felt it wasn't worth fighting his wife for. But I believe he always regretted his decision. Don't you, George?"

"I do, without a doubt," Mr. Merton said. He looked Juliette squarely in the eyes. "Now tell us what we can do for you."

"Ginny!" Mrs. Glenfield called out. "You're finished eating, so you can get washing those dishes. And, Susie, those fires'll need stoking, and Albert and Sally, you no doubt have some work to be done. So off with you, all of you!"

The four jumped up from the table without waiting for another word, but Juliette could tell now that it was a friendly, good-natured group, without hostility or resentments. Probably they were that much more harmonious, Juliette felt, because they were united in their dislike for Brenna.

She hoped she was right as she waited until the other servants were back to their work before she spoke. "Harriet, my mother's good friend, told me that my mother had hidden letters from William Banford in her room." Mrs. Glenfield's eyes had already lit up, and Juliette was thankful her mother had been so well-liked. "I realize it's not likely that the letters are still there, but if they are, they might do me a world of good. They're love letters and such, and they would prove pretty much beyond a doubt that William Banford *was* my father."

"Where in your mum's room?" Mrs. Glenfield cut in. "That would be Ginny's room now, and goodness knows no work has been done in the servants' quarters since before you were born, Juliette."

"She said it was under the bed, under a board," Juliette said. "All the way in the corner, where no one except an excellent maid would ever think to clean."

Mrs. Glenfield laughed. "That sounds like your mother."

Mrs. Glenfield stood up and brushed her hands off on her apron, then took off her apron and looked at the clock. "I can't say whether this is a good time or not to try because there's no schedule to speak of in this poor old household anymore. But most days we only see Miss Brenna in the morning room."

"Whatever you think," Juliette said. "And I have no idea where we're going, so if you can lead the way . . ."

The house was designed much along the same lines as Epping Place, and the stairs felt eerily familiar to Juliette—sharply ascending and winding, as dark as night because it was "only" for the servants.

As she followed Mrs. Glenfield, she thought about how her mother had used these very same steps, and she knew that trying to find the letters had been the correct path to take. She felt, oddly, as if her mother were watching her and encouraging her.

At the top landing, Mrs. Glenfield opened a door—low and compact, not tall enough to fit a grown man unless he bent over a good deal—and stepped into the little room that had been Kate Claypool's. It was one of those rooms in which everything barely fit: the rocking chair couldn't rock, there was no place for a chair to go with the dressing table, the bed was wedged into one end of the room.

*Let that mean no one has moved the bed.*

Mrs. Glenfield put her hands on her hips. "Here we are, then, and I imagine the easiest thing would be to move the bed—"

"But if Brenna hears—"

"Mmm," Mrs. Glenfield said, "true. I don't believe she's home—but you might be right."

"I'll just crawl under," Juliette said, getting down on her hands and knees. She didn't want to have to use a candle unless it was absolutely necessary—setting the attic on fire didn't sound like a particularly good idea. But if she felt around . . .

The floor was smooth, or rather, no seam felt different from any other. Now, would it have been near the foot, perhaps?

She slid down, ran her hand along the cool wooden floor, and found a seam that felt unnaturally wide. Prying it with the tips of her fingers, at first she didn't feel any give at all. *It's probably just a normal seam,* she thought. But she kept prying—it was the only part so far that had felt any different. And suddenly, it moved just a bit beneath her fingers.

She pulled harder, prying at the ends, which were about a foot apart.

And the board came up.

"It's out!" Juliette cried.

"We're moving the bed," Mrs. Glenfield proclaimed. "We can do it without making a sound if we lift it carefully."

Juliette crawled out from under the bed and took hold of one edge, while Mrs. Glenfield and Mr. Merton lifted the two ends. Carefully and silently, they lifted the bed and set it down gently so that they were all wedged between it and the back wall of the room.

Juliette climbed over the bed and looked into the hole. Down a few inches and covered by dust, lay a stack of letters tied with a dark blue ribbon.

"I don't believe it," she murmured.

"It was meant to be," Mrs. Glenfield said. "Let me get you something to wrap those in."

"No, I will," Mr. Merton said. "You both stay up here. The less commotion on the stairs, the better."

Mrs. Glenfield looked Juliette up and down again after Mr. Merton left the room. "You certainly are the picture of your mother," she mused. "You said you were in service in Epping Place?"

"I *was*; I was lady's maid to Miss Sarah Whitehall, the daughter of Lady Olivia and Lord Lionel Whitehall. But now I'm at Miss Glover's Designs in Regent Street."

Mrs. Glenfield was shaking her head. "What a shame your poor mum couldn't have lived to see you now. But then again, I imagine she's looking down on us, smiling out of those dark blue eyes."

They heard Mr. Merton's footsteps on the stairs, and a moment later, he came bustling into the room with some paper that looked much like the kind the Whitehalls used, and the servants reused, for gifts.

"Paper?" Mrs. Glenfield cried out. "What are you thinking? The poor girl can't leave here as if we've presented her with some sort of gift. What if Miss Brenna comes home?"

Mr. Merton looked incensed. "Miss Garrison is our guest," he blustered.

Mrs. Glenfield laughed and shook her head. "I'm afraid in his excitement over meeting Kate's daughter, our Mr. Merton has quite lost his head, Juliette. Let me get you something you can hide your letters in. Here, let's use this kerchief of Ginny's; I'll give her one of mine to replace it. I want you to leave this house as quickly as possible now that you've found what you came for. Miss Brenna is as unpredictable as an alley cat, if you ask me." She took the letters from Juliette's hands, wrapped them in her efficient, housekeeper's manner in the kerchief, then handed them to Juliette. "If I were you, dear, after we move the bed back, I would hide those somewhere in your dress. I would dearly hate to see Brenna get them after all you've gone through to find them."

"That's a good idea," Juliette said, setting them down on the small bedstand her mother had probably used when she had slept in this room.

Together, Juliette, Mrs. Glenfield, and Mr. Merton moved Ginny's bed back into position.

"Now, let's go downstairs and get you out of the house, Juliette. This has gone a mite too smoothly, in my opinion, and I'll breathe easily only when you're long gone, with your mum's letters safe and sound at your own little place."

Mr. Merton discreetly preceded them out of the room, and Juliette tucked the papers down against her stomach inside her dress. The waist was tight enough to hold them, she was fairly certain, and she would keep them in her dress until she was a good distance from Glendynn Place. "Thank you so much for all your help," Juliette said. "Truly, Mrs. Glenfield, I don't know what I would have done without your kindness."

"You can thank your mum for that," Mrs. Glenfield said, sounding emotional. "She was a wonderful girl who deserved better than she received. Now you go after what's yours, and don't let anyone stop you."

"I'll do my best," Juliette said, grateful once again that her mother had been so well loved by so many people.

She followed Mrs. Glenfield down the stairs and had just walked into the servants' dining room when she heard a most unwelcome voice.

"But this is completely unacceptable, Merton," Brenna Banford was saying. "I have an important guest and you're unable to find me the right wine. This never happened with my grandfather—"

"I believe I suggested a port," Mr. Merton was saying. "If that doesn't suit you, I can offer you something else. But in my opinion—"

"In *my* opinion, you've just interrupted me. I find your behavior quite surprising, Mr. Merton."

Juliette had been standing stock still, as had Mrs. Glenfield. Now Mrs. Glenfield motioned with her head for Juliette to back out toward the stairs. As Juliette took her first step, the floor creaked.

Brenna's head whipped around. Juliette would have thought her expression—open-mouthed and amazed—was comical if she hadn't been afraid of Brenna somehow finding the letters.

"What on earth—?" she sputtered. Her cheeks flushed nearly purple as she looked from Mrs. Glenfield to Mr. Merton. "One of you had better tell me the meaning of this instantly, or you shall both be out on your ears."

"They didn't know I was coming," Juliette said, stepping forward. She kept one hand as subtly as she could on her waist and walked up to Brenna as if she had been an invited guest. "If you insist on being irrational about my having come to see my own grandfather's house, take your feelings out on me, not on your servants, who had no idea I was coming."

"Why is your hand on your stomach?" Brenna demanded. "If you've come in and stolen something from this house—"

"I've done no such thing," Juliette said. She let her hand drop and puffed out her stomach so her dress would be as tight as possible. "And I have no intention of hanging about in order to be insulted. I wanted to take one last look at where my grandfather lived. If you must know, I pushed right past Mr. Merton and Mrs. Glenfield."

Brenna looked skeptical. "You're lucky I'm not firing you two on the spot. But I suppose you'll be looking soon enough in any case, now that my grandfather is no longer here."

"We shall be pleased to stay on until you know whether you're keeping Glendynn Place," Mr. Merton said.

Juliette was sure Brenna hadn't seen the look of surprise on Mrs. Glenfield's face, but she had. And she realized that Mr. Merton was probably planning to stay on in order to look out for her interests.

"Really," Brenna said, sounding understandably surprised.

"I must be going," Juliette said, beginning to move past Brenna.

"Just one minute there," Brenna said, reaching for Juliette's purse.

"Take your hands off my purse!" Juliette cried, grabbing at it. She shoved at Brenna and felt something next to her stomach shift. In the next moment she heard the packet of letters drop to the floor.

"What on earth—?" Brenna said, beginning to reach down.

But Juliette was faster. She reached down, scooped up the letters and pushed past Brenna. "You have no right to touch my property!" she called out, and ran to the servants' door, opened it, and dashed up the steps.

She hoped Mrs. Glenfield and Mr. Merton wouldn't get the sack; she desperately, truly hoped they wouldn't.

But she had to leave, and they wouldn't want her to have risked so much for no gain.

She had the letters, and if she were lucky, there would be some sort of proof in them that she could present to the solicitor. Harriet had wanted her to follow this path, and she was certain her mother's spirit wanted her to as well; it was time to try to right some of the wrongs the Banfords had committed.

# Chapter Twenty-one

"It's a ship that's designed to survive all conditions," Thomas was saying. "What we've developed is something completely new because it uses steam along with some of the older mechanisms. I can show you some sketches if you'd like."

Lord Harold Faraday looked as if he wished he was still at Hampton shooting grouse and tramping through the fields.

"I believe I'll pass on your offer," Lord Faraday said, standing up. "What I heard about the *Jessamine* isn't particularly favorable, in my opinion."

Thomas knew he had to choose his words carefully. Ships went down all the time, because of acts of God, acts of man, and everything in between.

*You should have gone back to Boston when you learned your crew survived.*

And he knew it was the truth. But then he never would have seen Juliette again.

"It's always a terrible thing when a ship goes down," he finally said. "What matters is that my crew survived."

"That's all well and good," Lord Faraday replied, "and your response reveals an admirable character in a man I might count as a friend. But as far as business goes, where would the loss of the *Jessamine* have left your investors?"

"Investment is a risk," Thomas said. "If a man invests in my company for the long term, I can promise he won't be disappointed. If a man expects to be made rich after a month in business with me, I promise nothing."

"I'm afraid it's simply not what I'm looking for." Lord Faraday held out his hand. "Best of luck, young man. I'm afraid you're going to need it."

*You should go back to Boston.*

Thomas thought of what he could accomplish when he did go. But then again, he had come to England to find investors; American maritime engineering was just a little ahead of British engineering, and the smart investors here knew it.

*You just want to be here because of Juliette.*

He thought of the day before, how he had never felt anything like that. . . .

"If you think you can come in here and move ahead of all of us who've been here for eons and eons, you're wrong," Emily Brownell said, speaking through gritted teeth and not even looking at Juliette.

"I'm not expecting to move ahead of anyone," Juliette said. "I'm trying to make enough money to live on, Emily—no more and no less. I didn't set out to displace anyone."

"Oh, I know your type. Pretty soon you'll think you can order us all about because you're in the senior position."

"I'm not in the senior position."

"But you will be now, won't you? As I said, I know your type—"

"And you know what? I know yours," Juliette spat out. "I've had just about enough of all your moaning and complaining. I don't see any of the other women whining about me. Go jump in a lake if my presence gets you so heated up and cross. It's no skin off *my* nose."

Out of the corner of her eye, she could see the corners of Alice Knowlton's mouth turn up. Some of the other women smiled as well, but everyone knew better than to say anything.

"Miss Glover, may I speak privately with you?" Emily called out as Miss Glover came into the room.

Miss Glover looked surprised and annoyed. "Can't you tell me here and now, Brownell? We're a day behind as it is."

"It's rather private, Miss Glover."

Now Miss Glover looked disgusted. "Very well, but make it quick. If it takes more than five minutes, I'm docking an hour from your pay."

"Whining little brat," Alice muttered under her breath. "You would think she'd have something better to do with her time than to worry about what everyone else is doing, but she doesn't—and I suppose that's why. It's all a big circle: She *has* no friends or family, because she *is* such a whining little brat."

"Now, now, Alice, not everyone can snare a Prince Charming like you found for yourself," said Christina Salem, probably the youngest seamstress of the group.

Alice's pale white cheeks suddenly turned scarlet, and she began to laugh. "A point well taken," she said.

"Prince Charming?" Juliette asked. "Tell me more."

"Oh, just that Alice landed the handsomest man to ever set foot in this place," Christina said. "Not everyone can have such luck."

"You only wish," Alice teased, still laughing and still blushing.

But her smile disappeared instantly, and Juliette followed her gaze.

Walking quickly toward her was Miss Glover, looking dour, followed by Emily Brownell—who also, Juliette was pleased to see, looked serious and subdued. Without a word, Emily sat back down in her chair and began to sew quickly and with exaggerated concentration.

Miss Glover stopped in front of Juliette, her arms crossed. "Is your name Juliette Maywood or Juliette Garrison?" she demanded.

So the game was up. It was one thing to rewrite her past when no one was asking any questions about it; but even she, an experienced bender of the truth from way back, knew that now was the time to tell the truth and look better, if only a bit, for having admitted her earlier lie.

"I am Juliette Garrison," she said.

She saw Miss Glover's cheek twitch ever so slightly. "What a disappointment," she said quietly. "If you'd like to hold on to your position here, I see no reason for anyone to know your true name. *I* shall certainly be the last person to reveal it."

Juliette could hardly believe her ears. No wonder Emily had slunk back to her chair like a chastened child. "Thank you, Miss Glover. I share your wish for discretion—obviously."

"Very well, Juliette." Miss Glover looked as if she was going to say something else, then apparently thought better of it and walked away.

After she had left the room, Alice leaned over toward Emily Brownell. "That's what you get for being a pathetic little tattler," she said. "It goes to show that skill is all, and yours just isn't up to snuff compared to Juliette's."

Emily, her face pinched and angry, said nothing.

Juliette sewed on, but she wished that Emily had chosen another day to reveal her identity. She had been planning on asking—or begging, really—Miss Glover to let her leave early so she could bring her mother's letters to the solicitor; if she had to work until ten o'clock or later every night, she would never be able to take them, and she didn't dare trust the mail. But now that Miss Glover had granted her this one enormous favor, it would hardly do to ask for another.

She sewed on until the end of the shift, watching with a sinking heart as the hours went by, knowing there wasn't a solicitor in London who would still be working in his office so late at night—and certainly no solicitor of Sir Roger Banford's would be.

At ten o'clock, Miss Glover finally said they could leave, and most women, as usual, left quickly. Juliette noticed that Emily Brownell was refusing to look up at anyone, her face bent over her sewing as if it were the most important thing in the world to her—and Juliette supposed that it was; but so what? People like

Emily Brownell had always caused trouble for her—women who couldn't mind their own business, for the most part—and she had no intention of trying to mend any fences; let there be a big, tall fence between Emily and all the other women, as far as she was concerned.

Out in the cold, dark night, Juliette began her long walk home. With every step she took, she was more conscious of what Harriet had warned her about so many times: "You've lost your street smarts, dearie, there's no two ways about it."

"Juliette," she heard from behind her.

She turned, and Thomas had already caught up with her. "You don't think I'd let you walk these streets alone, do you?"

"I lived on the streets for the first eleven years of my life," she snapped.

"But I didn't know you back then, did I?" he asked softly, taking her into his arms.

She wished—oh, how she wished—that it didn't feel so right and so wonderful to be wrapped in those warm, strong arms; and she wished she didn't love the smell of him and the feel of his soft, full lips against hers—but she did.

"We're engaged to be married," he murmured, ushering her toward a rented carriage. "Remember? Let's act the part. Now is there a reason you have to go home this moment?"

"I'm exhausted and I'm starved," she said, realizing that she had gotten extremely spoiled in the months she had worked in service. Back on the streets as a girl, she would have felt lucky having eaten breakfast that morning. Yet today, she had complained about her hunger along with all the other women at Miss Glover's, and she truly did feel as if she were nearly crazy, she was so famished.

"How do ham and potatoes and turkey sound?"

Juliette felt her stomach actually gurgle into activity just at the sound of the words, and her mouth was watering. She felt she would have done almost anything for the chance to eat a meal as delicious sounding as that.

But she was also annoyed. She had told Thomas she couldn't be with him anymore, and he was acting as if she had never said anything about it.

"I'll be fine," she managed to say, even though her stomach was practically screaming for food. "I'm sure there's food at our new place."

His gaze was penetrating. "I'm sure there isn't," he said.

His words were too much. Who did he think he was to always act as if he knew best and as if he knew more than she did?

"And you would know that because you've been there this evening?" she asked, moving out of his grasp. "Please don't tell me one more time that we have to act as if we're going to be married, Thomas. It doesn't look as if anyone is watching us out here in this dark street, and frankly, even if they were, I wouldn't care. I don't want you coming to meet me, and I don't want you acting as if we're going to be married any day now. I don't want your kisses, and I don't want you to offer me food as if I wouldn't be able to survive without you. I'm fine without you; I *belong* without you. I don't need this . . . this playacting any more."

By the faint light that emanated from the gaslights

of the carriage, she could see the features of his face shift, those beautiful eyes and soft lips change, and harden.

He was taking her at her word, accepting what she said. He wasn't going to pull her into his arms again, he wasn't going to argue with her, he wasn't going to say she was wrong. He looked as if he was at war with himself, as if there was something he wanted to say but couldn't. He took a slow, deep breath and gazed into her eyes for a long, long time. "Take the carriage," he finally said. "There's all sorts of food in it that I had thought we could eat on the way to Gregory's. Enjoy it and be safe, Juliette. I've already paid the driver."

He took off into the night, his long, strong strides somehow different looking. She hadn't even realized she'd memorized how he moved, how he walked, but she now knew that something in his gait had changed.

She couldn't dare hope that it had anything to do with her, that her words had affected him deeply. He had said his goodbye, caring though it may have been, and she truly was on her own.

# Chapter Twenty-two

Juliette could hardly sleep that night. She kept thinking about the oddness in Thomas's walk, how he had looked angry and alone and insulted. Did he know how much she loved him? Did he have any idea how she felt? But she couldn't have told him her true feelings.

She thought about what her mother had had to endure, listening to Lady Edith Banford's cruel prattling about William and Hazel Crichton's wedding, and she knew that compared to her mother, she had it easy.

But it hurt.

It hurt because Thomas was a better person than William Banford had been, and it hurt because she had warned herself not to fall in love, and then she had fallen as fast and deep as a stone in clear water.

*What if you had told him how you feel?*

She knew in her heart it wouldn't have made any difference. At every opportunity for an exchange of feelings, he had been uncommunicative, even gruff. "We're pretending," he had said over and over again. What they had shared was a great time, in his words—nothing more and nothing less.

The next day, at Miss Glover's, the hours stretched on endlessly, and for the first time, Juliette's fingers began to hurt as she sewed. Now she remembered the aches she had felt at her other sewing jobs, the feeling that her fingers couldn't make the needle form one more stitch, but on she sewed, until she was summoned, in the middle of the day, by Miss Glover, who looked pale and extremely upset.

"You must go to the back of the store, out into the alley and then onto the street," she said, her voice shaking.

"I beg your pardon, Miss Glover?" she asked.

"Do it now, Juliette," Miss Glover said, more loudly than Juliette had ever heard her say anything.

She walked out through the back room, out into the filthy alley, and then into the street. And her heart sank.

Inspector Hannigan was standing there, along with a London policeman.

Hannigan was giving Juliette a knowing, disgusted look. "This is your current place of employment?" he asked.

It *was,* Juliette thought; she doubted that Miss Glover had reacted enthusiastically to the sight of the police on her premises. "Yes, it's my new place of employment. Now that you've visited me here, I doubt I'll be employed after this morning."

Inspector Hannigan gave her a pained look. "You'd do well to learn to keep your opinions to yourself, Miss Garrison; I didn't ask for a prognostication on your part. Did I not tell you to keep us informed of your whereabouts?"

Juliette said nothing.

"Yes or no, Miss Garrison?"

"Does that mean I can now give an opinion, Inspector? I do believe it's an opinion and not a prognostication, but I want to be sure."

Now Inspector Hannigan's eyes were narrowed. "If you're trying not to annoy me, Miss Garrison, you are failing in your endeavor."

"I'm simply being truthful, Inspector, and sincere in my questions. And I daresay if I were guilty, I wouldn't have the nerve to do either one. I know I agreed to tell you of my whereabouts, but I'm still on probation here at Miss Glover's, and I only recently found a place to live. My dear aunt died, and I've not had a moment to go to a police station or even to write a note."

As she spoke, she realized how inadequate her words were. She'd had time to move her possessions, find a new job, go to the Banford house more than once. . . .

"I believe you should know that we've interviewed every other one of our suspects, Miss Garrison, and to a person, each can account for his or her whereabouts on that night."

"As can I," she cut in, "embarrassing and scandalous though some people may think it."

"Be that as it may," he went on, clearly unimpressed, "you don't seem to have taken my warning seriously."

"Because I'm innocent," she said, her voice louder than she had meant it to be.

Now Inspector Hannigan looked just plain angry.

"A concerned citizen took the time to report your whereabouts to me, and I came to warn you to keep me up to date. If I have to search for you again, Miss Garrison, I can promise you that you won't be happy with the results."

Juliette said nothing. She could just imagine who the "concerned citizen" was, none other than Miss Emily Brownell. She knew she would have to hold her tongue and ignore the blasted busybody; who even knew if she still had a job?

"I understand," she said, looking Inspector Hannigan in the eye.

"Now, I wouldn't suppose you would know how I might locate Mr. Jameson—?" *Hold your tongue! Or be more polite, at the very least.*

"Why wouldn't I know that when I'm engaged to marry the man?" she snapped, then forced a smile. "He's currently staying at the house of an acquaintance, a Mr. Gregory Chiswold, at Number Seventy Stamford Street."

Inspector Hannigan looked surprised. "Very good. Then I'll be contacting him quite shortly. And I assume you realize the gravity of your every action, Miss Garrison; if you change jobs or flats again—and I want you to jot down the address of your flat—I will take a dim view of it, indeed, if you don't contact me at once."

"Yes, Inspector Hannigan." She was tempted to ask him why the police felt the need to name her as a suspect in every newspaper article she had seen, yet all the other suspects consistently remained nameless.

But she knew that at best, he would tell her once again that she'd do well to keep her opinions to herself. At worst, he would tell her that the newspapers consistently named her because she was, in fact, their main suspect.

When she went back in—through the back, of course—Miss Glover called her into her office. "I wish I didn't have to do this," she began.

"I know," Juliette said. Miss Glover looked genuinely upset, and Juliette believed that she truly felt she had no choice other than to let her go.

"If the police hadn't come, it would have been different," Miss Glover said. "I was willing to hide everything and simply hope no one would wonder who was working in my back rooms. But now—"

"I know," Juliette said again, because she truly did understand.

Miss Glover stood. "Naturally, I'll pay you for the work you did; you definitely have talent, and I know that I'll kick myself in a year's time when you open a shop halfway down the street."

Juliette laughed. "I promise I'll make it farther away than that," she said. "And I do thank you for giving me a chance not everyone would have given me, Miss Glover."

They said goodbye, and Juliette quickly said her farewells to all the coworkers she liked. She and Alice promised to stay in touch and hugged each other, and then she stopped in front of Emily Brownell, who hadn't looked up from her sewing for even a moment.

"I do know you're the one who summoned the police, Emily, and don't think for a minute that I'll forget that fact."

Emily Brownell kept sewing. "I haven't the faintest idea what you're talking about," she said without looking up.

"That's neither here nor there, Emily, because

you're the only person who would have gone out of her way to focus attention on me. I hope you realize you had better watch your back, day and night."

Now Emily stopped sewing and looked up at Juliette, and Juliette almost had to laugh; the poor woman looked scared half to death.

"I mean it," Juliette said. "I've always said I was innocent, but you chose not to believe me." She leaned forward. "Who's to say you aren't right?" she whispered.

"Goodbye and good luck, everyone," she called out, and a moment later, she was out on the street.

Maybe it was meant to be, she said to herself. At least now, she had time to go see her grandfather's solicitor.

"Where did you get these?" Sir Harold Longley asked Juliette.

"I—" She hesitated. The truth was, she supposed, that she had stolen them from the Banford house. But weren't they hers, in one way, since they had belonged to her mother?

She took a deep breath and wondered whether she was about to sink her own ship. "I had heard from my mother's dear friend that William Banford and my mother—well, my parents—had written to each other quite a bit when my father went off to India."

Sir Harold Longley was looking at her carefully, and she couldn't read his expression at all. He had seemed quite friendly when she had first come in to his office, but maybe that was just his manner. . . .

"Miss Garrison," he finally said, steepling his fingers in front of himself on his desk. "I assume you know a little bit about your half-sister. She's hardly going to welcome what I consider conclusive proof that you're a legitimate descendant and heir of Sir Roger. Unless I can state where the letters were all these years and why they suddenly and miraculously appeared, I don't believe they'll carry much weight."

"Very well, then," Juliette said. "As I said, my mother's dear friend, the woman who raised me as her own daughter, told me about them. My mother had hidden them in her room at the Banford house, and she left without them when William made it clear he wanted nothing to do with her."

Sir Harold's eyebrows were raised. "And they were there all these years?"

"They were hidden under a floorboard beneath my mother's bed. I wondered whether they would still be there, but when I eventually found them, it was easy to see why no one had ever noticed them."

"So you went there and retrieved them?" he asked.

"A few days ago, sir. I wasn't able to bring them here sooner because I've been working until after ten o'clock every night."

Sir Harold was shaking his head. He put his pipe down and stood up. "I believe you have an excellent basis, Miss Garrison, for claiming a portion of the holdings of your grandfather's estate. And I can tell you right now that those holdings are quite substantial indeed."

"You'll need the money you earned sewing to pay back your friends at the Whitehall house," Polly said that evening when Juliette handed over her pay.

"But they all have jobs," Juliette said. "The money they lent us for Harriet's funeral was their savings. If we don't pay our rent, we'll all be out on our ears again."

Polly looked uncertain, her plump features shifting. "I suppose you're right, dear," she said, looking down at the money. "You made quite a good sum for a few days' work down there."

"I know," Juliette said. "It's one job I truly wish I could have held on to. Harriet's probably up there asking why I couldn't have kept my mouth shut just this once, but this time, I lost the job because of someone else—well, it's all water under the dam in any case. Have any of the others found jobs yet?"

"Sue Ann took slop work just to tide herself over. She says it's better than nothing, but I disagree; if she does it too long, she'll lose her eyesight and the use of those nimble fingers. And Louise took on a job at a button factory, but she says she'll be deaf before the week is out, what with the din in there."

"What about you?" Juliette asked.

Polly smiled for the first time since Harriet had died. "I followed Harriet's advice for the first time in my life, dear. I'm working as a shop assistant at a grocer's in Lipton Street, and I love every minute of it."

Juliette heard quick, purposeful footsteps on the stairs outside the flat, and a second later, a knock on the door.

"Quite late for a visitor," Polly said.

Juliette opened it and saw an unfamiliar-looking man—in his late thirties, perhaps, with the clothes of a footman.

"Yes?" Juliette said as the man looked straight at her.

"I'm told to ask for Miss Juliette Garrison and no other," he said.

"I'm Juliette Garrison."

His face took on a grave, distressed expression that seemed entirely sincere. "Miss Caroline Naughton is in urgent need of your attention," he said. "She lies in bed at Nottingham Hospital—"

"What happened?" Juliette asked.

"A terrible accident at Epping Place," he said. "A kitchen mishap involving boiling water and a new girl who didn't know what she was doing."

"Is Caroline going to be all right?" Juliette asked.

The man took a deep breath. "She's being aided by the doctors and the nurses, but she asked for you, and Lord Whitehall has sent me all over London. I've just come from that dress shop; they sent me here, but I've been gone from Epping Place a good three hours."

Juliette looked at Polly. "I must go to Caroline," she said, and she followed the man out the door and down the stairs.

# Chapter Twenty-three

"She'll be quite glad to see you," said the footman, whose name was John, as he helped Juliette into the carriage. "Quite glad indeed."

"When did it happen?" Juliette asked.

"Just this afternoon."

"I'm glad you found me," Juliette said as the man swung up into the driver's seat. "What happened to Hodgson, by the way?" Juliette asked, thinking of the Whitehalls' coachman, who had been with them for as long as any of the other servants could remember.

"It's a bit late in the day—or night, if you will—for old Hodgson," John called out over his shoulder. "Lady Whitehall has been asking me to do the honors every so often, and I'm happy to oblige, you might say. My favorite part of the day, it is, when I can drive a team like this."

"How long have you been at Epping Place?" Juliette asked.

It was the first time the words hadn't positively flowed from the man's mouth. "Oh, quite a short time, actually. Not long enough to bear any influence on the Whitehalls, that's for certain."

They traveled on in the darkness for a while, and Juliette thought about Caroline. She decided right then that when Caroline got better—if she got better—she would try to convince her to leave service and—

—and what? she wondered.

She didn't truly believe she would receive any of her grandfather's money; people in her position, with her history, never actually had things like that happen to them.

But she didn't need her grandfather's money to make changes in her life or to help Caroline make changes in hers. What she wanted was to introduce Caroline to the kind of independence people out of service experienced—yes, it was uncertain, and yes, there were undoubtedly times you had nothing, not even a roof over your head or a bite to eat, but you could see whom you wanted when you wanted, and that was perhaps worth everything.

*You can tell Caroline all this when she's better,* she told herself, *if indeed she gets better.*

"Do you know what the doctors have said about Caroline's condition?" she asked, just as John made the horses turn down a long, dark street.

"Don't know anything other than that Caroline wants to see you," he muttered, suddenly seemingly unwilling to say more than the minimum.

But Juliette wasn't thinking about whether John

wanted to talk or not anymore; she didn't understand why he had turned down Bretton Street, which she knew didn't lead to the hospital.

"Why did you turn down this street?" she asked. "I believe the hospital is that way," she said, pointing right. "If you make a right turn, you can get back in the correct direction."

John didn't say anything.

"Excuse me, but did you hear me?"

"I heard you," he said, snapping the reins to make the horses go faster.

"Then where are you taking me?"

"To the hospital," he said, without looking at her. He was looking straight ahead, at the horses and the dimly lit streets, but she had the feeling he was thinking of something else, and she suddenly felt extremely uneasy. Why was he going this way, and why wouldn't he look at her anymore?

"Excuse me," she said again. "John. I need to know what is happening—"

"I told you," he said in a flat, expressionless voice. "I'm taking you to see Caroline."

"But where? This is *not* the way to the hospital." She paused, and her heart was suddenly beating quickly and shallowly. "I demand to know where you're taking me. If you don't tell me, I'll get out—"

"Now, how're you going to get out with the horses going this fast? You'll break every bone in your body."

The horses were indeed nearly galloping, and fear closed around Juliette's heart and thoughts. What on earth had possessed her to blithely follow this man from the safety of her house out into the dark, dangerous night?

"Please tell me what you're doing!" she said, knowing it was absurd to think he was suddenly going to reveal all simply because she had asked him. "If I see someone out in the street, I shall scream—"

He shook his head. "You won't see a living soul," he called out over the clatter of the horses' hooves. He reached down, and Juliette was torn between trying to see what he was doing and watching, powerlessly, as the horses hurtled on in the night.

"There," he said, quickly straightening up and grabbing her wrist.

She felt something rough and felt a tug, and when she looked down, she nearly fainted. He had put a thick rope in a knot around her wrist and was holding the other end tightly in his hands.

Juliette felt as if the blood had stopped in her veins, as if her heart had stopped beating and she would never take another breath.

It was too late to wish she hadn't blithely followed this man, but she wished it nevertheless, and felt like kicking herself a hundred times over.

"Who are you and how do you know so much about me?" she asked. "Why are you doing this? I don't even know you!"

"Which is the way it's going to stay!" he called out.

In the distance, Juliette could see nothing but total darkness. She knew what that darkness held: the wharves.

When she was a child, she had been afraid of this area even on the brightest of days: Harriet had told her that the area held nothing but danger—"dark waters and quick-fingered thieves, child, and it'd please me no end if you never ventured down there even once in your life," she had said.

*Now I'm tied to a man who's taking me straight toward the wharves.*

But surely the fact that she was attached to the man was the worst part of all.

"What is it that you want from me?" she asked, though she was afraid the man's answer might be even worse than anything she might have already imagined.

"I don't want a thing at all from you," he said as he pulled the horses to a stop. "Now come out of the carriage with me."

"I'll do no such thing!" she said, her heart racing. She had no idea what she could do to fight him, but she had the feeling that the less cooperative she was, the better chance she had.

"You don't want to make this worse for yourself, believe me," he said as he left the carriage, wrenching her arm in his direction.

"Just pull and let's get this bloody well over with," came a voice—a man's voice—that it took Juliette a moment to recognize.

But then she knew, just as Randall Banford came into view and grabbed her other wrist.

"I told you I want no part beyond this point," John said. He handed the rope over to Randall Banford, and Juliette knew this might be her only chance to run.

*Think,* she said to herself.

But she should have moved instead of thought, she realized a moment later, after Randall had firmly jerked the rope close to his body.

Juliette suddenly felt as if she knew less than nothing, as if everything she had thought up until now had to be called into question. How could she have thought, for even a moment, that Randall Banford wouldn't want to hurt her?

Yet, even now, as she glimpsed his features in the moonlight, she couldn't quite believe that he meant her harm.

"You got yourself into this mess all by yourself," he muttered, yanking her as he spoke.

"I'm off and running and never saw nothing!" John called out over his shoulder. "And if you don't pay me by the morning, you know what's to happen."

"I'll pay you, I'll pay you," Randall grumbled, jerking at Juliette and pulling her toward the water.

"You can't honestly think the police won't go right to you," Juliette said, the pain in her wrist almost unbearable.

"They haven't been too intelligent up to this point, have they?" Randall asked.

She had stopped moving; it was insane, despite the pain, to move even one inch, Juliette had realized. And if Randall tried to pick her up, she would attempt to knock him off balance.

"You *are* a stubborn little bitch, aren't you?" he said, looking down at her. "Here I did my best to talk Brenna out of doing you any sort of harm, and it turns out she was right."

He yanked on her wrist again, and Juliette kicked at him, but he caught her other arm, shoved her to the ground and tied both wrists behind her back.

He was going to drag her to the water and throw her in; and even if he were caught later on, it would be too late for her. She would sink quickly and drown slowly, a death too horrible to imagine.

He began pulling her by her feet, and the cold, wet stones grated at her face, the pain even worse than the pain around her wrists.

*This can't be happening; I can't have survived this*

*long just to be killed by some money-hungry, spoiled ingrate.*

"I'll give you everything I have!" she yelled out.

Randall laughed. "I'd hardly expect you to say anything different," he said. "And it doesn't matter anyway, even if I did believe you; I can't have you running to the police."

Suddenly Juliette heard the clatter of horses' hooves, and she saw the faint light of a carriage down the street.

Randall tried to drag her faster, but he must have realized he wouldn't be able to get her as far as he wanted before the carriage arrived.

"Move or speak and you'll be sorry," he breathed, holding her down against the ground. He tried to roll her under his carriage, but she fought him so hard that he gave up and just held her immobile.

*I'll let him think I've given up and then I'll kick him,* she thought, but the new carriage had stopped and she saw a shape moving, running through the darkness.

Suddenly Randall was yanked from on top of her, thrown through the air, then subdued.

"Any last wishes?" Thomas asked, straddling Randall with one knee on top of his chest.

"I can't breathe," Randall wheezed.

"Good," Thomas snapped, leaning forward.

"Don't kill him!" Juliette called out.

Thomas didn't even turn his head. "Why not?" he asked, his voice sounding oddly distant. "I had to see you this evening. It just happened that I got to your rooms a little after this piece of garbage did and I was able to follow the carriage." He paused. "But I might have been too late. Easily. So you tell me why Randall Banford deserves to live."

"Because we're not like him and Brenna," Juliette cried. Every bone in her body ached and every inch of her skin burned, but she managed to roll onto her back and sit up.

Thomas rushed to her side. For a moment he just hugged her; then he cut the rope and freed her wrists, and held the knife up toward Randall Banford, who had begun to move.

"One more move and you *will* be dead," Thomas warned. "But I guess if you stay still and do what I say, we can save you for the police."

"Why would I want to do that?" Randall asked.

Thomas put the knife right against Randall Banford's throat. "I would have thought that was obvious," he said softly.

Juliette felt as if twelve hours had passed since "John," or whatever his name really was, had summoned her to help Caroline. Now, she stood in the area outside 24 Glendynn Place and thought how fitting a spot it actually was for her, neither upstairs nor down, an outsider in every respect.

Being near Thomas had been nearly too much for her; in his rescue of her, he had somehow become even more important to her in every way, and she felt breathless as he stood next to her, waiting for Brenna to come to the door.

Mr. Merton had evidently told Brenna that Randall was waiting outside to speak with her, because Brenna suddenly demanded, quite loudly, "Well, why on earth can't he come in?"

Juliette could only hear Mr. Merton's voice—not his words.

Then Randall spoke. "You wouldn't want me to come in like this now, would you, my dear?"

"Oh, my goodness," Brenna said from right inside the doorway. "That will be all, Merton. I believe I shall have to speak with Mr. Banford out here in the open air."

A moment later, she spoke again, and her voice sounded tentative to Juliette, afraid to ask the obvious question. "You're so dirty! So then—" She stopped.

"The deed is done," Randall said firmly. "As you wished."

Silence. Then: "I can hardly believe it," Brenna said, all stridency gone from her voice. "It's what we wanted, of course, but I can't say I truly wished her to *die*—"

"I believe it's *precisely* what you wished," Randall said, the tension obvious in his tone. "Exactly and precisely, Brenna."

"Well, yes, of course, because of the end result. It was necessary and unavoidable. But that doesn't mean I wished it to happen. Was it—did it take a very long time?"

"I'm afraid it did," Randall said. "Juliette put up quite a struggle. She's—she *was*—quite a strong young thing. I had to drag her, and she nearly pulled me right into the water. It did take quite a lot longer than I had wanted, but as I said, the deed is done, and your half-sister is no more."

Silence. "Well, then. That certainly calls for a drink. You'll have to go home and get cleaned up, of course, but then I would think a celebratory lunch later on tomorrow would be perfect."

Juliette could pretty much picture Randall staring

at Brenna. "You aren't really asking me to celebrate the death of your half-sister—?"

"I'm asking you to celebrate all that we've achieved. I don't have to share my inheritance, you don't have to share your inheritance, we don't have to endure all the dreadful, smug looks of everyone who would love to see me embroiled in a humiliating scandal—"

Juliette guessed that the policeman they had summoned had heard enough, because he was now emerging from the area and had begun walking up the steps. "You two can come with me now," he said. "Especially you," he added, grabbing Brenna's arm roughly.

"Do you know who I *am?*" she screeched. "Let me go! You can't grab me as if I'm some sort of criminal!"

Though Juliette was taking in every detail of this moment, she was suddenly intensely aware of Thomas's nearness, and she looked up at him.

He was looking down at her, and those deep, dark, long-lashed eyes were stormy with emotion.

But Thomas said nothing, and Juliette moved away and began walking up the steps.

She hadn't had much time to look forward to this moment, but she had hoped that even though the policeman was there, Brenna still hadn't guessed she was alive.

And she had been right.

The policeman had just handcuffed Brenna, and she had been struggling with him.

But when she saw Juliette, she stopped moving. Her mouth dropped open, and then she whirled around to look at Randall. "You fool!" she shrieked. "You complete and utter fool! How *could* you?"

"How could *you?*" Juliette asked. "I didn't need the money, Brenna. I would have been happy just to have a grandfather."

"You're a liar!" Brenna hissed. "This is absurd. You *must* let me go," she said breathlessly, looking desperately at the policeman. "You have no idea of all the absurd stories this—this *maid* has concocted. You can't possibly take her word over mine."

"I'm afraid it's a bit late for that, miss," the policeman said without emotion. "But you can tell all the stories you'd like to the judge and jury."

# Chapter Twenty-four

"It was entirely my cousin's idea!" Brenna was screaming, and Juliette had the feeling that Brenna had never raised her voice so loudly in her life.

Then again, she had never before been charged with murder and attempted murder, and the detectives and inspectors who had gathered around looked completely unimpressed and unconvinced.

"I loved my grandfather!" she cried out, and Juliette felt a rush of hatred. Brenna had killed their grandfather and tried to kill her for money, even though her entire life had been lived in utter luxury.

*I would have traded everything just to know my grandfather longer.*

"You're such a poor liar," Juliette said, her voice shaking. "And you robbed me of the chance to know Grandfather. All for money, when you've never worked a day in your life. But I guess now you'll finally have the chance at Newgate Prison, if you're not put to death."

Dark splotches of purple mottled Brenna's pale cheeks. "I should have gotten rid of you first!" she screeched. "How dare you talk about my grandfather as if he had any connection to you whatsoever? Did you honestly think I would have allowed people to think we're *related*? Did you honestly think I would have let a *maid* get her hands on money that was supposed to be mine?"

She suddenly stopped and looked around.

"Is there anything else you'd like to say in your defense?" one of the inspectors asked.

Brenna looked crushed, but she said nothing.

Randall had remained quiet—indeed silent—up to that point, but Juliette saw him raise his head. "May I ask a question?" he asked, his voice sounding exhausted and hopeless.

"Go ahead," one of the detectives said. "Perhaps you'll help our case as much as Miss Banford has already helped it."

"I should like to know if I can be tried separately from Miss Banford."

At these words, Brenna nearly broke out of her handcuffs. "You bastard!" she cried. "How dare you!" She began to cry, tears streaming down her face, her nose suddenly unceremoniously runny. "I hate you all! Every single person in this room. And when I'm set free, you shall all be sorry indeed."

One of the detectives laughed under his breath. "She's a dreamer, I'll give her that."

"May I ask another question?" Randall said.

"By all means," the chief detective answered. "Your cousin here has been so very helpful. The more questions you ask, the more certain we are to win the Crown's case."

Randall looked disgusted. "I'm well aware of how much information you already have. What I'd like to know is if I can add to it."

The chief detective looked surprised and suspicious. "Meaning what, exactly?"

"Meaning that if I help you, as a witness, will I get any sort of special treatment?"

"Special treatment?" Brenna cried. "Why should *he* get special treatment? He's the one who's ruined everything!"

"Would you be quiet for half a minute?" Randall snapped. "I'm not talking to you, Brenna, and I'm not asking you. I'm talking to the police."

The chief detective whispered something to one of the other men, who whispered to another man, who went into a back room and conferred with two others.

"This is absurd!" Brenna cried out. "My cousin should receive nothing—absolutely nothing!"

"If you say one more word, Brenna, I quite guarantee you will be sorrier than you can imagine," Randall called out.

A gray-haired man who introduced himself as Lord Graham sat down across from Randall. "In the interests of certain justice and spared expense to the Crown, we are prepared to offer you an arrangement. But the arrangement is conditional on its acceptance today, and today alone."

"*I* want an arrangement," Brenna cried. "Why should he get the arrangement?"

"Because he asked," Lord Graham answered, as if he were talking to a small child.

"What is the arrangement?" Randall asked.

"We would like you to testify to the events surrounding Sir Roger's death. You should be well aware, with the witnesses we have concerning your attempted murder of Miss Garrison, your conviction is assured. We would be willing to commute your certain death sentence to a sentence of life imprisonment if you admit to your role in Sir Roger Banford's death—if you did indeed play a role and have such knowledge."

"Done," Randall declared.

"Very well, then," Lord Graham said. "Though the public, I daresay, will demand our heads for depriving them of a colorful trial and execution, in the interests of the Court's knowledge of the true events surrounding Sir Roger Banford's death, we shall sentence you to life in prison."

"I demand the same treatment!" Brenna cried out. "I can supply you with the same information Randall can."

"Very well, then," Lord Graham said with an enigmatic smile. "You, too, Miss Banford, shall serve the rest of your living days in prison."

For a moment, Brenna looked stunned and confused, as if she had been rudely awakened from a dream.

Then she put her head in her hands and began to cry.

A few minutes later, Juliette was riding back to her rooms with Thomas in his carriage, and she felt as if all the aches and scrapes that were hurting and burning her body were nothing compared to the breaking of her heart.

Everything had come to an end too soon—her time in service, her time with her grandfather, her time with the man she knew she would love forever.

She had told him she could no longer pretend they were planning to be married, but now there was no more need to pretend. And she realized she would have preferred the pretense to having nothing at all.

"I still find it amazing you were able to find us at the wharves," she said, wanting to speak of what had happened so she wouldn't have to think of the separation she knew was coming.

"After you got into that carriage, I lost sight of it for a while. If it had been any earlier when more carriages are out, or in the daytime, I never would have found you."

"I wonder how he knew where to find me," Juliette mused.

"I would imagine Brenna found out where you were working. Whoever contacted the police probably contacted her too."

"Probably Emily Brownell, again," Juliette said.

She was annoyed with Emily for having stuck her nose where it didn't belong, but she knew, too, that this point was where fate had been leading her anyway. When she had lain in Thomas's arms and dreamed of a future with him, she had been a fool. When she had thought about how Thomas was so different, being American and all, and dreamed he could love a lady's maid, she had been a fool.

This was reality—an imminent goodbye, and deep, vivid memories that would last forever. She would have to forever live with the knowledge that if she had never approached her grandfather about their shared heritage, he would still be alive today.

"At least Emily Brownell's nosiness led to the police finding the real killers," Thomas said softly.

There was a long moment of near silence, in which

Juliette heard only the clatter of hooves and the beating of her own heart. She knew, somehow, that the next words Thomas was going to speak would be unwelcome.

"I'm going back to America tomorrow," he said softly. "Now that you're out of danger and no longer a suspect, I'm going to go back where I'm most needed."

"Of course," she said, feeling a small part of her heart close off and die.

"I don't have much of a company to return to," he went on. "No way to pay my men, no way to pay for materials, probably no way to raise any more money now that word has gotten out about my partner taking off." He paused. "When we met, I was a wealthy American shipping magnate, and now you're sitting next to a man who has nothing."

*I don't care,* she said to herself.

"Oh, you'll get back on your feet in no time," she said, her voice hollow. "You've been a survivor your whole life."

"It's just that now I'm responsible for putting food in the mouths of dozens of families," he said. He reached out and covered her sore cheeks with his palms, and Juliette willed her tears not to flow. "You know I'll never forget you," he said softly.

Juliette forced a smile. "I know." Though unwelcome, memories flooded her heart: "Miss Juliette Whitehall" and her social welfare project, the night out by the stream at Hampton, the night she and Thomas had shared that magnificent bed.

"And of course I shall never forget *you,*" she managed to say without crying, though she felt as if she were using every muscle in her body to stop herself.

"Oh, you'll be so busy you'll forget me in a week," he said. "You'll have your own shop, employees, and your fame and fortune and a string of men trying to catch your attention."

Juliette couldn't help smiling. "Aren't you getting ahead of yourself? I'd better find a new job first, wouldn't you think?"

Thomas's expression darkened. "Don't tell me that when all the complications of Sir Roger's estate get untangled, you're going to turn down the inheritance that's yours by law. He obviously wanted you to have that money."

"I know," Juliette said, although she did feel ambivalent about it and knew she always would. If Sir Roger had been poor and she had tracked him down, she would have ended up with the opposite: no money, but a grandfather to love. "I do know he wanted me to have it because he said as much. He was so honest about it, actually, telling me how one should never take fortune for granted. . . ." Her voice trailed off and was replaced by the tears she had tried to fight off. "If I do end up with the money, or even if I don't, I suppose I'll go on as Harriet always taught me—following my own path." She forced a smile. "Perhaps you'll even read about my world-famous dress shop in the American newspapers."

Thomas wiped a tear from Juliette's cheek and took her in his arms. This was what felt right—holding her, breathing in her scent, feeling her heart thud against his.

But she was on her way. He knew she had a wonderful future—even without Sir Roger's money, he believed she would be able to make her way.

But she would receive a substantial amount of money before long.

And now he was the one with nothing.

*You love this woman in a way you've never loved before.*

He looked back on that day when he had first seen her saving that little girl, and he knew.

Maybe, when she had been "exposed" as being a servant back at Hampton, when the Whitehalls' butler had pretty much ordered her to go downstairs, he should have told her how he felt.

But he hadn't understood at the time because he had been alone for so long.

Now it was too late, and it would be wrong. She was on her way to a bright future. He was on his way back to try to salvage a broken company.

"I'll tell you what," he said, wiping a tear with each of his thumbs. "When you're ready to open your shop, you let me know and I'll come see it. Who knows? I might even be able to straighten out Compton and Jameson, and I'll be back to try to find some more investors."

"Do you think you will?" she asked, her voice soft and broken. "I mean, do you think you'll be able to straighten things out?"

"I have no idea," he said, telling her the truth.

*What I know is that I wish I could offer you more. What I know is that I'll never forget you.*

*What I know is that I have to say goodbye to you so you can make your own way and I can find mine.*

When the carriage reached Juliette's house, Thomas walked Juliette up to her rooms. When she opened the door and her friends saw her wounds and scrapes, they were all over her, pulling her in and clucking like mother hens, full of a million questions as they cleaned her off and began bandaging what they could.

Thomas left before he could change his mind, before he put his emotions ahead of everything he knew was right.

Juliette had been given a new direction in her life, and it was time for him to go back to America and fix what was left of his.

# Chapter Twenty-five

"I realize that under the circumstances, congratulations are hardly appropriate," Sir Harold Longley said, setting down the sheaf of papers and steepling his fingers on top of them. "But you do know that your grandfather wished you to share in his holdings—the notes we found in the desk at Hampton made that clear. And now, with Brenna and Randall Banford sure to be convicted, you will be Sir Roger's sole heir."

Juliette could hardly believe his words. She had come to the office for practical reasons, feeling curious and reluctant, excited and saddened all at the same time. Sir Harold had already told her she would be sharing in the proceeds of her grandfather's estate, but she had no idea exactly what that would mean.

Now, Juliette stared as Sir Harold Longley turned a

piece of paper around on his desk so that it faced her. *350,000+ pounds,* she read.

"This is an approximation of the amount you'll be receiving, Juliette, after all Sir Roger's accounts and bills are paid. It's merely an approximation, but it gives you an idea."

He paused then, and looked her up and down. "I've been reading about you in the paper, of course. It must be quite an extraordinary feeling to be working as a maid one day and in a position to do whatever your heart desires on the next."

Whatever your heart desires.

What her heart desired was to be with Thomas again.

Would she have traded away the fortune she was about to receive in return for spending the rest of her life with the man she knew she would love forever?

In a heartbeat.

"It does feel quite unreal," she finally said, suddenly realizing that Sir Harold was waiting for some sort of response.

He smiled. "I can assure you it will be quite real in a few months' time. I can easily advance you some of the more available funds right now if you'd like."

For a moment, she was caught in a stream of memories, images she knew would burn in her heart forever: huddling under a bridge with Grace and Harriet, all nearly frozen to death; crying herself to sleep on too many nights from hunger; running into the street after an apple that had tumbled out of a costermonger's cart and nearly getting trampled by a team of horses. She had experienced so much hunger in her life. And now, she would never, ever be hungry again, or cold, or without a bed to sleep in and a roof over her head.

"That would be fine," she said, still feeling numb. If Sir Harold gave her ten or fifteen pounds, she could repay her friends at Epping Place and pay off Polly and the other women's rent for the next several months.

And then . . .

He handed her a sheaf of bills. She counted them—1,000 pounds—and realized she had never actually seen that much money in one place in her life. "I don't think I need this much," she said.

His smile was broad now and quite genuine. "Nonsense, Miss Garrison. Accustom yourself to the feeling of having money. Surely you've always had a dream."

*Indeed I have,* she said to herself, and she knew she would follow it. She just wished that the money had come to her under happier circumstances.

None of it felt right.

Thomas had arrived back in Boston and found his workers as loyal as ever and more faithful than he could have hoped for. "We know you'll find a way to pull through, Tommy," Hank had said. "You always have."

And indeed, with a loan from a newly formed Boston bank, he had begun to pick up the pieces. The suppliers who had been panicked about not getting their money were beginning to be paid, and the ones who had been especially patient had been rewarded with bigger orders. Thomas and Hank together had come up with their best design ever for an America's

Cup yacht, and Thomas had been able to make firm promises of bonuses for all the men who had survived the *Jessamine*'s ill-fated voyage.

He had heard bits and pieces about Cyrus Compton, rumors and half rumors that Compton had gone West, out to California or up the Oregon coast, that he had gambled away all the stolen money, that he had spent it and been killed.

He didn't know which to believe, but he cared less about catching the man than he did about moving forward. Moving forward without looking back was what he had always done best, and he wasn't planning on stopping now.

Except that there was one part of his life he didn't want to move away from, one person he thought about day and night, morning and evening, waking and sleeping and half dreaming and everything in between.

He had tried to act noble, telling himself if there were a chance he was going to be poor again, he had no right to lead on Juliette. But now that she was out of his life, he realized she *was* the passion of his life; that if he had to succeed again to give her what she needed, he would do whatever he had to in order to make that happen.

*You should never have left her.*

He had left her alone to deal with the setting of Sir Roger's estate, alone to pick up the pieces of her life.

And he had never once told her he loved her.

He walked into the office from the docks and looked down at his longtime secretary, Enid. With her gray hair and gray eyes, she had always had a calming influence on him, and she had always been able to recognize his moods, knowing when to keep quiet and when to offer advice.

Now she looked at him over her glasses with a knowing half smile. "You're going to look for Mr. Compton and you're telling me I'm going to have to hold down the fort—again—until you come back."

"Not exactly," he said, giving her an affectionate smile.

"You're going back to England to twist the arms of all the people who turned you down."

"You got the first part right," he said.

He hadn't told her much about Juliette—only that he had helped a young woman who had been accused of murder because he had been with her on the night the crime had occurred. Of course she had pried more details out of him, but he hadn't ever told her how he felt about Juliette because he hadn't even admitted it to himself.

Now she jumped out of her chair and nearly knocked him to the ground as she grabbed him by his upper arms. "It's that woman, the maid. It is, and don't you tell me any different."

Thomas had to laugh. "I wouldn't dream of telling you any different, Enid. Yes, it's Juliette. I'm going to see—well, I just hope I'm not too late."

Enid narrowed her eyes. "For as long as I've known you, Tommy, you've said you were a loner, and I haven't argued with you because there aren't enough hours in the day to convince you when you've made up your mind. But since you came back, you've been a *beastly* loner, and I think I know why. So you'd better not be too late, or you'll be a man without a secretary when you come back. Now when are you leaving?"

He couldn't help smiling. "Do you have to want to get rid of me that much? Couldn't you just pretend to be a little bit sorry to see me go?"

"No, I can't, Tommy, because this is too important. Now, make your arrangements and tell me what you need me to do. And if you change your mind, I swear I'll walk right out this door."

"I couldn't survive without you, Enid, so plan on my leaving in the morning."

She looked into his eyes. "Wonderful. You're less beastly already," she proclaimed.

Thomas smiled, but he knew that going back to London was only the first step.

# Chapter Twenty-six

It was a more perfect space than Juliette could ever have imagined, and she clutched Caroline's arm as the two women reached the back room. "We can have a dining area for all the seamstresses back here. Don't you think?" Juliette asked.

Caroline laughed. "Would you really want them to stain your creations? Imagine if someone spilled tea on a nearly finished gown."

"But they wouldn't," Juliette said. "There will be regular breaks for eating, and of course an area for washing one's hands."

Caroline was shaking her head. "I'm surprised you're not going to serve high tea out in the main shop."

"Do you know, I've honestly considered it? But I don't think I can trust the customers the way I'll be able to trust my employees. Speaking of which, Caroline: Have you given your notice to Lady Whitehall?"

Caroline's eyes were shining. "Just this morning. She was quite shocked when she heard I would be working for you. I think it will take them a very long time to get used to the idea of the two of us being out on our own. I do miss Sarah enormously. She's in America, apparently, with Andrew."

"You're joking!"

Caroline laughed. "Not a bit. I heard Lord and Lady Whitehall talking all morning of it. Sarah has completely thrown her upbringing out the window and she sounds quite happy, judging by the tone of her letter."

"Good," Juliette said. "I'm glad. She deserves it." She hesitated over her next words, for she still felt she had been an untrue friend for not having been able to tell Caroline what she had heard about Martin and Lady Foxcroft. "What about Martin?" she asked.

Caroline rolled her eyes. "Martin is no more. At least he's no longer in *my* life. Lady Foxcroft can have him all to herself, for all I care."

"What happened?"

"I went to visit him unannounced—Lady Whitehall had changed my afternoon off, and I thought I would surprise him. And I did quite surprise him when I found him romancing a little kitchen maid from his very own household. According to the staff there, it's been going on for quite some time. But I'm fine with it, really. I always suspected he was much more involved with Lady Foxcroft than he should have been, and the cook there, when I pressed her on it, hinted I had been right."

"I *am* sorry," Juliette said.

"Don't be. I quite mean it when I say I'm fine. And if, as you say, I'm soon to be manager of your dress shop, I'm quite a bit more than fine, Jules."

Juliette smiled and wished she could have as healthy and balanced an outlook on life as Caroline did. Here she was due to receive several lifetimes' worth of money, more than she could have ever imagined, and she couldn't shake her regret over what had happened between her and Thomas. Months had gone by since he had said goodbye to her, and she had thought that the feeling of missing him, the sharp sense that a part of her was gone, would lessen; but it now felt even deeper because Juliette was beginning to doubt her memories. When Thomas had seemed to love her, looking at her with so much affection in his eyes, had she only been imagining it? When he had seemed to care so much about her hopes and dreams for the future, had he cared only in her mind?

She knew she should never have expected their affair to turn into a permanent relationship; Thomas had told her he would always be alone, and she should have taken him at his word. Her deepest regret, she supposed, was that she had never told him she loved him because, somewhere in her heart, she couldn't help wondering if this would have made a difference.

"You're looking quite sad for someone who's about to open the shop of her dreams, Jules."

Juliette shook her head. "Don't mind me. I *am* quite happy—except for the sketch of the sign Mr. Scofield brought in. Did you like it?"

"Not a bit," Caroline said. "I think it has to be much more understated, much more elegant. I think he was so excited about what had happened to you that he put some of that excitement into the sign," she said with a laugh. "Do you know he took me aside and asked if you were 'smitten,' as he put it, with anyone? 'A maid what's got herself a whole new life,' he said. 'Now *that's* a lady I'd like to know.'"

Juliette smiled, and she wondered if this was the way Thomas had felt—a boy who had lost everything, who had become a man with a future. Had he worried all his life that women were after him for his fortune? She doubted it; he was a man women would have thrown themselves at no matter whether he was rich or poor.

But when he had lost everything, had he felt that he couldn't share his life with her, especially when she was going to end up with so much?

*He was a loner, and he'll always be a loner,* an inner voice said. Nothing she could have said would have made a difference to him.

"Well, let's get Mr. Scofield to tone down his enthusiasm a bit, don't you think?" she said. "'Garrison and Naughton Fine Designs' is all it has to say, without screamingly bright letters."

Caroline suddenly looked teary eyed. "You're certain you want me to be part of the business?"

"I'm certain I wouldn't want to do it without you, Caroline. I wouldn't have lasted a week at the Whitehalls' without your help."

Caroline laughed. "I won't argue with you about that," she said. "Do you think you'll ask Rachel to come work for us?"

"If we make a go of it, without a doubt. I think she'd enjoy it immensely. But I don't want to ask her until we know we'll succeed."

Caroline was staring at her. "Until we know? Jules,

we'll *make* it work. It's not as if we're starting with nothing."

"But I need the shop to work on its own merits," Juliette said. "It's just like with Thomas—he began from nothing, and he built an empire. I need to know that our shop has succeeded because we know what we're doing. Otherwise I don't want to do it. It's just the same with Polly and Sue Anne and Harriet's other friends; they're waiting, too, to see if we make a go of it."

"Oh, we'll make a go of it," Caroline said. "I promise you. And if we don't—"

She stopped, and Juliette looked at her. Caroline was standing at the glass counter they were planning to turn into an accessories display case, and she looked frozen for a moment, her mouth open, her hands and indeed her whole body stock still.

Then her cheeks darkened, and Juliette turned toward the doorway, where Caroline was staring.

Thomas had been standing there, but now he came forward, his eyes locked with Juliette's, and he didn't stop walking until he was holding her in his arms.

Juliette fought tears, but the feel of Thomas's embrace was too much for her. She breathed in his scent, her head against his chest, and he stroked her hair and tilted her face up toward his. "I've been away from you for too long," he murmured, and he brushed his lips against hers. He drew her into a kiss that thrilled her to her bones. Juliette couldn't believe that Thomas was actually here because this moment was so much like the dreams she'd had every single night.

He drew back and gazed into her eyes. "I made a mistake leaving you here," he said, brushing her hair back from her face. "And every day, I've wished that I hadn't. Do you know why I felt I had to leave?"

As much as she had yearned to see him, as much as she had felt as if a part of herself would be missing forever if she never saw Thomas again, now that he was here, she felt wary. How many times had he emphasized to her that they were only pretending? Now she felt all her vulnerabilities creeping back. "You said you had to save your company," she answered.

He was nodding. "Exactly. And my company is going to be fine. I guess I've been in business long enough that most everybody trusted me as far as starting up again. My ex-partner, Compton, is living it up in California, and as long as I can make the break from him legally, I'll be fine. Just let me have my men, and I don't care what Compton does. What isn't fine . . ." His voice trailed off, and for a moment, Juliette felt lost in his gaze. "I don't know if you understand how ingrained in me it was to be alone, Juliette; I hope you do. Because that was what was keeping me from seeing how much I love you."

She almost cried, but he went on. "I know you're on your way in the world, and that you can do it completely on your own. But if we got married, you could do what you're doing now, but with a husband in the background who's madly in love with you."

Out of the corner of her eye, she saw Caroline, and when she turned, Caroline did a mock swoon and went into the back room.

Juliette truly didn't know what to say, but she felt she had to object. How could Thomas suddenly be saying all these things she had wanted to hear for so long?

"I'm just getting started on my shop," she said. "And I'm setting up a charity for unwed mothers, a home where they can stay until they get on their feet.

And I'm . . . well, I'm in the middle of all sorts of projects."

He leaned down and brushed his lips against hers. "Then let me get in line as one of your projects," he murmured. "I know you can do it all on your own. But at least come home at night to a man who will be wild about you for the rest of his life."

"But what about *your* business?"

"I can go back and forth. I trust the people I've always trusted, Juliette. Now I just need to give them a little more responsibility." He looked into her eyes. "Say yes."

She almost couldn't believe it was really happening. Yet she believed that he loved her.

She had always felt that fate had played a large role in every part of their relationship, and fate had drawn him back to America. But Thomas himself had made the decision to come back to England; he had come back only to see her, and to ask her to marry him.

"Yes," she whispered, and she wrapped her arms around his strong, broad shoulders. She knew she would love him forever.

# Chapter Twenty-seven

"Yes, we would be able to make that by the fifteenth," Juliette said to Lady Bartlett. "If you come back on the tenth, we can do the final fittings, and you might even be able to receive the dress early."

Lady Bartlett smiled politely, thanked Juliette and left the shop. It had been a busy day so far, and Juliette and Caroline had spent almost as much time planning their one-year anniversary party as they had dealing with customers.

"Let's barricade the door," Juliette called out to Caroline with a laugh. "I want to set up all the food before anyone else comes in."

"But it isn't even one o'clock," Rachel said. "Won't today continue to be busy because of the regatta?"

Juliette smiled. Her staff members—Caroline, Rachel, Polly, and Sue Anne—were often more diligent than she was about the business. It had been an uphill battle attracting customers in the first two months—her notoriety had led to many walk-ins from the curious but few visits from women who actually wanted to buy dresses. But after she had sold her first few—Sarah had come back for a short visit, and she had helped spread the word—business had picked up. Lady Whitehall had even stopped in, though she had yet to order a dress.

But Juliette had found that even though she loved designing the dresses and loved that she had been able to employ so many women, her work with the charitable foundation she had set up was more rewarding. Their shelter was designed to house thirty women with their children, and Juliette was planning to open two more later in the year. She had dissolved her grandfather's private lending business and had quite a bit of money coming in from the men who still owed a debt. Lord Cornelian, one of the many men who had borrowed from her grandfather, had balked at the arrangement until she had threatened to make public the extent of his gambling debts; and now he paid her, reluctantly, a portion of his debt every week, with interest.

The front door of the shop opened, and Thomas and Violet walked in, each holding an armload of bags. "We've got supplies galore," Violet called out in her high, thin, street-urchin's voice, and Juliette couldn't get over how different Violet already looked from that long-ago day at the sweet shop. It had taken more than a month of searching, but Juliette had finally found Violet in the workhouse, and even though all Violet knew about her was that she had saved her from being arrested in the sweet shop, the girl had gone with her willingly, and then begged to stay. Juliette guessed that maybe it was because she and Thomas had both struggled so much as children that Violet had instantly felt comfortable with them and wanted to be part of their family.

Thomas drew Juliette into an embrace, then pulled back and gently put his hand on her stomach. "So how are my mama-to-be and baby?"

"Your mama-to-be is starving. I'd like to shut the doors right now, but Caroline and Rachel will have my head if we turn any well-paying customers away, so I guess I'll have to listen to them."

"I guess you will," Thomas murmured, brushing his lips against hers. "So now here you are, a year into having your own shop. Is it everything you had hoped for?"

Juliette thought back to that day she had pretended to be Miss Juliette Whitehall. So much had happened, so much had been gained and lost. She knew she would have traded every shilling she owned if she could only have Harriet and her grandfather back— every shilling and more. But of course she couldn't.

"I know who you're missing," Thomas said softly. "But they're looking down on all this and loving it, as are my parents and Quentin and everyone who's ever rooted for us. I just want to know that you're happy, Mrs. Jameson."

Juliette smiled. "More than I could have ever dreamed," she murmured, and it was the truth.

# SIGN OF THE WOLF

## ELAINE BARBIERI

It is an eerie howling in the night that only she can hear. As always, tragedy soon follows. This time, Letty Wolf will obey the teachings of her Kiowa heritage and bring back to New York her three estranged daughters…before it is too late.

Raised in fancy Eastern boarding schools, Letty's daughter Meredith is determined to return to Texas. Once there she is caught up in a whirlwind of mayhem. The only calm in the storm is Trace Stringer, who tracked Meredith down with a summons from her mother. In Trace's arms, Meredith begins to believe love might be possible, even for her.

------------------------------------------------

# The Mad, Bad Duke

## JENNIFER ASHLEY

Meagan Tavistock can easily see how Alexander earned the nickname Mad, Bad Duke. His deep blue eyes promise sinful pleasure and his rich voice intimates that as soon as they are skin to skin, he'll fulfill desires she isn't even aware of. When a love spell misses its intended target, Meagan can no longer resist the temptation...until the magic wears off, leaving the pair in a most compromising position. Their only option is a marriage that thrusts Meagan into a new world of high danger, dark secrets, and a passion so intense she can't help wondering: Is it the lingering power of the spell or true love at last?

------------------------------------------------------------